ODYSSEY
TO THE NORTH

ODYSSEY
TO THE NORTH

North-Western Stories

Edited by
JON TUSKA

Five Star • Waterville, Maine

First Edition
First Printing: December 2003

Published in 2003 in conjunction with Golden West Literary Agency.

Set in 11 pt. Plantin by Al Chase.

Printed in the United States on permanent paper.

Library of Congress Cataloging-in-Publication Data

Odyssey to the north : north-western stories / edited by
   Jon Tuska.—1st ed.
       p. cm.
     "A Five Star western"—T.p. verso.
     Contents: An odyssey of the north / by Jack London—
The call of the wild / by Robert Service—North fifty-three /
by Rex Beach—The match / by James Oliver Curwood—
Carcajou's Trail / by Max Brand®—Voyageur of the
wasteland / by Frederick L. Nebel—The craft of ka-yip /
by Dan Cushman—Maintien le droit / by Tim Champlin.
   ISBN 0-7862-3805-4 (hc : alk. paper)
   1. Western stories.   2. Klondike River Valley (Yukon)—
Fiction.   3. American fiction—20th century.
4. Northwest, Canadian—Fiction.   5. Adventure stories,
American.   6. Alaska—Fiction.   I. Tuska, Jon.
PS648.W4O39 2003
813'.01083278—dc21   2003052877

276

ODYSSEY
TO THE NORTH

Table of Contents

Foreword

Jon Tuska

The last great gold rush the world was to know began in the Klondike, and in 1897 at twenty-one years of age Jack London, who had been living in San Francisco, joined the stampede. He spent the winter of 1897–1898 in the Yukon. When he returned to San Francisco, he began writing a series of imaginative stories based on his experiences.

Bret Harte, a generation before Jack London, had won an international reputation for his Western stories set during the California gold rush of 1849. "It *was* a very special world, that gold-rush world," Walter Van Tilburg Clark wrote in his Foreword to *Bret Harte: Stories of the Early West* (Platt & Munk, 1964), "with ways of living, thinking, feeling, and acting so particularly its own that there has never been anything quite like it anywhere, before or since. Which is what the literary histories mean when they call Bret Harte a local-color writer." In *San Francisco's Literary Frontier* (Knopf, 1939), Franklin Walker gave credit where credit was due when he observed that "with situations in which what was said was only less forceful than what was implied, Harte created the land of a million Westerns, a land in which gun play was chronic, vigilante committees met before breakfast, and death was as common as a rich strike in the diggings." Walker felt Harte's stories "succeeded in turning the gold-rush days into what he called 'an era replete with a certain heroic Greek poetry'. Roaring Camp, Poker Flat, Sandy Bar, Wingdam, and Red Gulch were mythical towns inhabited by a society grown in two decades almost as romantic as Camelot or Bagdad." What Walker did not point out, but well could have, is that the geography was nearly as mythical as the place names themselves.

Jack London in his own way did with his stories of the far North what Bret Harte earlier had done with his stories of the far West, and the first of them appeared in the same magazine that had carried Bret Harte's early stories, *The Overland Monthly*. It seemed that Jack London created a new and mythical world filled with characters and events no one ever had read before. Also like Harte, London populated this new world with characters that would recur in story after story. Malemute Kid is a character with a major rôle in London's "To the Man on the Trail" in *The Overland Monthly* (1/99), in "The White Silence" in *The Overland Monthly* (2/99), in "An Odyssey of the North" in *The Atlantic Monthly* (1/00), and he is mentioned in passing in "The Son of the Wolf" in *The Overland Monthly* (4/99). In "The Son of the Wolf" Scuff Mackenzie seeks to take as his wife Zarinska, the comely daughter of Chief Thling-Tinneh of the Upper Tanana Sticks. The chief tells Mackenzie of his other daughter who has already married a white man named Mason. Mason's death is narrated in "The White Silence", and Mackenzie relates to Chief Thling-Tinneh how Mason's wife, called Ruth by the white men, and her son with Mason took Mason's gold and went south to live where there is " 'no biting frost, no snow, no summer's midnight sun, no winter's noonday night!' "

Stanley Price in "To the Man on the Trail" is described as "a young mining expert who had been in two years"—where being "in" means having lived in the far North. In "An Odyssey of the North" Price is living with Malemute Kid and the two listen as the Indian Naass tells the story of how his bride was taken from him on his wedding night. Father Roubeau is the Jesuit mentioned in "To the Man on the Trail" as having married Mason and Ruth after they had fled the Tananas. In "The Men of Forty-Mile" in *The Overland Monthly* (5/99) Father Roubeau and Malemute Kid are among the *dramatis personae,* as is Scuff Mackenzie, and the reader learns that Mackenzie's marriage to Zariska has prospered.

On the other hand, some of London's most familiar far North stories have characters that, of necessity, are seen but once. Perhaps his most famous short story is "To Build a Fire" which first appeared in *The Youth's Companion* (5/29/02). London himself later expanded and polished this story, and it appeared under the same title in *The Century Magazine* (8/08). "In a Far Country" in *The Overland Monthly* (6/99) is probably the London short story that has been most anthologized after "To Build a Fire". It is a tale of two shirkers in the far North for the first time who find themselves isolated in an Arctic cabin for an entire winter with dire results.

Five of London's novels are set in the Klondike region of Yukon Territory during the 1896–1898 gold rush. The most celebrated of these is *The Call of the Wild* (Macmillan, 1903), a 32,000-word short novel originally serialized in *The Saturday Evening Post*. It sold 10,000 copies on its first day of issue in book form. London, desperate for money, made one of the biggest mistakes in his professional writing career by acceding to Macmillan's "best" offer for what they considered a "dog" story—$2,000 for an outright purchase of the copyright without royalties. He had received $700 from the *Post* for the magazine serialization, and, while $2,700 was a sizable sum in 1903, London would have earned a small fortune in royalties from this book alone for the next forty-two years, the maximum period of protection provided by the

Copyright Act in effect at that time. London said he wrote the short novel as a sort of species-redeeming sequel to his "Bâtard", first published as "Diable—A Dog" in *Cosmopolitan* (6/02), a grim Yukon tale of a dog who finds sweet revenge after being brutalized by his master. Ostensibly *The Call of the Wild* is the story of Buck, a domestic dog who is stolen, taken into the Yukon wilderness, starved and beaten into submission until he becomes later, in turn, a great sled animal, a vicious killer, the property of a kindly gold hunter, and, after the murder of this man by Indians, a ghostly legend as leader of a wolf pack. For all of its apparent simplicity, *The Call of the Wild* portrays vividly a naturalistic view of the brutality of life controlled by biological and environmental impulses. Yet the eerily lyrical, romantic prose of this novel also suggests a significant ambiguity on the author's part, the terror of surrender to a wholly naturalistic universe. This, for me, is the theological quandary Jack London sought to confront, even if the confrontation is oblique, and it is easily misinterpreted. So much theology depends on the notion of a benevolent Deity that can, and upon occasion will, intervene and suspend the laws of His own creation. In the far North, I believe, it occurred to Jack London that it is very possible that, even if He is all-powerful, God has chosen from the beginning of time to act only within the laws of His own creation. This does provide a great latitude, however, for quite possibly the so-called laws of the universe at base may very well be merely a matter of hazard, and the probability of even such a common occurrence as the sun rising tomorrow, no matter how many days in the past it may have arisen, still remains only one out of two. It could simply be that God has infinitely more imagination than any of His creatures. It could also be that the truly mortal sin for which Prometheus was pinioned and tormented and Adam and Eve exiled from the

12

Garden of Eden might actually have been the all-too-human belief that knowledge is power, rather than imagination—for, truly, imagination is the essence of all creation. London studied Nietzsche extensively, and it was Nietzsche in *Die Geburt der Tragödie* [*The Birth of Tradgedy*] who asked: ". . . is what is incomprehensible to me then not also unintelligible? Perhaps there is a realm of prudent wisdom from which the logician is banished? Perhaps art is actually a necessary correlative and supplement to rational intelligence?"

A year after *The Call of the Wild* was published, London announced to his publisher that he had decided to write a "complete antithesis" and "companion book" to his bestseller. *White Fang* (Macmillan, 1906), an even more naturalistic story than its predecessor, takes a sort of reverse twist on *The Call of the Wild*. Fang is a wolf dog, born in the Yukon wilderness, brutalized by his masters but eventually domesticated. A remarkable feature of this novel is London's depiction of the white silence of the Arctic wilderness in even more forbidding terms than he had described it previously: "Life is an offense to it, for life is movement, and the Wild aims always to destroy movement. It freezes the water to prevent it running to the sea; it drives the sap out of the trees till they are frozen to their mighty hearts; and most ferociously and terribly of all does the Wild harry and crush into submission man—man, who is the most restless of life. . . ."

Burning Daylight (Macmillan, 1910) is London's most important North-Western story in terms of his development as a writer and social thinker. It is a sprawling narrative of a legendary Klondike king of El Dorado named Elam Harnish who has spent thirteen years searching for gold in the Yukon before the great rush and who now takes his hard-won millions outside to face a far different world than the one of trusting, faithful, work-hardened men to which he is accustomed. London's other extended works set in the Northland include *A Daughter of the Snows* (Lippincott, 1902) and a series of interconnected stories titled *Smoke Bellew* (Century, 1912) about an effete litterateur who finds manhood among the rough-and-tumble miners of the Klondike.

Robert Service in his ballads about life in the far North and the one novel he wrote about the Klondike added further imaginative dimensions to this new literary world. In the spirit of Vergil before him who had opened his epic paean of Rome in *The Æneid* with the words— *"Arma virumque cano"*— Robert Service sang of "The Law of the Yukon":

> **Send me the best of your breeding,**
> **lend me your chosen ones;**
> **Them will I take to my bosom,**
> **them will I call my sons;**
> **Them will I gild with my treasure,**
> **them will I glut with my meat;**
> **But the others—the misfits, the failures—**
> **I trample under my feet.**

Service was born two years before Jack London and spent his boyhood in Glasgow. He became apprenticed as a bank clerk but was restless and sailed to Canada to seek his fortune. In 1904 he took the position of a bank clerk in Whitehorse, and later the Canadian Bank of Commerce transferred him to its branch in the former roaring camp of Dawson where he lived in a little bungalow. The days of the gold rush were over by then, but he retold and embellished tales he had heard, transforming them into legends. His first collection of poetry, *Songs of a Sourdough* (Stern and Company, 1907), contained "The Shooting of Dan McGrew" and "The Cremation of Sam McGee", ballads that soon became two of the most-often memorized poems in the English language. The lines I have quoted above come from this first book of ballads.

Service was able with the money he earned from this volume to quit his bank job and pursue the career of an author. *Ballads of a Cheechako* (Stern and Company, 1909) followed. In Jack London's stories this Siwash word for a greenhorn (literally a person from Chicago, *i.e.,* Chicagoan) was rendered *Che-cha-qua*. By the time Robert Service used it, his rendering of it had become a part of the English language.

In *Jack London and the Klondike: The Genesis of an American Writer* (Huntington Library, 1966) Franklin Walker provided an invaluable commentary on Jack London's life in the far North compared with the stirring evocation of the far North in his Northwest fiction. Such a study has never been made with regard to the images of the far North in Robert Service's poetry and fiction. Yet in his case there is an equally indispensable book titled *The Best of Robert Service* (Running Press, 1990) with a brief Preface by Tam Mossman. It consists of most of Service's finest ballads illustrated with photographs taken around the time and in the places that Service used as settings or background for his narratives. Just as motion pictures can capture beyond a person's lifetime the movements, facial expressions, gestures, and spoken words of actors and actresses, giving them in this sense a practical, albeit incorporeal, immortality which they might never have imagined, so photographs can capture forever images and impressions. It is even possible for us by this means to journey to a remote valley in the Canadian North-West Territories and capture forever the brief blooming of lush moss campion and flowers amid the granite spires of the Logan Mountains that surround these treeless and usually barren meadows.

In *The Spoilers* (Universal, 1942) Marlene Dietrich,

playing saloon-owner Cherry Malotte, passes the second-floor tables in her Nome saloon and pauses briefly at one of them to have a word with a poet sitting there writing. His name is Robert Service. The author, of course, of the novel, *The Spoilers* (Harper, 1905), on which this and several other film versions were based was Rex Beach. He came to be called the "Victor Hugo of the North" for his North-Western novels that were avidly read by many of the same readers who loved Jack London's Northland stories. Beach went to Rampart City in Alaska at the turn of the century, and for three years he worked in various mines before returning to the States. Seeing there was an avid market for fiction set in the North, he sold his first story, "The Thaw at Slisco", to *McClure's Magazine* (11/04) for fifty dollars and followed it with numerous other stories and novels. He was a master at capturing accents, that of the Yukon natives as well as French-Canadians and Russians. In his autobiography, *Personal Exposures* (Harper, 1940), Beach wrote of his own work and a writer's responsibilities that "however fertile may be his inevitable genius, it seems to me that he owes it to his readers to respect the realities of his environment and, if he proposes to make use of facts, he should see that they are accurate. All of which is perhaps another way of saying that I'm a sort of long-hand cameraman."

In terms of the era of the great gold rush, James Oliver Curwood came upon the scene after London, Service, and Beach, but I rather suspect he had more first-hand experience of the terrain than any of them. For two years he was employed by the Canadian government as an explorer and a descriptive writer. It was in this capacity that he lived among the Eskimos as well as traveled thousands of miles by canoe, snowshoes, and pack train through the Hudson's Bay country. His love for the wild Northland and his intimate knowledge of its ways were reflected in the backgrounds and settings for his many novels, the first of which to appear was *The Courage of Captain Plum* (Bobbs-Merrill, 1908). Frequently Curwood's protagonists were red coats in the Royal North-West Mounted Police, heroes who are strong, handsome, and morally above reproach and his heroines beautiful, innocent, and intelligent. His plots seem today to be too often contrived and even sentimental. But it would be wrong to dismiss all of what he wrote as flat or two-dimensional, because amid these romantic and flamboyant characterizations there remain his exuberant descriptions of the land and the elements that still are capable of mesmerizing a reader.

Given such a powerful and provocative impetus, by the 1920s the North-Western story had become a legitimate variety of the Western story, and it was commonplace to find North-Western stories appearing regularly in such magazines as Street & Smith's *Western Story Magazine*, some of the best of them written by Frank Richardson Pierce and Robert Ormond Case. Fiction House, replacing an unsuccessful pulp magazine called *Illustrated Novelets* (there were no illustrations!) but continuing the volume and issue numbers, launched *North-West Stories* with the issue dated May, 1925. About half of the stories in each issue are set in the Northland. Unlike its predecessor, this new magazine proved so popular with readers that by the end of the year it began being issued bi-weekly. Walt Coburn, the cowboy author from Montana who was the headliner in other Fiction House magazines like *Action Stories* and *Lariat Story Magazine*, at the request of Jack Kelly, editor of all the company's magazines, tried his hand at a North-Western story in the third issue, "Superstition House" (7/25). Coburn, however, writing a story about a Mounted Policeman in the Northland was out of his element, and most of his stories in later issues were set in either Montana or the Southwest. More successful, however, were stories by Frederick L. Nebel, A. De Herries Smith, Jack Bechdolt, Dex Volney, and Victor Rousseau.

With Jack Kelly's death in 1932, Fiction House closed down all of its magazines, and publication was resumed very slowly after 1934, one magazine at a time. Shortly after *North-West Stories* came back, beginning with the Fall, 1938 issue, it had a new editor, Malcolm Reiss, and was given a new name: *North-West Romances*. This magazine differed from the former one in more than title. All of the stories in it were set in the Northland. *North-West Romances* was continuously published as a quarterly magazine until the issue dated Winter, 1953, coming near the end of the era of all pulp magazines. Many of the same authors were back as well, Frederick L. Nebel who wrote his best Northland fiction in the late 1930s for *North-West Romances*, Jack Bechdolt, Victor Rousseau, as well as a newcomer, John Starr. When Starr retired from writing fiction to pursue a career as a book editor, Fiction House, which had done so much to showcase his name, bought the rights to use John Starr as a house name. That is how years later, when Dan Cushman would have two stories in one issue, his own name was used as the byline for one of them, John Starr his byline for the other. Les Savage, Jr., who headlined many Fiction House magazines in the 1940s, as did Dan Cushman, also wrote extensively for *North-West Romances* in that decade, along with Tom W. Blackburn, William Heuman, Jim Kjelgaard, Curtis Bishop, and Verne Athanas. Many of their stories can still be read with pleasure. Limitations due to space have confined me to select exemplary stories from this period by Frederick L. Nebel and Dan Cushman. Les Savage, Jr., is not included only because all of his North-Western fiction may be found in the collection, *In the Land of Little Sticks* (Five Star Westerns,

2000). By the late 1940s *North-West Romances* began including reprints of stories by Jack London and ballads by Robert Service in many issues. "The League of the Old Men" by Jack London was reprinted in the issue dated Fall, 1948. In that same issue is also found "The Law of the Yukon" by Robert Service.

The late 1930s may be regarded as a halcyon period for stories of the Northwest in magazines. *Complete Northwest Novel Magazine* was launched in 1935 by the Double-Action pulp group as a bi-monthly. In addition to reprints of short stories by James Oliver Curwood, new novel-length stories were regularly published in its pages by authors like William Byron Mowery, some of which were later published in book form, and reprints of North-Western fiction that had previously appeared only in book form, such as *Royce of the Royal Mounted* (Macaulay, 1932) by Amos Moore, pseudonym for George Hubbard, which appeared in the February, 1937 issue under the title "The Mountie from Texas". Double-Action also launched *Real Northwest Adventures* in late 1935 with reprints of James Oliver Curwood's stories and new Northwest fiction by William Byron Mowery and Frank Richardson Pierce.

James B. Hendryx, although he did travel to the Klondike, did not actually write North-Western fiction until *The Promise: A Tale of the Great Northwest* (Putnam, 1915). For nearly four decades he continued to write Northland stories, many featuring his series characters, Corporal Downey of the Royal North-West Mounted Police and Black John, a miner and trapper in the frontier town of Halfaday Creek. Hendryx's short novels and short stories appeared in magazines like *Short Stories* and were later welded into picaresque novels published by Doubleday, Doran.

However, beyond this necessarily sketchy survey of

North-Western fiction published in the hundred years since the last great gold rush, I should not wish to leave my subject without at least a word about the direction we take in all of the stories in this collection. From the dawn of civilization, human beings have watched the heavens at night and tried to understand the meaning of the universe in terms of the celestial motion of the planets and stars visible to the naked eye. Johannes Kepler, the 16th-Century German astronomer who first formulated laws mathematically for the motions of the planets, created a trigon diagram he called *Schema magnarum Coniunctionum Saturni et Jovis* concerned with the conjunctions of Saturn with Jupiter. His trigonic series illustrated how every 794 1/3 years, or after forty such conjunctions, the triangle had turned through one-third of the ecliptic and thus will appear to be in the same position as at the beginning. However, to move through the entire zodiac, one of the angles of the trigon requires 2,383 years.

Before this alliance of mathematics and astronomy gave mankind the means to chart and codify celestial motion and precession of the equinoxes, human beings had to resort to other ways, of which perhaps the most captivating remains the technical language encoded in mythology. The Greek name for Saturn was Kronos and for Jupiter it was Zeus. Greek legend tells us that there was once a great battle between Kronos and Zeus and that Zeus emerged the victor. By looking into the heavens over a sufficient period of time we can see how in the conjunction of Jupiter with Saturn—Jupiter being larger than Saturn and closer to the Earth—it would appear to the naked eye that Jupiter had engulfed Saturn because, truly, for a time from the Earth's perspective Saturn disappears behind the greater planet.

In the ancient Near East, the Persian Magi saw, in the return of the conjunction of Jupiter with Saturn to Pisces, the

20

dawn of a new age—as the defeat of Kronos by Zeus had once meant the dawn of a new age for the Greeks—and so they set forth, following the "star in the east" to find the new king of the new age. In Christendom that event is still observed annually in what in the northern hemisphere is the cold time following the winter solstice. In Andean myth the god Viracocha "left the earth" in the northwest, and so a new age was ushered in. In fact, all mythologies, no matter their geographical origin, seem to agree that northwest is the direction in which one must travel to have access to the land of the gods. In this collection of stories of the far North it is no coincidence that northwest is, indeed, the direction in which these authors take us. Yet the land of the midnight sun can be more than a locus. It can be a metaphor for an odyssey of the human soul.

An Odyssey of the North
Jack London

Jack London (1876–1916) was born John Griffith Chaney in San Francisco, California. The surname he later adopted was that of his stepfather, John London, a farmer from Pennsylvania, who married Jack's mother, Flora Wellman, the year Jack was born. His stories of the Northwest, beginning with "To the Man on the Trail" in *The Overland Monthly* (1/99), won him immediate popularity with readers and created a wholly different kind of story. By this I do not mean merely the physical setting of his far North fiction, but rather the added dimension to be found in London's finest stories. Earle Labor, one of London's finest critics, put it well in his Introduction to *The Great Short Works of Jack London* (Harper, 1965): "When London writes that 'like giants they toiled, days flashing on the heels of days like dreams as they heaped the treasure up,' he is obviously modulating his imagery in terms of a farther and deeper music than that of the ordinary phenomenal world . . . a world of the *un*conscious (Jung called it the 'collective unconscious'), the primordial world against which modern man has erected inhibiting barriers of rationality and the social ethic but nonetheless a real world to which he would return, in dreams, to find his soul." In London's best stories this deeper music is to be heard as a subtext co-existing with the action embodied in surface events

—what it all *means* to the human soul is a tale he tells simultaneously with what happens in a story. At the same time, London realized that perhaps all we can ever know is only part of a tale and, quite possibly, not the most important part. "An Odyssey of the North" first appeared in *The Atlantic Monthly* (January, 1900). The story was obviously influenced by London's having read Nietzsche, since in it we encounter the "blond beast" and a moral dilemma that is "beyond good and evil".

I

The sleds were singing their eternal lament to the creaking of the harness and the tinkling bells of the leaders, but the men and dogs were tired and made no sound. The trail was heavy with new-fallen snow, and they had come far, and the runners, burdened with flint-like quarters of frozen moose, clung tenaciously to the unpacked surface and held back with a stubbornness almost human. Darkness was coming on, but there was no camp to pitch that night. The snow fell gently through the pulseless air, not in flakes, but in tiny frost crystals of delicate design. It was very warm—barely ten below zero—and the men did not mind. Meyers and Bettles had raised their earflaps, while Malemute Kid had even taken off his mittens.

The dogs had been fagged out early in the afternoon, but they now began to show new vigor. Among the more astute there was a certain restlessness—an impatience at the restraint of the traces, an indecisive quickness of movement, a sniffing of snouts and pricking of ears. These became incensed at their more phlegmatic brothers, urging them on with numerous sly nips on their hinder quarters. Those, thus chidden, also contracted and helped spread the contagion. At last the leader of the foremost sled uttered a sharp whine of satisfaction, crouching lower in the snow and throwing himself against the collar. The rest followed suit. There was an ingathering of back-bands, a tightening of traces; the sleds leaped forward, and the men clung to the gee poles, violently accelerating the uplift of their feet that they might escape going under the runners. The weariness of the day fell from them, and they whooped encouragement to the dogs. The an-

imals responded with joyous yelps. They were swinging
through the gathering darkness at a rattling gallop.

"Gee! Gee!" the men cried, each in turn, as their sleds
abruptly left the main trail, heeling over on single runners like
luggers on the wind.

Then came a hundred yards' dash to the lighted parch-
ment window, which told its own story of the home cabin, the
roaring Yukon stove, and the steaming pots of tea. But the
home cabin had been invaded. Threescore Huskies chorused
defiance, and as many furry forms precipitated themselves
upon the dogs which drew the first sled. The door was flung
open, and a man, clad in the scarlet tunic of the North-West
Police, waded knee-deep among the furious brutes, calmly
and impartially dispensing soothing justice with the butt end
of a dog whip. After that the men shook hands, and in this
wise was Malemute Kid welcomed to his own cabin by a
stranger.

Stanley Prince, who should have welcomed him and who
was responsible for the Yukon stove and hot tea aforemen-
tioned, was busy with his guests. There were a dozen or so of
them, as nondescript a crowd as ever served the Queen in the
enforcement of her laws or the delivery of her mails. They
were of many breeds, but their common life had formed of
them a certain type—a lean and wiry type, with trail-hard-
ened muscles and sun-browned faces and untroubled souls
that gazed frankly forth, clear-eyed and steady. They drove
the dogs of the Queen, wrought fear in the hearts of her enemies, ate of her meager fare, and were happy. They had seen
life and done deeds and lived romances, but they did not
know it.

They were very much at home. Two of them were
sprawled upon Malemute Kid's bunk, singing chansons that
their French forebears sang in the days when first they en-

tered the Northwest land and mated with its Indian women. Bettles's bunk had suffered a similar invasion, and three or four lusty *voyageurs* worked their toes among its blankets as they listened to the tale of one who had served on the boat brigade with Wolseley when he fought his way to Khartoum. When he tired, a cowboy told of courts and kings and lords and ladies he had seen when Buffalo Bill toured the capitals of Europe. In a corner two half-breeds, ancient comrades in a lost campaign, mended harnesses and talked of the days when the Northwest flamed with insurrection and Louis Riel was king.

Rough jests and rougher jokes went up and down, and great hazards by trail and river were spoken of in the light of commonplaces, only to be recalled by virtue of some grain of humor or ludicrous happening. Prince was led away by these uncrowned heroes who had seen history made, who regarded the great and the romantic as but the ordinary and the incidental in the routine of life. He passed his precious tobacco among them with lavish disregard, and rusty chains of reminiscence were loosened, and forgotten odysseys resurrected for his special benefit.

When conversation dropped and the travelers filled the last pipes and lashed their tight-rolled sleeping furs, Prince fell back upon his comrade for further information.

"Well, you know what the cowboy is," Malemute Kid answered, beginning to unlace his moccasins, "and it's not hard to guess the British blood in his bed partner. As for the rest, they're all children of the *coureurs du bois,* mingled with God knows how many other bloods. The two turning in by the door are the regulation 'breeds or *bois brûles*. That lad with the worsted breech scarf . . . notice his eyebrows and the turn of his jaw . . . shows a Scotchman wept in his mother's smoky teepee. And that handsome-looking fellow putting the capote under his head is a French half-breed . . . you heard him talking . . . he doesn't like the two Indians turning in next to him. You see, when the 'breeds rose under Riel, the full-bloods kept the peace, and they've not lost much love for one another since."

"But, I say, what's that glum-looking fellow by the stove? I'll swear he can't talk English. He hasn't opened his mouth all night."

"You're wrong. He knows English well enough. Did you follow his eyes when he listened? I did. But he's neither kith nor kin to the others. When they talked their own patois, you could see he didn't understand. I've been wondering myself what he is. Let's find out. . . . Fire a couple of sticks into the stove!" Malemute Kid commanded, raising his voice and looking squarely at the man in question.

He obeyed at once.

"Had discipline knocked into him somewhere," Prince commented in a low tone.

Malemute Kid nodded, took off his socks, and picked his way among recumbent men to the stove. There he hung his damp footgear among a score or so of mates.

"When do you expect to get to Dawson?" he asked tentatively.

The man studied him a moment before replying. "They say seventy-five mile. So? Maybe two days."

The very slightest accent was perceptible, while there was no awkward hesitancy or groping for words.

"Been in the country before?"

"No."

"North-West Territory?"

"Yes."

"Born there?"

"No."

"Well, where the devil were you born? You're none of these." Malemute Kid swept his hand over the dog drivers, even including the two policemen who had turned into Prince's bunk. "Where did you come from? I've seen faces like yours before, though I can't remember just where."

"I know you," he irrelevantly replied, at once turning the drift of Malemute Kid's questions.

"Where? Ever see me?"

"No . . . your partner, him priest, Pastilik, long time ago. Him ask me if I see you, Malemute Kid. Him give me grub. I no stop long. You hear him speak 'bout me?"

"Oh! You're the fellow that traded the otter skins for the dogs?"

The man nodded, knocked out his pipe, and signified his disinclination for conversation by rolling up in his furs. Malemute Kid blew out the slush lamp and crawled under the blankets with Prince.

"Well, what is he?"

"Don't know . . . turned me off, somehow, and then shut up like a clam. But he's a fellow to whet your curiosity. I've heard of him. All the coast wondered about him eight years ago. Sort of mysterious, you know. He came down out of the North, in the dead of winter, many a thousand miles from here, skirting Bering Sea and traveling as though the devil were after him. No one ever learned where he came from, but he must have come far. He was badly travel-worn when he got food from the Swedish missionary on Golovin Bay and asked the way south. We heard of all this afterward. Then he abandoned the shoreline, heading right across Norton Sound. Terrible weather, snowstorms and high winds, but he pulled through where a thousand other men would have died, missing Saint Michael's and making the land at Pastilik. He'd lost all but two dogs, and was nearly gone with starvation.

"He was so anxious to go on that Father Roubeau fitted him out with grub, but he couldn't let him have any dogs, for he was only waiting my arrival, to go on a trip himself. Mister Ulysses knew too much to start out without animals, and fretted around for several days. He had on his sled a bunch of beautifully cured otter skins . . . sea otters, you know . . . worth their weight in gold. There was also at Pastilik an old Shylock of a Russian trader, who had dogs to kill. Well, they didn't dicker very long, but when the Strange One headed south again, it was in the rear of a spanking dog team. Mister Shylock, by the way, had the otter skins. I saw them, and they were magnificent. We figured it up and found the dogs brought him at least five hundred apiece. And it wasn't as if the Strange One didn't know the value of sea otter. He was an Indian of some sort, and what little he talked showed he'd been among white men.

"After the ice passed out of the sea, word came up from Nunivak Island that he'd gone in there for grub. Then he dropped from sight, and this is the first heard of him in eight years. Now where did he come from? . . . and what was he doing there? . . . and why did he come from there? He's Indian, he's been nobody knows where, and he's had discipline, which is unusual for an Indian. Another mystery of the North for you to solve, Prince."

"Thanks awfully, but I've got too many on hand as it is," he replied.

Malemute Kid was already breathing heavily, but the young mining engineer gazed straight up through the thick darkness, waiting for the strange orgasm which stirred his blood to die away. When he did sleep, his brain worked on, and for the nonce he, too, wandered through the white unknown, struggled with the dogs on endless trails, and saw men live, and toil, and die like men.

★ ★ ★ ★ ★

The next morning, hours before daylight, the dog drivers and policemen pulled out for Dawson. But the powers that saw to Her Majesty's interests and ruled the destinies of her lesser creatures gave the mailmen little rest, for a week later they appeared at Stuart River, heavily burdened with letters for Salt Water. However, their dogs had been replaced by fresh ones; but, then, they were dogs.

The men had expected some sort of a layover in which to rest up; besides, this Klondike was a new section of the Northland, and they had wished to see a little something of the Golden City where dust flowed like water and dance halls rang with never-ending revelry. But they dried their socks and smoked their evening pipes with much the same gusto as on their former visit, though one or two bold spirits speculated on desertion and the possibility of crossing the unexplored Rockies to the east, and thence, by the Mackenzie Valley, of gaining their old stamping grounds in the Chippewyan country. Two or three even decided to return to their homes by that route when their terms of service had expired, and they began to lay plans forthwith, looking forward to the hazardous undertaking in much the same way a city-bred man would to a day's holiday in the woods.

He of the Otter Skins seemed very restless, though he took little interest in the discussion, and at last he drew Malemute Kid to one side and talked for some time in low tones. Prince cast curious eyes in their direction, and the mystery deepened when they put on caps and mittens and went outside. When they returned, Malemute Kid placed his gold scales on the table, weighed out the matter of sixty ounces, and transferred them to the Strange One's sack. Then the chief of the dog drivers joined the conclave, and certain business was transacted with him. The next day the gang went on upriver, but

He of the Otter Skins took several pounds of grub and turned his steps back toward Dawson.

"Didn't know what to make of it," said Malemute Kid in response to Prince's queries, "but the poor beggar wanted to be quit of the service for some reason or other . . . at least it seemed a most important one to him, though he wouldn't let on what. You see, it's just like the army . . . he signed for two years, and the only way to get free was to buy himself out. He couldn't desert and then stay here, and he was just wild to remain in the country. Made up his mind when he got to Dawson, he said, but no one knew him, hadn't a cent, and I was the only one he'd spoken two words with. So he talked it over with the lieutenant-governor, and made arrangements in case he could get the money from me . . . loan, you know. Said he'd pay back in the year, and, if I wanted, would put me onto something rich. Never'd seen it, but he knew it was rich.

"And talk! why, when he got me outside he was ready to weep. Begged and pleaded, got down in the snow to me till I hauled him out of it. Palavered around like a crazy man. Swore he's worked to this very end for years and years, and couldn't bear to be disappointed now. Asked him what end, but he wouldn't say. Said they might keep him on the other half of the trail and he wouldn't get to Dawson in two years, and then it would be too late. Never saw a man take on so in my life. And when I said I'd let him have it, had to yank him out of the snow again. Told him to consider it in the light of a grubstake. Think he'd have it! No, sir! Swore he'd give me all he found, make me rich beyond the dreams of avarice, and all such stuff. Now a man who puts his life and time against a grubstake ordinarily finds it hard enough to turn over half of what he finds. Something behind all this, Prince, just you make a note of it. We'll hear of him if he stays in the country. . . ."

"And if he doesn't?"

"Then my good nature gets a shock, and I'm sixty some odd ounces out."

The cold weather had come on with the long nights, and the sun had begun to play his ancient game of peek-a-boo along the southern snow line ere aught was heard of Malemute Kid's grubstake. And then, one bleak morning in early January, a heavily laden dog train pulled into his cabin below Stuart River. He of the Otter Skins was there, and with him walked a man such as the gods have almost forgotten how to fashion. Men never talked of luck and pluck and five-hundred-dollar dirt without bringing in the name of Axel Gunderson, nor could tales of nerve or strength or daring pass up and down the campfire without the summoning of his presence. When the conversation flagged, it blazed anew at mention of the woman who shared his fortunes.

As has been noted, in the making of Axel Gunderson the gods had remembered their old-time cunning and cast him after the manner of men who were born when the world was young. Full seven feet he towered in his picturesque costume that marked a king of El Dorado. His chest, neck, and limbs were those of a giant. To bear his three hundred pounds of bone and muscle, his snowshoes were greater by a generous yard than those of other men. Rough-hewn, with rugged brow and massive jaw and unflinching eyes of palest blue, his face told the tale of one who knew but the law of might. Of the yellow of ripe corn silk, his frost-incrusted hair swept like day across the night and fell far down his coat of bearskin. A vague tradition of the sea seemed to cling about him as he swung down the narrow trail in advance of the dogs, and he brought the butt of his dog whip against Malemute Kid's door as a Norse sea rover, on southern foray, might thunder for admittance at the castle gate.

Prince bared his womanly arms and kneaded sourdough bread, casting as he did so many a glance at the three guests—three guests the like of which might never come under a man's roof in a lifetime. The Strange One, who Malemute Kid had surnamed Ulysses, still fascinated him, but his interest chiefly gravitated between Axel Gunderson and Axel Gunderson's wife. She felt the day's journey, for she had softened in comfortable cabins during the many days since her husband mastered the wealth of frozen pay streaks, and she was tired. She rested against his great breast like a slender flower against a wall, replying lazily to Malemute Kid's good-natured banter, and stirring Prince's blood strangely with an occasional sweep of her deep, dark eyes. For Prince was a man, and healthy, and had seen few women in many months. She was older than he, and an Indian besides, but she was different from all native wives he had met. She had traveled—had been in his country among others, he gathered from the conversation, and she knew most of the things the women of his own race knew, and much more that it was not in the nature of things for them to know. She could make a meal of sun-dried fish or a bed in the snow, yet she teased them with tantalizing details of many-course dinners, and caused strange internal dissensions to arise at the mention of various quondam dishes which they had well-nigh forgotten. She knew the ways of the moose, the bear, and the little blue fox, and of the wild amphibians of the Northern seas. She was skilled in the lore of the woods, and the streams, and the tale writ by man and bird and beast upon the delicate snow crust was to her an open book, yet Prince caught the appreciative twinkle in her eye as she read the Rules of the Camp. These rules had been fathered by the Unquenchable Bettles at a time when his blood ran high and were remarkable for the terse simplicity of their humor. Prince always turned them to the wall before the arrival of ladies, but who could suspect that this native wife—well, it was too late now.

This, then, was the wife of Axel Gunderson, a woman whose name and fame had traveled with her husband's, hand-in-hand, through all the Northland. At table, Malemute Kid baited her with the assurance of an old friend, and Prince shook off the shyness of first acquaintance and joined in. But she held her own in the unequal contest, while her husband, slower in wit, ventured naught but applause. He was very proud of her; his every look and action revealed the magnitude of the place she occupied in his life. He of the Otter Skins ate in silence, forgotten in the merry battle, and long ere the others were done he pushed back from the table and went out among the dogs. Yet all too soon his fellow travelers drew on their mittens and parkas and followed him.

There had been no snow for many days, and the sleds slipped along the hard-packed Yukon trail as easily as if it had been glare ice. Ulysses led the first sled; with the second came Prince and Axel Gunderson's wife, while Malemute Kid and the yellow-haired giant brought up the third.

"It's only a hunch, Kid," he said, "but I think it's straight. He's never been there, but he tells a good story, and shows a map I heard of when I was in the Kootenay country years ago. I'd like to have you go along, but he's a strange one and swore pointblank to throw it up if anyone was brought in. But when I come back, you'll get first tip, and I'll stake you next to me, and give you a half share in the town site besides.

"No! no!" he cried, as the other strove to interrupt. "I'm running this, and before I'm done it'll need two heads. If it's all right, why, it'll be a second Cripple Creek, man, do you hear? . . . a second Cripple Creek! It's quartz, you know, not placer, and, if we work it right, we'll corral the whole thing . . . millions upon millions. I've heard of the place before, and so have you. We'll build a town . . . thousands of workmen . . . good waterways . . . steamship lines . . . big carrying trade . . . light-draft steamers for headreaches . . . survey a railroad, perhaps . . . sawmills . . . electric light plant . . . do your own banking . . . commercial company . . . syndicate. . . . Say! . . . just you hold your hush till I get back!"

The sleds came to a halt where the trail crossed the mouth of Stuart River. An unbroken sea of frost, its wide expanse stretched away into the unknown east. The snowshoes were withdrawn from the lashings of the sleds. Axel Gunderson shook hands and stepped to the fore, his great webbed shoes sinking a fair half yard into the feathery surface and packing the snow so the dogs would not wallow. His wife fell in behind the last sled, betraying long practice in the art of handling the awkward footgear. The stillness was broken with cheery farewells; the dogs whined, and He of the Otter Skins talked with his whip to a recalcitrant wheeler.

An hour later the train had taken on the likeness of a black pencil crawling in a long straight line across a mighty sheet of foolscap.

II

One night, many weeks later, Malemute Kid and Prince fell to solving chess problems from the torn page of an ancient magazine. The Kid had just returned from his Bonanza properties and was resting up preparatory to a long moose hunt. Prince, too, had been on creek and trail nearly all winter, and had grown hungry for a blissful week of cabin life.

"Interpose the black knight, and force the king. No, that won't do. See, the next move. . . ."

"Why advance the pawn two squares? Bound to take it in transit, and with the bishop out of the way. . . ."

"But, hold on! That leaves a hole, and. . . ."

"No, it's protected. Go ahead! You'll see it works."

It was very interesting. Somebody knocked at the door a second time before Malemute Kid said: "Come in." The door swung open. Something staggered in. Prince caught one square look and sprang to his feet. The horror in his eyes caused Malemute Kid to whirl about, and he, too, was startled, although he had seen bad things before. The thing tottered blindly toward them. Prince edged away till he reached the nail from which hung his Smith & Wesson.

"My God, what is it?" he whispered to Malemute Kid.

"Don't know. Looks like a case of freezing and no grub," replied the Kid, sliding away in the opposite direction. "Watch out! It may be mad," he warned, coming back from closing the door.

The thing advanced to the table. The bright flame of the slush lamp caught its eye. It was amused, and gave voice to eldritch cackles that betokened mirth. Then, suddenly, he—for

37

it was a man—swayed back, with a hitch to his skin trousers, and began to sing a chantey, such as men lift when they swing around the capstan circle and the sea snorts in their ears:

Yan-kee ship come down de ri-ib-er
Pull! my bully boys! Pull!
D'yeh want . . . to know de captain ru-uns her?
Pull! my bully boys Pull!!
Jon-a-than Jones ob South Caho-li-in-a,
Pull! my bully. . . .

He broke off abruptly, tottered with a wolfish snarl to the meat shelf, and before they could intercept was tearing with his teeth at a chunk of raw bacon. The struggle was fierce between him and Malemute Kid, but his mad strength left him as suddenly as it had come, and he weakly surrendered the spoil. Between them they got him upon a stool, where he sprawled with half his body across the table. A small dose of whiskey strengthened him, so that he could dip a spoon into the sugar caddy that Malemute Kid placed before him. After his appetite had been somewhat cloyed, Prince, shuddering as he did so, passed him a mug of weak beef tea.

The creature's eyes were alight with a somber frenzy, which blazed and waned with every mouthful. There was very little skin to the face. The face, for that matter, sunken and emaciated, bore little likeness to human countenance. Frost after frost had bitten deeply, each depositing its stratum of scab upon the half-healed scar that went before. This dry, hard surface was of a bloody-black color, serrated by grievous cracks wherein the raw red flesh peeped forth. His skin garments were dirty and in tatters, and the fur of one side was singed and burned away, showing where he had lain upon his fire.

Malemute Kid pointed to where the sun-tanned hide had been cut away, strip by strip—the grim signatures of famine.

"Who . . . are . . . you?" slowly and distinctly enunciated the Kid.

The man paid no heed.

"Where do you come from?"

"Yan-kee ship come down de ri-ib-er," was the quavering response.

"Don't doubt the beggar came down the river," the Kid said, shaking him in an endeavor to start a more lucid flow of talk.

But the man shrieked at the contact, clapping a hand to his side in evident pain. He rose slowly to his feet, half leaning on the table.

"She laughed at me . . . so . . . with the hate in her eye, and she . . . would . . . not . . . come."

His voice died away, and he was sinking back when Malemute Kid gripped him by the wrist and shouted: "Who? Who would not come?"

"She, Unga. She laughed, and struck at me, so, and so. And then. . . ."

"Yes?"

"And then. . . ."

"And then what?"

"And then he lay very still in the snow a long time. He is . . . still in . . . the . . . snow."

The two men looked at each other helplessly.

"Who is in the snow?"

"She, Unga. She looked at me with the hate in her eye, and then. . . ."

"Yes, yes."

"And then she took the knife, so . . . and once, twice . . . she was weak. I traveled very slow. And there is much gold in that place, very much gold."

"Where is Unga?" For all Malemute Kid knew, she might be dying a mile away. He shook the man savagely, repeating again and again: "Where is Unga? Who is Unga?"

"She . . . is . . . in . . . the . . . snow."

"Go on!" The Kid was pressing his wrist cruelly.

"So . . . I . . . would . . . be . . . in . . . the . . . snow . . . but I had a debt to pay. It . . . was . . . heavy . . . I . . . had . . . a . . . debt . . . to . . . pay. I had. . . ." The faltering monosyllables ceased as he fumbled in his pouch and drew forth a buckskin sack. "A . . . debt . . . to . . . pay . . . five . . . pounds . . . of . . . gold . . . grub . . . stake . . . Malemute Kid . . . I. . . ." The exhausted head dropped upon the table, nor could Malemute Kid rouse it again.

"It's Ulysses'," he said quietly, tossing the bag of dust on the table. "Guess it's all day with Axel Gunderson and the woman. Come on, let's get him between the blankets. He's Indian. He'll pull through and tell a tale besides."

As they cut his garments from him, near his right breast could be seen two unhealed, hard-lipped knife thrusts.

III

"I will talk of the things which were, in my own way, but you will understand. I will begin at the beginning, and tell of myself and the woman, and, after that, of the man."

He of the Otter Skins drew over to the stove as do men who have been deprived of fire and are afraid the Promethean gift may vanish at any moment. Malemute Kid picked up the slush lamp and placed it so its light might fall upon the face of the narrator. Prince slid his body over the edge of the bunk and joined them.

"I am Naass, a chief, and the son of a chief, born between a sunset and a rising, on the dark seas, in my father's oomiak. All of a night the men toiled at the paddles, and the women cast out the waves that threw in upon us, and we fought with the storm. The salt spray froze upon my mother's breast till her breath passed with the passing of the tide. But I . . . I raised my voice with the wind and the storm, and lived. We dwelt in Akatan. . . ."

"Where?" asked Malemute Kid.

"Akatan, which is in the Aleutians, Akatan, beyond Chignik, beyond Kardalak, beyond Unimak. As I say, we dwelt in Akatan, which lies in the midst of the sea on the edge of the world. We farmed the salt seas for the fish, the seal, and the otter, and our homes shouldered about one another on the rocky strip between the rim of the forest and the yellow beach where our kayaks lay. We were not many, and the world was very small. There were strange lands to the east . . . islands like Akatan, so we thought all the world was islands and did not mind.

"I was different from my people. In the sands of the beach were the crooked timbers and wave-warped planks of a boat such as my people built, and I remember on the point of the island which overlooked the ocean three ways there stood a pine tree which never grew there, smooth and straight and tall. It is said the two men came to that spot, turn about, through many days, and watched with the passing of the light. These two men came from out of the sea in a boat that lay in pieces on the beach. And they were white like you, and weak as the little children when the seal have gone away and the hunters come home empty. I know of these things from the old men and the old women, who got them from their fathers and mothers before them. These strange white men did not take kindly to our ways at first, but they grew strong, what of the fish and the oil, and fierce. And they built them each his own house, and took the pick of our women, and in time children came. Thus he was born who was to become the father of my father's father.

"As I said, I was different from my people, for I carried the strong, strange blood of this white man who came out of the sea. It is said we had other laws in the days before these men, but they were fierce and quarrelsome, and fought with our men till there were no more left who dared to fight. Then they made themselves chiefs, and took away our old laws, and gave us new ones, insomuch that the man was the son of his father, and not his mother, as our way had been. They also ruled that the man, first-born, should have all things which were his father's before him, and that the brothers and sisters should shift for themselves. And they gave us other laws. They showed us new ways in the catching of fish and the killing of bear that were thick in the woods, and they taught us to lay by bigger stores for the time of famine. And these things were good.

"But when they had become chiefs, and there were no more men to face their anger, they fought, these strange white men, each with the other. And the one whose blood I carry drove his seal spear the length of an arm through the other's body. Their children took up the fight, and their children's children, and there was great hatred between them, and black doings, even to my time, so that in each family but one lived to pass down the blood of them that went before. Of my blood I was alone. Of the other man's there was but a girl. Unga, who lived with her mother. Her father and my father did not come back from the fishing one night, but afterward they washed up on the beach on the big tides, and they held very close to each other.

"The people wondered, because of the hatred between the houses, and the old men shook their heads and said the fight would go on when children were born to her and children to me. They told me this as a boy, till I came to believe, and to look upon Unga as a foe, who was to be the mother of children that were to fight with mine. I thought of these things day by day, and, when I grew to a stripling, I came to ask why this should be so. And they answered . . . 'We do not know, but that in such way your fathers did.' And I marveled that those who were to come should fight the battles of those that were gone, and in it I could see no right. But the people said it must be, and I was only a stripling.

"And they said I must hurry, that my blood might be the older and grow strong before hers. This was easy, for I was head man, and the people looked up to me because of the deeds and the laws of my fathers, and the wealth which was mine. Any maiden would come to me, but I found none to my liking. And the old men and the mothers of maidens told me to hurry, for even then were the hunters bidding high to the mother of Unga and should her children grow strong before

43

mine, mine would surely die.

"Nor did I find a maiden till one night coming back from the fishing. The sunlight was lying so, low and full in the eyes, the wind free, and the kayaks racing with the white seas. Of a sudden the kayak of Unga came driving past me, and she looked upon me, so, with her black hair flying like a cloud of night and the spray wet on her cheek. As I say, the sunlight was full in the eyes, and I was a stripling, but somehow it was all clear, and I knew it to be the call of kind to kind. As she whipped ahead, she looked back within the space of two strokes . . . looked as only the woman Unga could look . . . and again I knew it as the call of kind. The people shouted as we ripped past the lazy oomiaks and left them far behind. But she was quick at the paddle, and my heart was like the belly of a sail, and I did not gain. The wind freshened, the sea whitened, and, leaping like the seals on the windward breech, we roared down the golden pathway of the sun."

Naass was crouched half out of his stool, in the attitude of one driving a paddle, as he ran the race anew. Somewhere across the stove he beheld the tossing kayak and the flying hair of Unga. The voice of the wind was in his ears, and its salt beat freshly upon his nostrils.

"But she made the shore, and ran up the sand, laughing, to the house of her mother. And a great thought came to me that night . . . a thought worthy of him that was chief over all the people of Akatan. So, when the moon was up, I went down to the house of her mother, and looked upon the goods of Yash-Noosh, which were piled by the door . . . the goods of Yash-Noosh, a strong hunter who had it in mind to be the father of the children of Unga. Other young men had piled their goods there and taken them away again, and each young man had made a pile greater than the one before.

"And I laughed to the moon and the stars, and went to my

own house where my wealth was stored. And many trips I made, till my pile was greater by the fingers of one hand than the pile of Yash-Noosh. There were fish, dried in the sun and smoked, and forty hides of the hair seal, and half as many of the fur, and each hide was tied at the mouth and big-bellied with oil, and ten skins of bear which I killed in the woods when they came out in the spring. And there were beads and blankets and scarlet cloths, such as I got in trade from the people who lived to the east, and who got them in trade from the people who lived still beyond in the east. And I looked upon the pile of Yash-Noosh and laughed, for I was head man in Akatan, and my wealth was greater than the wealth of all my young men, and my fathers had done deeds, and given laws, and put their names for all time in the mouths of the people.

"So, when the morning came, I went down to the beach, casting out of the corner of my eye at the house of the mother of Unga. My offer yet stood untouched. And the women smiled, and said sly things, one to the other. I wondered, for never had such a price been offered, and that night I added more to the pile, and put beside it a kayak of well-tanned skins which never yet had swam in the sea. But in the day it was yet there, open to the laughter of all men. The mother of Unga was crafty, and I grew angry at the shame in which I stood before my people. So that night I added till it became a great pile, and I hauled up my oomiak, which was of the value of twenty kayaks. And in the morning there was no pile.

"Then made I preparation for the wedding, and the people that lived even to the east came for the food of the feast and the potlatch token. Unga was older than I by the age of four suns in the way we reckoned the years. I was only a stripling, but then I was a chief, and the son of a chief, and it did not matter.

"But a ship shoved her sails above the floor of the ocean, and grew larger with the breath of the wind. From her scuppers she ran clear water, and the men were in haste and worked hard at the pumps. On the bow stood a mighty man, watching the depth of the water and giving commands with a voice of thunder. His eyes were of the pale blue of the deep waters, and his head was maned like that of a sea lion. And his hair was yellow, like the straw of a southern harvest or the manila rope yarns which sailormen plait.

"Of late years we had seen ships from afar, but this was the first to come to the beach of Akatan. The feast was broken, and the women and children fled to the houses, while we men strung our bows and waited with spears in hand. But when the ship's forefoot smelled the beach, the strange men took no notice of us, being busy with their own work. With the falling of the tide they careened the schooner and patched a great hole in her bottom. So the women crept back, and the feast went on.

"When the tide rose, the sea wanderers kedged the schooner to deep water and then came among us. They bore presents and were friendly, so I made room for them, and out of the largeness of my heart gave them tokens such as I gave all the guests, for it was my wedding day, and I was head man in Akatan. And he with the mane of the sea lion was there, so tall and strong that one looked to see the earth shake with the fall of his feet. He looked much and straight at Unga, with his arms folded, so, and stayed till the sun went away and the stars came out. Then he went down to his ship. After that I took Unga by the hand and led her to my own house. And there was singing and great laughter, and the women said sly things, after the manner of women at such times. But we did not care. Then the people left us alone and went home.

"The last noise had not died away when the chief of the sea

wanderers came in by the door. And he had with him black bottles, from which we drank and made merry. You see, I was only a stripling, and had lived all my days on the edge of the world. So my blood became as fire, and my heart as light as the froth that flies from the surf to the cliff. Unga sat silent among the skins in the corner, her eyes wide, for she seemed to fear. And he with the mane of the sea lion looked upon her straight and long. Then his men came in with bundles of goods, and he piled before me wealth such as was not in all Akatan. There were guns, both large and small, and powder and shot and shell, and bright axes and knives of steel, and cunning tools, and strange things the like of which I had never seen. When he showed me by sign that it was all mine, I thought him a great man to be so free, but he showed me, also, that Unga was to go away with him in his ship. Do you understand? . . . that Unga was to go away with him in his ship. The blood of my fathers flamed hot on the sudden, and I made to drive him through with my spear. But the spirit of the bottles had stolen the life from my arm, and took me by the neck, so, and knocked my head against the wall of the house. And I was made weak like a newborn child, and my legs would no more stand under me. Unga screamed, and she laid hold of the things of the house with her hands, till they fell all about us as he dragged her to the door. Then he took her in his great arms and, when she tore at his yellow hair, laughed with a sound like that of the big bull seal in the rut.

"I crawled to the beach and called upon my people, but they were afraid. Only Yash-Noosh was a man, and they struck him on the head with an oar, till he lay with his face in the sand and did not move. And they raised the sails to the sound of their songs, and the ship went away on the wind.

"The people said it was good, for there would be no more war of the bloods in Akatan, but I never said a word, waiting till the time of the full moon, when I put fish and oil in my kayak and went away to the east. I saw many islands and many people, and I, who had lived on the edge, saw that the world was very large. I talked by signs, but they had not seen a schooner or a man with the mane of a sea lion, and they pointed always to the east. And I slept in queer places, and ate odd things, and met strange faces. Many laughed, for they thought me light of head, but sometimes old men turned my face to the light and blessed me, and the eyes of the young women grew soft as they asked me of the strange ship, and Unga, and the men of the sea.

"And in this manner, through rough seas and great storms, I came to Unalaska. There were two schooners there, but neither was the one I sought. So I passed on to the east, with the world growing ever larger, and in the island of Unamok there was no word of the ship, nor in Kodiak, or in Atognak. And so I came one day to a rocky land, where men dug great holes in the mountain. And there was a schooner, but not my schooner, and men loaded upon it the rocks that they dug. This I thought childish, for all the world was made of rocks, but they gave me food and set me to work. When the schooner was deep in the water, the captain gave me money and told me to go, but I asked which way he went, and he pointed south. I made signs that I would go with him, and he laughed at first, but then, being short of men, took me to help work the ship. So I came to talk after their manner, and to heave on ropes, and to reef the stiff sails in sudden squalls, and to take my turn at the wheel. But it was not strange, for the blood of my fathers was the blood of the men of the sea.

"I had thought it an easy task to find him I sought, once I got among his own people, and, when we raised the land one day and passed between a gateway of the sea to a port, I looked for perhaps as many schooners as there were fingers to my hands. But the ships lay against the wharves for miles, packed like so many little fish, and, when I went among them to ask for a man with the mane of a sea lion, they laughed and answered me in the tongues of many peoples. And I found that they hailed from the uttermost parts of the earth.

"And I went into the city to look upon the face of every man. But they were like the cod when they run thick on the banks, and I could not count them. And the noise smote upon me till I could not hear, and my head was dizzy with much movement. So I went on and on, through the lands which sang in the warm sunshine where the harvests lay rich on the plains, and where great cities were fat with men that lived like women, with false words in their mouths and their hearts black with the lust of gold. And all the while my people of Akatan hunted and fished, and were happy in the thought that the world was small.

"But the look in the eyes of Unga coming home from the fishing was with me always, and I knew I would find her when the time was met. She walked down quiet lanes in the dusk of the evening, or led me chases across the thick fields wet with the morning dew, and there was a promise in her eyes such as only the woman Unga could give.

"So I wandered through a thousand cities. Some were gentle and gave me food, and others laughed, and still others cursed, but I kept my tongue between my teeth and went strange ways and saw strange sights. Sometimes I, who was a chief and the son of a chief, toiled for men . . . men rough of speech and hard as iron, who wrung gold from the sweat and sorrow of their fellow men. Yet no word did I get out of my quest till I came back to the sea like a homing seal to the rookeries. But this was at another port, in another country that lay to the north. And there I heard dim tales of the yellow-haired sea wanderer, and I learned that he was a hunter of seals, and

49

that even then he was abroad on the ocean.

"So I shipped on a seal schooner with the lazy Siwashes, and followed his trackless trail to the north where the hunt was then warm. And we were away weary months, and spoke with many of the fleet, and heard much of the wild doings of him I sought, but never once did we raise him above the sea. We went north, even to the Pribilofs, and killed the seals in herds on the beach, and brought their warm bodies aboard till our scuppers ran grease and blood and no man could stand upon the deck. Then were we chased by a ship of slow steam that fired upon us with great guns. But we put on sail till the sea was over our decks and washed them clean, and lost ourselves in a fog.

"It is said, at this time, while we fled with fear at our hearts, that the yellow-haired sea wanderer put in to the Pribilofs, right to the factory, and, while the part of his men held the servants of the company, the rest loaded ten thousand green skins from the salt houses. I say it is said, but I believe, for in the voyages I made on the coast with never a meeting the northern seas rang with his wildness and daring, till the three nations that have lands there sought him with their ships. And I heard of Unga, for the captains sang loud in her praise, and she was always with him. She had learned the ways of his people, they said, and was happy. But I knew better . . . knew that her heart harked back to her own people by the yellow beach of Akatan.

"So, after a long time, I went back to the port which is by a gateway of the sea, and there I learned that he had gone across the girth of the great ocean to hunt for the seal to the east of the warm land which runs south from the Russian seas. And I, who was become a sailorman, shipped with men of his own race, and went after him in the hunt of the seal. And there were few ships off that new land, but we hung on the flank of the seal pack and harried it north through all the spring of the year. And when the cows were heavy with pup and crossed the Russian line, our men grumbled and were afraid. For there was much fog, and every day men were lost in the boats. They would not work, so the captain turned the ship back toward the way it came. But I knew the yellow-haired sea wanderer was unafraid and would hang by the pack, even to the Russian Isles, where few men go. So I took a boat, in the black of night, when the look-out dozed on the fo'c'slehead, and went alone to the warm, long land. And I journeyed south to meet the men by Yeddo Bay, who are wild and unafraid. And the Yoshiwara girls were small, and bright like steel, and good to look upon, but I could not stop, for I knew that Unga rolled on the tossing floor by the rookeries of the north.

"The men by Yeddo Bay had met from the ends of the earth, and had neither gods nor homes, sailing under the flag of the Japanese. And with them I went to the rich beaches of Copper Island, where our salt piles became high with skins. And in that silent sea we saw no man till we were ready to come away. Then one day the fog lifted on the edge of a heavy wind, and there jammed down upon us a schooner, with close in her wake the cloudy funnels of a Russian man-of-war. We fled away on the beam of the wind, with the schooner jamming still closer and plunging ahead three feet to our two. And upon her poop was the man with the mane of the sea lion, pressing the rails under with the canvas and laughing in his strength of life. And Unga was there . . . I knew her on the moment . . . but he sent her below when the cannons began to talk across the sea. As I say, with three feet to our two, till we saw the rudder lift green at every jump . . . and I swinging on to the wheel and cursing, with my back to the Russian shot. For we knew he had it in mind to run before us, that he might get away while we were caught. And they knocked our masts out of us till we dragged into the wind like a wounded gull, but he went on over the edge of the skyline . . . he and Unga.

"What could we? The fresh hides spoke for themselves. So they took us to a Russian port, and after that to a lone country, where they set us to work in the mines to dig salt. And some died, and . . . and some did not die."

Naass swept the blanket from his shoulders, disclosing the gnarled and twisted flesh, marked with the unmistakable striations of the knout. Prince hastily covered him, for it was not nice to look upon.

"We were there a weary time and sometimes men got away to the south, but they always came back. So, when we who hailed from Yeddo Bay rose in the night and took the guns from the guards, we went to the north. And the land was very large, with plains, soggy with water, and great forests. And the cold came, with much snow on the ground, and no man knew the way. Weary months we journeyed through the endless forest . . . I do not remember, now, for there was little food and often we lay down to die. But at last we came to the cold sea, and but three were left to look upon it. One had shipped from Yeddo as captain and he knew in his head the lay of the great lands, and of the place where men may cross from one to the other on the ice. And he led us . . . I do not know . . . it was so long . . . till there were but two. When we came to that place, we found five of the strange people that live in that country, and they had dogs and skins, and we were very poor. We fought in the snow until they died, and the captain died, and the dogs and the skins were mine. Then I crossed on the ice, which was broken, and once I drifted till a gale from the west put me upon the shore. And after that, Golovin Bay, Pastilik, and the priest. Then south, south, to the warm sun lands where first I wandered.

"But the sea was no longer fruitful, and those who went upon it after the seal went to little profit and great risk. The fleets scattered, and the captains and the men had no word of those I sought. So I turned away from the ocean that never rests, and went among the lands, where the trees, the houses, and the mountains sit always in one place and do not move. I journeyed far, and came to learn many things, even to the way of reading and writing from books. It was well that I should do this, for it came upon me that Unga must know these things, and that someday, when the time was met . . . we . . . you understand, when the time was met?

"So I drifted, like those little fish which raise a sail to the wind but cannot steer. But my eyes and my ears were open always, and I went among men who traveled much, for I knew they had but to see those I sought to remember. At last there came a man, fresh from the mountains, with pieces of rock in which the free gold stood to the size of peas, and he had heard, he had met, he knew them. They were rich, he said, and lived in the place where they drew the gold from the ground.

"It was in a wild country, and very far away, but in time I came to the camp, hidden between the mountains, where men worked night and day, out of the sight of the sun. Yet the time was not come. I listened to the talk of the people. He had gone away . . . they had gone away . . . to England, it was said, in the matter of bringing men with much money together to form companies. I saw the house they had lived in, more like a palace, such as one sees in the old countries. In the nighttime I crept in through a window that I might see in what manner he treated her. I went from room to room and in such way thought kings and queens must live, it was all so very good. And they all said he treated her like a queen, and many marveled as to what breed of woman she was for there was other blood in her veins, and she was different from the women of Akatan, and no one knew her for what she was. Aye, she was a queen, but I was a chief, and the son of a chief, and I had paid for her an untold price of skin and boat and bead.

"But why so many words? I was a sailorman, and knew the way of the ships on the seas. I followed to England, and then to other countries. Sometimes I heard of them by word of mouth, sometimes I read of them in the papers, yet never once could I come by them, for they had much money, and traveled fast, while I was a poor man. Then came trouble upon them, and their wealth slipped away one day like a curl of smoke. The papers were full of it at the time, but after that nothing was said, and I knew they had gone back where more gold could be got from the ground.

"They had dropped out of the world, being now poor, and so I wandered from camp to camp, even north to the Kootenay country, where I picked up the cold scent. They had come and gone, some said this way and some that, and still others that they had gone to the country of the Yukon. And I went this way, and I went that, ever journeying from place to place, till it seemed I must grow weary of the world that was so large. But in the Kootenay I traveled a bad trail, and a long trail, with a 'breed of the Northwest, who saw fit to die when the famine pinched. He had been to the Yukon by an unknown way over the mountains and, when he knew his time was near, gave me the map and the secret of the place where he swore by his gods there was much gold.

"After that all the world began to flock into the North. I was a poor man. I sold myself to be a driver of dogs. The rest you know. I met him and her in Dawson. She did not know me, for I was only a stripling, and her life had been large, so she had no time to remember the one who had paid for her an untold price.

"So? You bought me from my term of service. I went back to bring things about in my own way, for I had waited long, and now that I had my hand upon him was in no hurry. As I say, I had it in mind to do my own way, for I read back in my life, through all I had seen and suffered, and remembered the cold and hunger of the endless forest by the Russian seas. As you know, I led him into the east . . . him and Unga . . . into the east where many have gone and few returned. I led them to the spot where the bones and the curses of men lie with the gold that they may not have.

"The way was long and the trail unpacked. Our dogs were many and ate much, nor could our sleds carry till the break of spring. We must come back before the river ran free. So here and there we cached grub, that our sleds might be lightened and there be no chance of famine on the back trip. At the McQuestion there were three men, and near them we built a cache, as also did we at the Mayo, where was a hunting camp of a dozen Pellys that had crossed the divide from the south. After that, as we went on into the east, we saw no men, only the sleeping river, the moveless forest, and the White Silence of the North. As I say, the way was long and the trail unpacked. Sometimes, in a day's toil, we made no more than eight miles, or ten, and at night we slept like dead men. And never once did they dream that I was Naass, head man of Akatan, the righter of wrongs.

"We now made smaller caches, and in the nighttime it was a small matter to go back on the trail we had broken and change them in such way that one might deem the wolverines the thieves. Again there be places where there is a fall to the river, and the water is unruly, and the ice makes above and is eaten away beneath. In such a spot the sled I drove broke through, and the dogs, and to him and Unga it was ill luck, but no more. And there was much grub on that sled, and the dogs the strongest. But he laughed, for he was strong of life, and gave the dogs that were left little grub till we cut them from the harnesses one by one and fed them to their mates. We would go home light, he said, traveling and eating from cache to cache, with neither dogs nor sleds, which was true, for our grub was very short, and the last dog died in the traces the night we came to the gold and the bones and the curses of men.

"To reach that place . . . and the map spoke true . . . in the heart of the great mountains, we cut ice steps against the wall of a divide. One looked for a valley beyond, but there was no valley, the snow spread away, level as the great harvest plains, and here and there about us mighty mountains shoved their white heads among the stars. And midway on that strange plain that should have been a valley, the earth and the snow fell away, straight down toward the heart of the world. Had we not been sailormen our heads would have swung 'round with the sight, but we stood on the dizzy edge that we might see a way to get down. And on one side, and one side only, the wall had fallen away till it was like the slope of the decks in a topsail breeze. I do not know why this thing should be so, but it was so. 'It is the mouth of hell,' he said. 'Let us go down.' And we went down.

"And on the bottom there was a cabin, built by some man, of logs which he had cast down from above. It was a very old cabin, for men had died there alone at different times, and on pieces of birch bark that were there we read their last words and their curses. One had died of scurvy, another's partner had robbed him of his last grub and powder and stolen away, a third had been mauled by a bald-face grizzly, a fourth had hunted for game and starved . . . and so it went, and they had been loath to leave the gold, and had died side-by-side of it in one way or another. And the worthless gold they had gathered yellowed the floor of the cabin like in a dream.

"But his soul was steady, and his head clear, this man I had led thus far. 'We have nothing to eat,' he said, 'and we will only look upon this gold, and see whence it comes and how much there be. Then we will go away quick, before it gets into our eyes and steals away our judgment. And in this way we may return in the end, with more grub, and possess it all.' So we looked upon the great vein, which cut the wall of the pit as a true vein should, and we measured it, and traced it from above and below, and drove the stakes of the claims and blazed the trees in token of our rights. Then, our knees shaking with lack of food, and a sickness in our bellies, and our hearts chugging close to our mouths, we climbed the mighty wall for the last time and turned our faces to the back trip.

"The last stretch we dragged Unga between us, and we fell often, but in the end we made the cache. And, lo, there was no grub. It was well done, for he thought it the wolverines, and damned them and his gods in one breath. But Unga was brave, and smiled, and put her hand in his, till I turned away that I might hold myself. 'We will rest by the fire,' she said, 'till morning, and we will gather strength from our moccasins.' So we cut the tops of our moccasins in strips, and boiled them half of the night, that we might chew them and swallow them. And in the morning we talked of our chance. The next cache was five days' journey. We could not make it. We must find game.

" 'We will go forth and hunt,' he said.

" 'Yes,' said I, 'we will go forth and hunt.'

"And he ruled that Unga stay by the fire and save her strength. And we went forth, he in quest of the moose and I to the cache I had changed. But I ate little, so they might not see in me much strength. And in the night he fell many times as

57

he drew into camp. And I, too, made to suffer great weakness, stumbling over my snowshoes as though each step might be my last. And we gathered strength from our moccasins.

"He was a great man. His soul lifted his body to the last, nor did he cry aloud, save for the sake of Unga. On the second day I followed him, that I might not miss the end. And he lay down to rest often. That night he was near gone, but in the morning he swore weakly and went forth again. He was like a drunken man, and I looked many times for him to give up, but his was the strength of the strong, and his soul the soul of a giant, for he lifted his body through all the weary day. And he shot two ptarmigan, but would not eat them. He needed no fire. They meant life, but his thought was for Unga, and he turned toward camp. He no longer walked, but crawled on hand and knee through the snow. I came to him, and read death in his eyes. Even then it was not too late to eat the ptarmigan. He cast away his rifle and carried the birds in his mouth like a dog. I walked by his side, upright. And he looked at me during the moments he rested, and wondered that I was so strong. I could see it, though he no longer spoke, and, when his lips moved, they moved without sound. As I say, he was a great man, and my heart spoke for softness, but I read back in my life, and remembered the cold and hunger of the endless forest by the Russian seas. Besides, Unga was mine, and I had paid for her an untold price of skin and boat and bead.

"And in this manner we came through the white forest, with the silence heavy upon us like a damp sea mist. And the ghosts of the past were in the air and all about us, and I saw the yellow beach of Akatan, and the kayaks racing home from the fishing, and the houses on the rim of the forest. And the men who had made themselves chiefs were there, the law-givers whose blood I bore and whose blood I had wedded in

58

Unga. Aye, and Yash-Noosh walked with me, the wet sand in his hair, and his war spear, broken as he fell upon it, still in his hand. And I knew the time was met, and saw in the eyes of Unga the promise.

"As I say, we came thus through the forest, till the smell of the camp smoke was in our nostrils. And I bent above him, and tore the ptarmigan from his teeth. He turned on his side and rested, the wonder mounting in his eyes, and the hand that was under slipping slow toward the knife at his hip. But I took it from him, smiling close in his face. Even then he did not understand. So I made to drink from black bottles, and to build high upon the snow a pile of goods, and to live again the things that had happened on the night of my marriage. I spoke no word, but he understood. Yet was he unafraid. There was a sneer on his lips, and cold anger, and he gathered new strength slow. Once he lay so long I turned him over and gazed into his eyes. And sometimes he looked forth, and sometimes death. And when I loosed him, he struggled on again. In this way we came to the fire. Unga was at his side on the instant. His lips moved without sound, then he pointed at me, that Unga might understand. And after that he lay in the snow, very still, for a long while. Even now is he there in the snow.

"I said no word till I had cooked the ptarmigan. Then I spoke to her, in her own tongue, which she had not heard in many years. She straightened herself, so, and her eyes were wonder-wide, and she asked who I was, and where I had learned that speech.

" 'I am Naass,' I said.

" 'You?' she said. 'You?' And she crept close that she might look upon me.

" 'Yes,' I answered, 'I am Naass, head man of Akatan, the last of the blood, as you are the last of the blood.'

"And she laughed. By all the things I have seen and the deeds I have done may I never hear such a laugh again. It put the chill to my soul, sitting there in the White Silence, alone with death and this woman who laughed.

" 'Come!' I said, for I thought she wandered. 'Eat of the food and let us be gone. It is a far fetch from here to Akatan.'

"But she shoved her face in his yellow mane, and laughed till it seemed the heavens must fall about our ears. I had thought she would be overjoyed at the sight of me, and eager to go back to the memory of old times, but this seemed a strange form to take.

" 'Come!' I cried, taking her strong by the hand. 'The way is long and dark. Let us hurry!'

" 'Where?' she asked, sitting up, and ceasing from her strange mirth.

" 'To Akatan,' I answered, intent on the light to grow on her face at the thought. But it became like his, with a sneer to the lips, and cold anger.

" 'Yes,' she said, 'we will go, hand-in-hand, to Akatan, you and I. And we will live in the dirty huts, and eat of the fish and oil, and bring forth a spawn . . . a spawn to be proud of all the days of our life. We will forget the world and be happy, very happy. It is good, most good. Come! Let us hurry. Let us go back to Akatan.'

"And she ran her hand through his yellow hair, and smiled in a way which was not good. And there was no promise in her eyes.

"I sat silent, and marveled at the strangeness of woman. I went back to the night when he dragged her from me and she screamed and tore at his hair . . . at his hair that now she played with and would not leave. Then I remembered the price and the long years of waiting, and I gripped her close, and dragged her away as he had done. And she held back, even as on that night, and fought like a she-cat for its whelp. And when the fire was between us and the man, I loosed her, and she sat and listened. And I told her of all that lay between, of all that had happened to me on strange seas, of all that I had done in strange lands, of my weary quest, and the hungry years, and the promise which had been mine from the first. Aye, I told all, even to what had passed that day between the man and me, and in the days yet young. And as I spoke, I saw the promise grow in her eyes, full and large like the break of dawn. And I read pity there, the tenderness of woman, the love, the heart and the soul of Unga. And I was a stripling again, for the look was the look of Unga as she ran up the beach, laughing, to the home of her mother. The stern unrest was gone, and the hunger, and the weary waiting. The time was met. I felt the call of her breast, and it seemed there I must pillow my head and forget. She opened her arms to me, and I came against her. Then, sudden, the hate flamed in her eye, her hand was at my hip. And once, twice, she passed the knife.

" 'Dog!' she sneered, as she flung me into the snow. 'Swine!' And then she laughed till the silence cracked, and went back to her dead.

"As I say, once she passed the knife, and twice, but she was weak with hunger, and it was not meant that I should die. Yet was I minded to stay in that place, and to close my eyes in the last long sleep with those whose lives had crossed with mine and led my feet on unknown trails. But there lay a debt upon me that would not let me rest.

"And the way was long, the cold bitter, and there was little grub. The Pellys had found no moose, and had robbed my cache. And so had the three white men, but they lay thin and dead in their cabins as I passed. After that I do not remember, till I came here, and found food and fire . . . much fire."

As he finished, he crouched closely, even jealously, over the stove. For a long while the slush lamp shadows played tragedies upon the wall.

"But Unga!" cried Prince, the vision still strong upon him.

"Unga? She would not eat of the ptarmigan. She lay with her arms about his neck, her face deep in his yellow hair. I drew the fire close, that she might not feel the frost, but she crept to the other side. And I built a fire there, yet it was little good, for she would not eat. And in this manner they still lie up there in the snow."

"And you?" asked Malemute Kid.

"I do not know, but Akatan is small, and I have little wish to go back and live on the edge of the world. Yet is there small use in life. I can go to Constantine, and he will put irons upon me, and one day they will tie a piece of rope, so, and I will sleep good. Yet . . . no, I do not know."

"But, Kid," protested Prince, "this is murder!"

"Hush!" commanded Malemute Kid. "There be things greater than our wisdom, beyond our justice. The right and the wrong of this we cannot say, and it is not for us to judge."

Naass drew yet closer to the fire. There was a great silence, and in each man's eyes many pictures came and went.

The Call of the Wild
Robert Service

Robert (William) Service (1874–1958) was born in Preston, a city about twenty-five miles from Liverpool, but like his narrator in the novel, *The Trail of '98* (Dodd, Mead, 1910), he spent his boyhood in Glasgow. He emigrated to the Pacific Northwest and eventually came to work as a bank teller in Dawson. Only in two collections of ballads and *The Trail of '98* did Service attempt to capture the Klondike and the Yukon in the days of the great gold rush. During the Great War, he became a foreign correspondent for the Toronto *Star* and was sent to the Balkans. Later, in part because he had long been an admirer of the life and fiction of Robert Louis Stevenson, he wandered to the South Seas, and finally he came to reside in France where he lived until his death. There is a Gothic romance at the center of *The Trail of '98* that might not appeal to a modern reader, but its images of the gold rush, of the people and places, remain imperishable. Much of his poetry has never been out of print. Like Coleridge, Service in his ballads favored internal rhymes, and, since meter is essential to meaning in his poetry, the verses that follow break only according to their meter, as the poet intended —a concern not always shown by his various publishers. "The Call of the Wild" first appeared in *The Spell of the Yukon and Other Verses* (Edward Stern, 1907).

Robert Service

Have you gazed on naked grandeur
where there's nothing else to gaze on,
Set pieces and drop-curtain scenes galore,
Big mountains heaved to heaven,
which the blinding sunsets blazon,
Black cañons where the rapids rip and roar?
Have you swept the visioned valley
with the green stream streaking through it,
Searched the Vastness for a something you have lost?
Have you strung your soul to silence?
Then for God's sake go and do it;
Hear the challenge, learn the lesson, pay the cost.

Have you wandered in the wilderness,
the sagebrush desolation,
The bunch-grass levels where the cattle graze?
Have you whistled bits of ragtime
at the end of all creation,
And learned to know the desert's little ways?
Have you camped upon the foothills,
have you galloped o'er the ranges,
Have you roamed the arid sun-lands through and through?
Have you chummed up with the mesa?
Do you know its moods and changes?
Then listen to the Wild—it's calling you.

Have you known the Great White Silence,
not a snow-gemmed twig aquiver?
(Eternal truths that shame our soothing lies.)
Have you broken trail on snowshoes,
mushed your Huskies up the river,
Dared the unknown, led the way, and clutched the prize?
Have you marked the map's void spaces,

mingled with the mongrel races,
Felt the savage strength of brute in every thew?
And though grim as hell the worst is,
can you round it off with curses?
Then hearken to the Wild—it's wanting you.

Have you suffered, starved, and triumphed,
groveled down, yet grasped at glory,
Grown bigger in the bigness of the whole?
"Done things" just for the doing,
letting babblers tell the story,
Seeing through the nice veneer the naked soul?
Have you seen God in His splendors,
heard the text that nature renders—
(You'll never hear it in the family pew.)
The simple things, the true things,
the silent men who do things?
Then listen to the Wild—it's calling you.

They have cradled you in custom,
they have primed you with their preaching,
They have soaked you in convention through and through;
They have put you in a showcase;
you're a credit to their teaching.
But can't you hear the Wild?—it's calling you.

Let us probe the silent places,
let us seek what luck betides us.
Let us journey to a lonely land I know.
There's a whisper on the night wind,
there's a star agleam to guide us,
And the Wild is calling, calling . . . let us go.

North of Fifty-Three
Rex Beach

Rex Beach (1877–1949) was born in Atwood, Michigan, but at an early age was taken to Florida by his parents where they became "squatters" under the Homestead Act on a deserted military base near Tampa. Before venturing to Alaska, Beach attended the Kent College of Law in Chicago. *The Spoilers* was published in 1905 and became a best seller. This novel, *The Barrier* (Harper, 1908), and *The Silver Horde* (Harper, 1909)—all set in Alaska—comprise his best work and may still be read with enjoyment to this day. He was the first American author to include a clause in all his book contracts reserving film rights, and his aptitude for business was in turn reflected by the success he later enjoyed as a film producer. The last two years of his life were fraught with suffering from inoperable cancer of the throat and increasing blindness. He shot himself on December 7, 1949. "North of 'Fifty-Three" was first published in *McClure's Magazine* (May, 1904). It was subsequently collected in book form by the author in *Pardners* (McClure, 1905).

Big George was drinking, and the activities of the little Arctic mining camp were paralyzed. Events invariably ceased their progress and marked time when George became excessive, and now nothing of public consequence stirred except the quicksilver, which was retiring fearfully into its bulb at the song of the wind that came racing over the lonesome, bitter, northward waste of tundra.

He held the center of the floor at the Northern Club and proclaimed his modest virtues in a voice as pleasant as the cough of a bull walrus.

"Yes, me! Little Georgie! I did it. I've licked 'em all from Herschel Island to Dutch Harbor, big 'uns and little 'uns. When they didn't suit, I made 'em over. I'm the boss carpenter of the Arctic and I own this camp, don't I, Slim? Hey? Answer me!" he roared at the emaciated bearer of the title, whose attention seemed wandering from the inventory of George's startling traits toward a card game.

"Sure ye do." Slim nervously smiled, frightened out of a heart solo as he returned to his surroundings.

"Well, then, listen to what I'm saying. I'm the big chief of the village, and, when I'm stimulated and happy, them fellers I don't like hides out and lets me and Nature operate things. Ain't that right?" He glared inquiringly at his friends.

Red, the proprietor, explained over the bar in a whisper to Captain, the new man from Dawson: "That's Big George, the whaler. He's a squawman and sort of a bully . . . see? When he's sober, he's on the level strictly, an' we all likes him fine, but when he gets to fightin' the pain-killer, he ain't altogether a gentleman. Will he fight? Oh! Will he fight? Say! He's there, with chimes, he is! Why, Doc Miller's made a grubstake rebuildin' fellers that's had a lingerin' doubt cached away about that, an' now, when he gets the booze up his nose, them patched-up guys oozes away an' hibernates till the gas dies out in him. Afterwards, he's sore on himself an' apologizes to everybody. Don't get into no trouble with him, 'cause he's two checks past the limit. They don't make 'em as bad as him any more. He busted the mold."

George turned and, spying the newcomer, approached, eyeing him with critical disfavor.

Captain saw a bear-like figure, clad *cap-â-pie* in native fashion. Reindeer pants, with the hair inside, clothed legs like rock pillars, while out of the loose squirrel parka a corded neck rose, brown and strong, above which darkly gleamed a rugged face seamed and scarred by the hate of Arctic winters. He had kicked off his deerskin socks and stood barefooted on the cold and drafty floor, while the poison he had imbibed showed only in his heated face. Silently he extended a cracked and hardened hand, which closed like the armored claw of a crustacean and tightened on the crunching fingers of the other. Captain's expression remained unchanged and, gradually slackening his grip, the sailor roughly inquired: "Where'd you come from?"

"Just got in from Dawson yesterday," politely responded the stranger.

"Well! What're you goin' to do now you're here?" he demanded.

"Stake some claims and go to prospecting, I guess. You see, I wanted to get in early before the rush next spring."

"Oh! I s'pose you're going to jump some of our ground, hey? Well, you ain't! We don't want no claim jumpers here," disagreeably continued the seaman. "We won't stand for it.

70

This is my camp . . . see? I own it, and these is my little children." Then, as the other refused to debate with him, he resumed, groping for a new ground of attack.

"Say! I'll bet you're one of them eddicated dudes, too, ain't you? You talk like a feller that had been to college," and, as the other assented, he scornfully called to his friends, saying: "Look here, fellers! Pipe the jellyfish! I never see one of these here animals that was worth a cuss. They plays football an' smokes cigarettes at school, then, when they're weaned, they come off up here an' jump our claims 'cause we can't write a location notice proper. They ain't no good. I guess I'll stop it."

Captain moved toward the door, but the whaler threw his bulky frame against it and scowlingly blocked the way.

"No, you don't. You ain't goin' to run away till I've had the next dance, Mister Eddication! *Humph!* I ain't begun to tell ye yet what a useless little barnacle you are."

Red interfered, saying: "Look 'ere, George, this guy ain't no playmate of yourn. We'll all have a jolt of this disturbance promoter, an' call it off." Then, as the others approached, he winked at Captain and jerked his head slightly toward the door.

The latter, heeding the signal, started out, but George leaped after him and, seizing an arm, whirled him back, roaring: "Well, of all the cussed impudence I ever see! You're too high-toned to drink with us, are you? You don't get out of here now till you take a lickin' like a man."

He reached over his head and, grasping the hood of his fur shirt, with one movement he stripped it from him, exposing a massive naked body whose muscles swelled and knotted beneath a skin as clear as a maiden's, while a map of angry scars strayed across the heavy chest.

As the shirt sailed through the air, Red lightly vaulted to

the bar and, diving at George's naked middle, tackled beauti-fully, crying to Captain: "Get out quick! We'll hold him."

Others rushed forward and grasped the bulky sailor, but Captain's voice replied: "I sort of like this place, and I guess I'll stay a while. Turn him loose."

"Why, man, he'll kill ye," excitedly cried Slim. "Get out!"

The captive hurled his peacemakers from him and, shaking off the clinging arms, drove furiously at the insolent stranger. In the cramped limits of the corner where he stood, Captain was unable to avoid the big man, who swept him with a crash against the plank door at his back, grasping hungrily at his throat. As his shoulders struck, however, he dropped to his knees and, before the raging George could seize him, he avoided a blow which would have strained the rivets of a strength-tester and ducked under the other's arms, leaping to the cleared center of the floor.

Seldom had the big man's rush been avoided, and, whirling, he swung a boom-like arm at the agile stranger. Before it landed, Captain stepped in to meet his adversary and, with the weight of his body behind the blow, drove a clenched and bony fist crashing into the other's face. The big head with its blazing shock of hair snapped backward and the whaler drooped to his knees at the other's feet.

The drunken flush of victory swept over Captain as he stood above the swaying figure, then, suddenly, he felt the great bare arms close about his waist with a painful grip. He struck at the bleeding face below him and wrenched at the circling hands that wheezed the breath from his lungs, but the whaler squeezed him, writhing, across the floor and in a shiver of broken glass fell crashing against the bar and to the floor.

As the struggling men writhed upon the planks, the door opened at the hurried entrance of an excited group, which paused at the sight of the ruin, then, rushing forward, tore the men apart. The panting berserker strained at the arms about his glistening body, while Captain, with sobbing sighs, relieved his aching lungs and watched his enemy, who frothed at the interference.

"It was George's fault," explained Slim to the questions of the arrivals. "This feller tried to make a getaway, but George had to have his amusement."

A newcomer addressed the squawman in a voice as cold as the wind. "Cut this out, George! This is a friend of mine. You're making this camp a reg'lar hell for strangers, and now I'm goin' to tap your little snap. Cool off . . . see?"

Jones's reputation as a bad gunman went hand in hand with his name as a good gambler, and his scanty remarks invariably evoked attentive answers, so George explained: "I don't like him, Jones, and I was jus' makin' him over to look like a man. I'll do it yet, too," he flashed wrathfully at his quiet antagonist.

" 'Pears to me like he's took a hand in the remodeling himself," replied the gambler, "but if you're lookin' for something to do, here's your chance. Windy Jim just drove in and says Barton and Kid Sullivan are adrift on the ice."

"What's that?" questioned eager voices, and, forgetting the recent trouble at the news, the crowd pressed forward anxiously.

"They was crossin' the bay and got carried out by the off-shore gale," explained Jones. "Windy was follerin' 'em when the ice ahead parted and begun movin' out. He tried to yell to 'em, but they was too far away to hear in the storm. He managed to get back to land and followed the shore ice around. He's over at Hunter's cabin now, 'most dead, face and hands froze pretty bad."

A torrent of questions followed and many suggestions as to the fate of the men.

"They'll freeze before they can get ashore," said one.

"The ice pack'll break up in this wind," added another, "and, if they don't drown, they'll freeze before the floe comes in close enough for them to land."

From the first announcement of his friends' peril, Captain had been thinking rapidly. His body, sore from his long trip and aching from the hug of his recent encounter, cried woefully for rest, but his voice rose calm and clear: "We've got to get them off," he said. "Who will go with me? Three is enough."

The clamoring voices ceased, and the men wheeled at the sound, gazing incredulously at the speaker. "What! In this storm?" "You're crazy," many voices said.

He gazed appealingly at the faces before him. Brave and adventurous men he knew them to be, jesting with death, and tempered to perils in this land where hardship rises with the dawn, but they shook their ragged heads hopelessly.

"We *must* save them!" resumed Captain hotly. "Barton and I played as children together, and, if there's not a man among you who's got the nerve to follow me . . . I'll go alone, by heavens!"

In the silence of the room, he pulled the cap about his ears and, tying it snugly under his chin, drew on his huge fur mittens, then with a scornful laugh he turned toward the door.

He paused as his eye caught the swollen face of Big George. Blood had stiffened in the heavy creases of his face like rusted stringers in a ledge, while his mashed and discolored lips protruded thickly. His hair gleamed red, and the sweat had dried upon his naked shoulders, streaked with dirt and flecked with spots of blood, yet the battered features shone with the unconquered, fearless light of a rough, strong man.

Captain strode to him with outstretched hand. "You're a

man," he said. "You've got the nerve, George, and you'll go with me, won't you?"

"What! Me?" questioned the sailor vaguely. His wondering glance left Captain and drifted round the circle of shamed and silent faces—then he straightened stiffly and cried: "Will I go with you? Certainly! I'll go to hell with you."

Ready hands harnessed the dogs, dragged from protected nooks where they sought cover from the storm that moaned and whistled through the low houses. Endless ragged folds of sleet whirled out of the north, then writhed and twisted past, vanishing into the gray veil that shrouded the landscape in a twilight gloom.

The fierce wind sank the cold into the aching flesh like a knife and stiffened the face to a whitening mask, while a fusillade of frozen ice particles beat against the eyeballs with blinding fury.

As Captain emerged from his cabin, furred and hooded, he found a long train of crouching, whining animals harnessed and waiting, while muffled figures stocked the sled with robes and food and stimulants.

Big George approached through the whirling white, a great squat figure with fluttering squirrel tails blowing from his parka, and at his heels there trailed a figure, skin-clad and dainty.

"It's my wife," he explained briefly to Captain. "She won't let me go alone."

They gravely bade farewell to all, and the little crowd cheered lustily against the whine of the blizzard as, with cracking whip and hoarse shouts, they were wrapped in the closely winding sheet of snow.

Arctic storms have an even sameness: the intense cold, the heartless wind which augments tenfold the chill of the temperature, the air thick and dark with stinging flakes rushing by in an endless cloud. A drifting, freezing, shifting eternity of snow, driven by a ravening gale that sweeps the desolate, bald wastes of the Northland.

The little party toiled through the smother till they reached the igloos under the breast of the tall, coast bluffs, where coughing Eskimos drilled patiently at ivory tusks and gambled the furs from their backs at stud-horse poker.

To George's inquiries they answered that their largest canoe was the three-holed bidarka on the cache outside. Owing to the small circular openings in its deck, this was capable of holding but three passengers, and Captain said: "We'll have to make two trips, George."

"Two trips, eh?" answered the other. "We'll be doin' well if we last through one, I'm thinking."

Lashing the unwieldy burden upon the sled, they fought their way along the coast again till George declared they were opposite the point where their friends went adrift. They slid their light craft through the ragged wall of ice hummocks guarding the shore pack and dimly saw, in the gray beyond them, a stretch of angry waters mottled by drifting cakes and floes.

George spoke earnestly to his wife, instructing her to keep the team in constant motion up and down the coast a rifle shot in either direction, and to listen for a signal of the return. Then he picked her up as he would a babe, and she kissed his storm-beaten face.

"She's been a good squaw to me," he said, as they pushed their dancing craft out into the breath of the gale, "and I've always done the square thing by her. I s'pose she'll go back to her people now, though."

The wind hurried them out from land, while it drove the sea water in freezing spray over their backs and changed their fur garments into scaly armor, as they worked through the ice cakes, peering with strained eyes for a sign of their friends.

The sailor, with deft strokes, steered them between the grinding bergs, raising his voice in long signals like the weird cry of a siren. Twisting back and forth through the floes, they held to their quest, now floating with the wind, now paddling desperately in a race with some drifting mass which dimly towered above them and splintered hungrily against its neighbor close in their wake.

Captain emptied his six-shooter till his numbed fingers grew rigid as the trigger, and always at his back swelled the deep shouts of the sailor, who, with practiced eye and mighty strokes, forced their way through the closing lanes between the jaws of the ice pack.

At last, beaten and tossed, they rested, disheartened and hopeless. Then, as they drifted, a sound struggled to them against the wind—a faint cry, illusive and fleeting as a dream voice—and, still doubting, they heard it again.

"Thank God! We'll save 'em yet," cried Captain, and they drove the canoe boiling toward the sound.

Barton and Sullivan had fought the cold and wind stoutly hour after hour, till they found their great floe was breaking up in the heaving waters. Then the horror of it had struck Kid, till he raved and cursed up and down their little island, as it dwindled gradually to a small acre. He had finally yielded to the weight of the cold that crushed resistance out of him and settled, despairing and listless, upon the ice. Barton dragged him to his feet and forced him around their rocking prison, begging him to brace up, to fight it out like a man, till the other insisted on resting, and dropped to his seat again.

The older man struck deliberately at the whitening face of his freezing companion, who recognized the well-meant insult and refused to be roused into activity. Then to their ears had come the faint cries of George, and, in answer to their screams, through the gloom they beheld a long, covered, skin canoe and the anxious faces of their friends.

Captain rose from his cramped seat, and, ripping his crackling garments from the boat where they had frozen, he wriggled out of the hole in the deck and grasped the weeping Barton.

"Come, come, old boy! It's all right now," he said.

"Oh, Charlie, Charlie!" cried the other. "I might have known you'd try to save us. You're just in time, though, for Kid's about all in."

Sullivan apathetically nodded and sat down again.

"Hurry up there. This ain't no G.A.R. encampment, and you ain't got no time to spare," said George, who had dragged the canoe out and, with a paddle, broke the sheets of ice that covered it. "It'll be too dark to see anything in half an hour."

The night, hastened by the storm, was closing rapidly, and they realized another need of haste, for, even as they spoke, a crack had crawled through the ice floe where they stood and, widening as it went, left but a heaving cake supporting them.

George spoke quietly to Captain, while Barton strove to animate Kid. "You and Barton must take him aside and hurry him down to the village. He's 'most gone now."

"But you?" questioned the other. "We'll have to come back for you, as soon as we put him ashore."

"Never mind me," roughly interrupted George. "It's too late to get back here. When you get ashore, it'll be dark. Besides, Sullivan's freezing, and you'll have to rush him through quick. I'll stay here."

"No! No! George!" cried Captain, as the meaning of it bore in upon him. "I got you into this thing, and it's my place to stay here. You must go. . . ."

But the big man had hurried to Sullivan and, seizing him in his great hands, shook the drowsy one like a rat, cursing and beating a goodly share of warmth back into him. Then he dragged the listless burden to the canoe and forced him to a seat in the middle opening.

"Come, come," he cried to the others, "you can't spend all night here! If you want to save Kid, you've got to hurry. You take the front seat there, Barton," and, as he did so, George turned to the protesting Captain: "Shut up, curse you, and get in!"

"I won't do it," rebelled the other. "I can't let you lay down your life in this way, when I made you come."

George thrust a cold face within an inch of the other's and grimly said: "If they hadn't stopped me, I'd've beat you into dog meat this morning, and, if you don't quit this sniveling, I'll do it yet. Now get in there and paddle to beat hell or you'll never make it back. Quick!"

"I'll come back for you then, George, if I live to the shore!" Captain cried, while the other slid the burdened canoe into the icy waters.

As they drove the boat into the storm, Captain realized the difficulty of working their way against the gale. On him fell the added burden of holding their course into the wind and avoiding the churning ice cakes. The spray whipped into his face like shot and froze as it clung to his features. He strained at his paddle till the sweat soaked out of him and the cold air filled his aching lungs.

Unceasingly the merciless frost cut his face like a keen blade, till he felt the numb paralysis that told him his features were hardening under the touch of the cold. An arm's length ahead the shoulders of Kid protruded from the deck hole where he had sunk again into the death sleep, while Barton, in the forward seat, leaned wearily on his ice-clogged paddle, moaning as he strove to shelter his face from the sting of the blizzard.

An endless time they battled with the storm, slowly gaining, foot by foot, till in the darkness ahead they saw the wall of shore ice and swung into its partial shelter.

Dragging the now unconscious Sullivan from the boat, Captain rolled and threshed him, while Barton, too weak and exhausted to assist, feebly strove to warm his stiffened limbs.

In answer to their signals, the team appeared, maddened by the lash of the squaw. Then they wrapped Sullivan in warm robes and forced scorching brandy down his throat, till he coughed weakly and begged them to let him rest.

"You must hurry him to the Indian village," directed Captain. "He'll only lose some fingers and toes now, maybe, but you've got to hurry!"

"Aren't you coming, too?" queried Barton. "We'll hire some Eskimos to go after George. I'll pay 'em anything."

"No, I'm going back to him now. He'd freeze before we could send help, and, besides, they wouldn't come out in the storm and the dark."

"But you can't work that big canoe alone. If you get out there and don't find him, you'll never get back. Charlie! Let me go, too," he said, then apologized. "I'm afraid I won't last, though. I'm too weak."

The squaw, who had not questioned the absence of her lord, now touched Captain's arm. "Come," she said, "I will go with you." Then addressing Barton: "You quick go Indian house. White man die, mebbe. Quick! I go Big George."

"Ah, Charlie, I'm afraid you'll never make it!" cried Barton, and, wringing his friend's hand, he staggered into the darkness behind the sled wherein lay the fur-bundled Sullivan.

Captain felt a horror of the starving waters rise up in him and a panic shook him fiercely, till he saw the silent squaw waiting for him at the ice edge. He shivered as the wind searched through his dampened parka and hardened the wet clothing next to his body, but he took his place and dug the paddle fiercely into the water, till the waves licked the hair of his gauntlets.

The memory of that scudding trip through the darkness was always cloudy and visioned. Periods of keen alertness alternated with moments when his weariness bore upon him till he stiffly bent to his work, wondering what it all meant.

It was the woman's sharpened ear which caught the first answering cry, and her hands which steered the intricate course to the heaving berg where the sailor crouched, for, at their approach, Captain had yielded to the drowse of weariness and, in his relief at the finding, the blade floated from his listless hands.

He dreamed quaint dreams, broken by the chilling lash of spray from the strokes of the others, as they drove the craft back against the wind, and he only partly awoke from his lethargy when George wrenched him from his seat and forced him down the rough trail toward warmth and safety.

Soon, however, the stagnant blood tingled through his veins, and under the shelter of the bluffs they reached the village, where they found the anxious men waiting.

Skilful natives had worked the frost from Sullivan's members, and the stimulants in the sled had put new life into Barton as well. So, as the three crawled wearily through the dog-filled tunnel of the igloo, they were met by two wet-eyed and thankful men, who silently wrung their hands or uttered broken words.

When they had been despoiled of their frozen furs, and the welcome heat of whiskey and fire had met in their blood, Captain approached the whaler, who rested beside his mate.

"George, you're the bravest man I ever knew, and your woman is worthy of you," he said. He continued slowly: "I'm sorry about the fight this morning, too."

The big man rose and, crushing the extended palm in his grasp, said: "We'll just let that go double, partner. You're as game as I ever see." Then he added: "It *was* too bad them fellers interfered jest when they did . . . but we can finish it up whenever you say," and as the other, smiling, shook his head, he continued: "Well, I'm glad of it, 'cause you'd sure beat me the next time."

The Match
James Oliver Curwood

James Oliver Curwood (1879–1927) was born in Owosso,
Michigan. He was expelled from school at sixteen, although
later he would attend the University of Michigan, 1898–1900.
He was first employed as a reporter for the *Detroit News-Tribune*,
and, before he resigned to work for the Canadian government,
he became the managing editor. His novel, *Kazan* (Cosmopolitan Book Corporation, 1914), is probably his best-known work
because of the number of motion pictures based on this canine
character. In fact, even more than for Rex Beach, it was motion-
picture adaptations that brought Curwood his greatest success
and, in time, they exceeded even the number of books he published in his lifetime. In all justice to Curwood, although he was
credited and paid for the stories, the screen adaptations often
have nothing more to do with his fiction than that they are set in
the Canadian Northwest and have Royal North-West Mounted
Policemen as protagonists. Curwood died at a relatively early
age, and his popularity with readers did not extend far beyond
the 1930s when stories reprinted in pulp magazines and in
economy hard-cover editions kept his name alive. Judith A.
Eldridge has provided a biography of the man and his work in
God's Country and the Man (Bowling Green Popular Press,
1993). Jack London was the author Curwood most sought to

emulate—sometimes he would labor all day to write twelve lines that were acceptable to himself. "The Match" first appeared in *Collier's* (January 18, 1913).

Sergeant Brokaw was hatchet-faced, with shifting pale blue eyes that had a glint of cruelty in them. He was tall, and thin, and lithe as a cat. He belonged to the Royal North-West Mounted Police and was one of the best men on the trail that had ever gone into the North. His business was manhunting. Ten years of seeking after human prey had given to him many of the characteristics of a fox. For six of those ten years he had represented law north of fifty-three. Now he had come to the end of his last hunt, close up to the Arctic Circle. For one hundred and eighty-seven days he had been following a man. The hunt had begun in midsummer, and it was now midwinter. Billy Loring, who was wanted for murder, had been a hard man to find. But he was caught at last, and Brokaw was keenly exultant. It was his greatest achievement. It would mean a great deal for him down at headquarters.

In the rough and dimly lighted cabin his man sat opposite him, on a bench, his manacled hands crossed over his knees. He was a younger man than Brokaw—thirty, or a little better. His hair was long, reddish, and untrimmed. A stubble of reddish beard covered his face. His eyes, too, were blue—of the deep, honest blue that one remembers and most frequently trusts. He did not look like a criminal. There was something almost boyish in his face, a little hollowed by long privation. He was the sort of man that other men liked. Even Brokaw, who had a heart like flint in the face of crime, had melted a little.

"*Ugh!*" he shivered. "Listen to that heady wind! It means three days of storm." Outside a gale was blowing straight

85

down from the Arctic. They could hear the steady moaning of it in the spruce tops over the cabin, and now and then there came one of those raging blasts that filled the night with strange, shrieking sounds. Volleys of fine, hard snow beat against the one window with a rattle like gunshots. In the cabin it was comfortable. It was Billy's cabin. He had built it, deep in a swamp, where there were lynx and fisher cat to trap, and where he had thought that no one could find him. The sheet-iron stove was glowing hot. An oil lamp hung from the ceiling. Billy was sitting so that the glow of this fell on his face. It scintillated on the rings of steel about his wrists. Brokaw was a cautious man, as well as a clever one, and he took no chances.

"I like storms . . . when you're inside, an' close to a stove," replied Billy. "Makes me feel sort of . . . safe." He smiled a little grimly. Even at that it was not an unpleasant smile.

Brokaw's snow-reddened eyes gazed at the other. "There's something in that," he said. "This storm will give you at least three more days of life."

"Won't you drop that?" asked the prisoner, turning his face a little, so that it was shaded from the light. "You've got me now, an' I know what's coming as well as you do." His voice was low and quiet with the faintest trace of a broken note in it, deep down in his throat. "We're alone, old man, and a long way from anyone. I ain't blaming you for catching me. I haven't got anything against you. So let's drop this other thing . . . what I'm going down to . . . and talk of something pleasant. I know I'm going to hang. That's the law. It'll be pleasant enough when it comes, don't you think? Let's talk about . . . about . . . home. Got any kids?"

Brokaw shook his head, and took his pipe from his mouth. "Never married," he said shortly.

"Never married," mused Billy, regarding him with a curious softening of his blue eyes. "You don't know what you've missed, Brokaw. Of course, it's none of my business, but you've got a home . . . somewhere. . . ."

Brokaw shook his head again. "Been in the service ten years," he said. "I've got a mother living with my brother somewhere down in New York state. I've sort of lost track of them. Haven't seen 'em for five years."

Billy was looking at him steadily. Slowly he rose to his feet, lifted his manacled hands, and turned down the light. "Hurts my eyes," he said, and he laughed frankly as he caught the suspicious glint in Brokaw's eyes. He seated himself again, and leaned over toward the other. "I haven't talked to a white man for three months," he added, a little hesitatingly. "I've been hiding . . . close. I had a dog for a time, but he died, an' I didn't dare go hunting for another. I knew you fellows were pretty close after me. But I wanted to get enough fur to take me to South America. Had it all planned, an' *she* was going to join me there . . . with the kid. Understand? If you'd kept away another month. . . ." There was a husky break in his voice, and he coughed to clear it. "You don't mind if I talk, do you . . . about her, an' the kid? I've got to do it, or bust, or go mad. I've got to because . . . today . . . she was twenty-four . . . at ten o'clock in the morning . . . an' it's our wedding day. . . ."

The half gloom hid from Brokaw what was in the other's face, and then Billy laughed almost joyously. "Say, but she's been a true little pardner," he whispered proudly, as there came a lull in the storm. "She was just born for me, an' everything seemed to happen on her birthday, an' that's why I can't be down-hearted even *now*. It's her birthday, you see, an' this morning, before you came, I was just so happy that I set a plate for her at the table, an' put her picture and a curl of her hair beside it . . . set the picture up so it was looking at me

. . . an' so we had breakfast together. Look here. . . ."

He moved to the table, with Brokaw watching him like a cat, and brought something back with him, wrapped in a soft piece of buckskin. He unfolded the buckskin tenderly, and drew forth a long curl that rippled a dull red and gold in the lamp glow, and then he handed a photograph to Brokaw.

"That's her," he whispered.

Brokaw turned so that the light fell on the picture. A sweet, girlish face smiled at him from out of a wealth of flowing, disheveled curls.

"She had it taken that way just for me," explained Billy, with the enthusiasm of a boy in his voice. "She's always worn her hair in curls . . . an' a braid . . . for me, when we're home. I love it that way. Guess I may be silly, but I'll tell you why. *That* was down in New York state, too. She lived in a cottage, all grown over with honeysuckle an' morning glory, with green hills and valleys all about it . . . and the old apple orchard just behind. That day we were in the orchard, all red an' white with bloom, and she dared me to a race. I let her beat me, and, when I came up, she stood under one of the trees, her cheeks like the pink blossoms and her hair all tumbled about her like an armful of gold, shaking loose apple blossoms down on her head. I forgot everything then, and I didn't stop until I had her in my arms, an' . . . an' she's been my little pardner ever since. After the baby came, we moved up into Canada, where I had a good chance in a new mining town. An' then. . . ." A furious blast of the storm sent the overhanging spruce tops smashing against the top of the cabin. Straight overhead the wind shrieked almost like human voices, and the one window rattled as though it were shaken by human hands. The lamp had been burning lower and lower. It began to flicker now, the quick sputter of the wick lost in the noise of the gale. Then it went out. Brokaw leaned over and opened the door of the big box stove, and the red glow of the fire took the place of the lamplight. He leaned back and re-lighted his pipe, eyeing Billy. The sudden blast, the going out of the light, the opening of the stove door, had all happened in a minute, but the interval was long enough to bring a change to Billy's voice. It was cold and hard when he continued. He leaned over toward Brokaw, and the boyishness had gone from his face.

"Of course, I can't expect you to have any sympathy for this other business, Brokaw. Sympathy isn't in your line, an' you wouldn't be the big man you are in the service if you had it. But I'd like to know what *you* would have done. We were up there six months, and we'd both grown to love the big woods, and she was growing prettier and happier every day . . . when Thorne, the new superintendent, came up. One day she told me that she didn't like Thorne, but I didn't pay much attention to that and laughed at her, and said he was a good fellow. After that, I could see that something was worrying her, and pretty soon I couldn't help from seeing what it was, and everything came out. It was Thorne. He was persecuting her. She hadn't told me, because she knew it would make trouble and I'd lose my job. One afternoon I came home earlier than usual, and found her crying. She put her arms around my neck and just cried it all out, with her face snuggled in my neck, and kissin' me. . . ."

Brokaw could see the cords in Billy's neck. His manacled hands were clenched.

"What would you have done, Brokaw?" he asked huskily. "What if *you* had a wife, an' she told you that another man had insulted her and was forcing his attentions on her, and she asked you to give up your job and take her away? Would you have done it, Brokaw? No, you wouldn't. You'd have hunted up the man. That's what I did. He had been drinking

. . . just enough to make him devilish, and he laughed at me . . . I didn't mean to strike so hard . . . but it happened. I killed him. I got away. She and the baby are down in the little cottage again . . . down in New York state . . . an' I know she's awake this minute . . . our wedding day . . . thinking of me, an' praying for me, and counting the days between now and spring. We were going to South America then."

Brokaw rose to his feet, and put fresh wood into the stove. "I guess it must be pretty hard," he said, straightening himself, "but the law up here doesn't take them things into account . . . not very much. It may let you off with manslaughter . . . ten or fifteen years. I hope it does. Let's turn in."

Billy stood up beside him. He went with Brokaw to a bunk built against the wall, and the sergeant drew a fine steel chain from his pocket. Billy lay down, his hands over his breast, and Brokaw deftly fastened the chain about his ankles.

"And I suppose you think *this* is hard, too," he added. "But I guess you'd do it if you were me. Ten years of this sort of work teaches you not to take chances. If you want anything in the night, just whistle." It had been a hard day with Brokaw, and he slept soundly. For an hour Billy lay awake, thinking of home, and listening to the wail of the storm. Then he, too, fell into sleep—a restless, uneasy slumber filled with troubled visions. For a time there had come a lull in the storm, but now it broke over the cabin with increased fury. A hand seemed slapping at the window, threatening to break it. The spruce boughs moaned and twisted overhead, and a volley of wind and snow shot suddenly down the chimney, forcing open the stove door, so that a shaft of ruddy light cut like a red knife through the dense gloom of the cabin. In varying ways the sounds played a part in Billy's dreams. In all those dreams, and segments of dreams, the girl—his wife—was present. Once they had gone for wildflowers and had

90

been caught in a thunderstorm, and had run to an old and disused barn in the middle of a field for shelter. He was back in that barn again, with *her*—and he could feel her trembling against him, and he was stroking her hair, as the thunder crashed over them and the lightning filled her eyes with fear. After that there came to him a vision of the early autumn nights when they had gone corn roasting, with other young people. He had always been afflicted with a slight nasal trouble, and smoke irritated him. It set him sneezing, and kept him dodging about the fire, and she had always laughed when the smoke persisted in following him about, like a young scamp of a boy bent on tormenting him. The smoke was unusually persistent tonight. He tossed in his bunk, and buried his face in the blanket that answered for a pillow. The smoke reached him even there, and he sneezed chokingly. In that instant the girl's face disappeared. He sneezed again— and awoke.

A startled gasp broke from his lips, and the handcuffs about his wrists clanked as he raised his hands to his face. In that moment his dazed senses adjusted themselves. The cabin was full of smoke. It partly blinded him, but through it he could see tongues of fire shooting toward the ceiling. He could hear the crackling of burning pitch, and he yelled loudly to Brokaw. In an instant the sergeant was on his feet. He rushed to the table, where he had placed a pail of water the evening before, and Billy heard the hissing of the water as it struck the flaming wall.

"Never mind that!" he shouted. "The shack's built of pitch cedar. We've got to get out!"

Brokaw groped his way to him through the smoke and began fumbling at the chain about his ankles. "I can't . . . find . . . the key . . ." he gasped chokingly. "Here . . . grab hold of me!"

He caught Billy under the arms and dragged him to the door. As he opened it, the wind came in with a rush and behind them the whole cabin burst into a furnace of flame. Twenty yards from the cabin he dropped Billy in the snow, and ran back. In that seething room of smoke and fire was everything on which their lives depended: food, blankets, even their coats and caps and snowshoes. But he could go no farther than the door. He returned to Billy, found the key in his pocket, and freed him from the chain about his ankles. Billy stood up. As he looked at Brokaw, the glass in the window broke and a sea of flame spouted through. It lighted up their faces. The sergeant's jaw was set hard. His leathery face was curiously white. He could not help from shivering. There was a strange smile on Billy's face and a strange look in his eyes. Neither of the two men had undressed for sleep, but their coats and caps and heavy mittens were in the flames. Billy rattled his handcuffs.

Brokaw looked him squarely in the eyes. "You ought to know this country," he said. "What'll we do?"

"The nearest post is sixty miles from here," said Billy.

"I know that," replied Brokaw. "And I know that Thoreau's cabin is only twenty miles from here. There must be some trapper or Indian shack nearer than that. Is there?"

In the red glare of the fire Billy smiled. His teeth gleamed at Brokaw. It was in a lull of the wind, and he went close to Brokaw, and spoke quietly, his eyes shining more and more with that strange light that had come into them.

"This is going to be a big sight easier than hanging, or going to jail for half my life, Brokaw . . . an' you don't think I'm going to be fool enough to miss the chance, do you? It ain't hard to die of cold. I've almost been there once or twice. I told you last night why I couldn't give up hope . . . that something good for me always came on her birthday, or near to it. An' it's come. It's forty below, an' we won't live the day out. We ain't got a mouthful of grub. We ain't got clothes enough on to keep us from freezing inside the shanty, unless we had a fire. Last night I saw you fill your match bottle and put it in your coat pocket. Why, man, *we ain't even got a match!*"

In his voice there was a thrill of triumph. Brokaw's hands were clenched, as if someone had threatened to strike him. "You mean . . . ?" he gasped.

"Just this," interrupted Billy, and his voice was harder than Brokaw's now. "The God you used to pray to when you were a kid has given me a chance, Brokaw, an' I'm going to take it. If we stay by this fire, an' keep it up, we won't die of cold, but starvation. We'll be dead before we get halfway to Thoreau's. There's an Indian shack that we could make, but you'll never find it . . . not unless you unlock these irons and give me that revolver at your belt. Then I'll take you over there as *my* prisoner. That'll give me another chance for South America . . . an' the kid an' home."

Brokaw was buttoning the thick collar of his shirt close up about his neck. On his face, too, there came for a moment a grim and determined smile. "Come on," he said, "we'll make Thoreau's or die."

"Sure," said Billy, stepping quickly to his side. "I suppose I might lie down in the snow an' refuse to budge. I'd win my game, then, wouldn't I? But we'll play it . . . on the square. It's Thoreau's, or die. And it's up to you to find Thoreau's."

He looked back over his shoulder at the burning cabin as they entered the edge of the forest, and in the gray darkness that was preceding dawn he smiled to himself. Two miles to the south, in a thick swamp, was Indian Joe's cabin. They could have made it easily. On their way to Thoreau's they would pass within a mile of it. But Brokaw would never know.

And they would never reach Thoreau's. Billy knew that. He looked at the manhunter as he broke trail ahead of him—at the pugnacious hunch of the shoulders, his long stride, the determined clench of his hands, and wondered what the soul and the heart of a man like this must be, who in such an hour would not trade life for life. For almost three-quarters of an hour Brokaw did not utter a word. The storm had broken. Above the spruce tops the sky began to clear. Day came slowly. It was growing steadily colder. The swing of Brokaw's arms and shoulders kept the blood in them circulating, while Billy's manacled wrists held a part of his body almost rigid. He thought that his hands were already frozen. His arms were numb, and, when at last Brokaw paused for a moment on the edge of a frozen stream, Billy thrust out his hands and *clanked* the steel rings.

"It must be getting colder," he said. "Look at that."

The cold steel had seared his wrists like hot iron and had pulled off patches of skin and flesh.

Brokaw looked and hunched his shoulders. His lips were blue. His cheeks, ears, and nose were frostbitten. There was a curious thickness in his voice when he spoke. "Thoreau lives on this creek," he said. "How much farther is it?"

"Fifteen or sixteen miles," replied Billy. "You'll last just about five, Brokaw. I won't last that long unless you take these things off and give me the use of my arms."

"To knock out my brains when I ain't looking," growled Brokaw. "I guess . . . before long . . . you'll be willing to tell where the Indian's shack is."

He kicked his way through a drift of snow to the smoother surface of the stream. There was a breath of wind in their faces, and Billy bowed his head to it. In the hours of his greatest loneliness and despair Billy had kept up his fighting spirit by thinking of pleasant things, and now, as he followed in Brokaw's trail, he began to think of home. It was not hard for him to bring up visions of the young wife who would probably never know how he had died. He forgot Brokaw. He followed in the trail mechanically, failing to notice that his captor's pace was growing steadily slower and that his own feet were dragging more and more like leaden weights. He was back among the old hills again, and the sun was shining, and he heard laughter and song. He saw Jeanne standing at the gate in front of the little white cottage, smiling at him, and waving Baby Jeanne's tiny hand at him as he looked back over his shoulder from down the dusty road. His mind did not often travel as far as the mining camp, and he had completely forgotten it now. He no longer felt the sting and pain of the intense cold. It was Brokaw who brought him back into the reality of things. The sergeant stumbled and fell into a drift, and Billy fell over him. For a moment the two men sat half buried in the snow, looking at each other without speaking.

Brokaw moved first. He rose to his feet with an effort. Billy made an attempt to follow him. After three efforts he gave it up, and blinked up into Brokaw's face with a queer laugh. The laugh was almost soundless. There had come a change in Brokaw's face. Its determination and confidence were gone. At last the iron mask of the law was broken, and there shone through it something of the emotions and the brotherhood of man. He was fumbling in one of his pockets and drew out the key to the handcuffs. It was a small key, and he held it between his stiffened fingers with difficulty. He knelt down beside Billy. The keyhole was filled with snow. It took a long time—ten minutes—before the key was fitted in and the lock *clicked*. He helped to tear off the cuffs. Billy felt no sensation as bits of skin and flesh came with them. Brokaw gave him a hand, and assisted him to rise.

For the first time he spoke. "Guess you've got me best,

Billy," he said. "Where's the Indian's?"

He drew the revolver from its holster and tossed it in the snowdrift. The shadow of a smile passed grimly over his face. Billy looked about him. They had stopped where the frozen path of a small stream joined the creek. He raised one of his stiffened arms and pointed to it.

"Follow that creek . . . four miles . . . and you'll come to Indian Joe's shack," he said.

"And a mile is just about our limit."

"Just about yours," replied Billy. "I can't make another half. If we had a fire. . . ."

"If . . . ," wheezed Brokaw.

"If we had a fire," continued Billy, "we could warm ourselves, an' make the Indian's shack easy, couldn't we?"

Brokaw did not answer. He had turned toward the creek when one of Billy's pulseless hands fell heavily on his arm.

"Look here, Brokaw."

Brokaw turned. They looked into each other's eyes.

"I guess mebby you're a man, Brokaw," said Billy quietly. "You've done what you thought was your duty. You've kept your word to th' law, an' I believe you'll keep your word with me. If I say the word that'll save us now, will you go back to headquarters an' report me dead?"

For a full half minute their eyes did not waver.

Then Brokaw said: "No."

Billy dropped his hand. It was Brokaw's hand that fell on his arm now.

"I can't do that," he said. "In ten years I ain't run out the white flag once. It's something that ain't known in the service. There ain't a coward in it, or a man who's afraid to die. But I'll play you square. I'll wait until we're both on our feet again and then I'll give you twenty-four hours the start of me."

Billy was smiling now. His hand reached out. Brokaw's met it, and the two joined in a grip that their numb fingers scarcely felt.

"Do you know," said Billy softly, "there's been somethin' runnin' in my head ever since we left the burning cabin. It's something my mother taught me. 'Do unto others as you'd have others do unto you.' I'm a damned fool, ain't I? But I'm goin' to try the experiment, Brokaw, an' see what comes of it. I could drop in a snowdrift an' let you go on . . . to die. Then I could save myself. But I'm going to take your word . . . an' do the other thing. *I've got a match.*"

"*A match?*"

"Just one. I remember dropping it in my pants pocket yesterday when I was out on trail. It's in *this* pocket. Your hand is in better shape than mine. Get it."

Life had leaped into Brokaw's face. He thrust his hand into Billy's pocket, staring at him as he fumbled, as if fearing that he had lied. When he drew his hand out, the match was between his fingers.

"Ah!" he whispered excitedly.

"Don't get nervous," warned Billy. "It's the only one."

Brokaw's eyes were searching the low timber along the shore.

"There's a birch tree!" he cried. "Hold it . . . while I gather a pile of bark!"

He gave the match to Billy, and staggered through the snow to the bank. Strip after strip of the loose bark he tore from the tree. Then he gathered it in a heap in the shelter of a low-hanging spruce, and added dry sticks and still more bark to it. When it was ready, he stood with his hands in his pockets and looked at Billy.

"If we had a stone, an' a piece of paper . . . ," he began.

Billy thrust a hand that felt like lifeless lead inside his shirt, and fumbled in a pocket he had made there. Brokaw watched him with red, eager eyes. The hand reappeared, and in it was the buckskin wrapped photograph he had seen the night before. Billy took off the buckskin. About the picture there was a bit of tissue paper. He gave this and the match to Brokaw.

"There's a little gun file in the pocket the match came from," he said. "I had it mending a trap chain. You can scratch the match on that."

He turned so Brokaw could reach into the pocket, and the manhunter thrust in his hand. When he brought it forth, it held the file. There was a smile on Billy's frostbitten face as he held the picture for a moment under Brokaw's eyes. Billy's own hands had ruffled up the girl's shining curls an instant before the picture was taken and she had been laughing at him when the camera clicked.

"It's all up to her, Brokaw," Billy said gently. "I told you that last night. It was she who woke me up before the fire got us. If you ever prayed . . . pray a little now. *For she's going to strike that match!*"

He still looked at the picture as Brokaw knelt beside the pile he had made. He heard the scratch of the match on the file, but his eyes did not turn. The living, breathing face of the most beautiful thing in the world was speaking to him from out of that picture. His mind was dazed. He swayed a little. He heard a voice, low and sweet and so distant that it came to him like the faintest whisper. *I am coming . . . I am coming, Billy . . . coming . . . coming . . . coming. . . .* A joyous cry surged up from his soul, but it died on his lips in a strange gasp. A louder cry brought him back to himself for a moment. It was from Brokaw. The sergeant's face was terrible to behold. He rose to his feet, swaying, his hands clutched at his breast. His voice was thick—hopeless.

"That match . . . went . . . out. . . ." He staggered up to Billy, his eyes like a madman's.

Billy swayed dizzily. He laughed, even as he crumpled down in the snow. As if in a dream he saw Brokaw stagger off in the frozen trail. He saw him disappear in his hopeless effort to reach the Indian's shack, and then a strange darkness closed him in, and in that darkness he heard still the sweet voice of his wife. It spoke his name again and again, and it urged him to wake up—wake up—*wake up!* It seemed a long time before he could respond to it. But at last he opened his eyes. He dragged himself to his knees, and looked first to find Brokaw. But the manhunter had gone—forever. The picture was still in his hand. Less distinctly than before he saw the girl smiling at him. And then—at his back—he heard a strange and new sound. With an effort he turned to discover who it was.

The match had hidden an unseen spark from Brokaw's eyes. From out of the pile of fuel was rising a pillar of smoke and flame.

Carcajou's Trail
Max Brand

Frederick Faust (1892–1944) was born in Seattle, Washington, but grew up in California. He was a most creative and fecund author who wrote in his lifetime the equivalent of 500 books under various pen names, of which at least 300 were Western stories. The name by which he is best known is Max Brand, and much about his life and work, including a comprehensive bibliography, can be found in *The Max Brand Companion* (Greenwood Press, 1996) that Vicki Piekarski and I edited. Among his finest Western stories are actually those set in the Northwest. The earliest of these to be published in book form was *The White Wolf* (Putnam, 1926). Four decades later it was followed by the equally fine *Mighty Lobo* (Dodd, Mead, 1962) and *Torture Trail* (Dodd, Mead, 1965). More recently in the Five Star Westerns there have appeared *Sixteen in Nome* (1995), the Prologue to *Sixteen in Nome*, "Alec the Great", in *Outlaws All: A Western Trio* (1996), *The Lightning Warrior* (1996), *Chinook* (1998), and *The Masterman* (2000). "Carcajou's Trail" first appeared in Street & Smith's *Western Story Magazine* (March 26, 1932). Faust no less than Jack London was influenced by Nietzsche in his Northland fiction. Nietzsche introduced the idea of the blond beast in *On the Genealogy of Morality* (1887): ". . . These men enjoy freedom from all social constraint, in the wilderness they are repaid for the tension that a long confinement and being enclosed in the precincts of society engender, they fall *back* into the innocence of the beast of prey, like a rejoicing monster who is convinced, perhaps coming back from a ghastly sequence of murder, arson, rape, torture with bravado and psychic equipoise, as if merely having carried out a student prank, that the poets now have again something to sing about and to celebrate. At the very depths of all these aristocratic races is the beast of prey, the unmistakable, magnificent, rampaging *blond beast* lusting after plunder and victory; it is needed for the eruption of these very concealed depths, that the brute must again be let outside, must again venture back into the wilderness:— Roman, Arabian, German, Japanese aristocracy, Homeric heroes, Scandinavian Vikings—they are all the same in having this need." This is an idea to keep in mind when it comes Carcajou who in many ways is an embodiment of the blond beast.

I

"BACK-THROW"

Two boats were just in from Juneau, and Dyea was filled with excited men and howling dogs. Over in Chilkoot Pass, where misery and folly crowded in together, men were laboring, but no one between the mountains and the sea could realize the importance of the man who stood at Steuermann's Bar in Dyea. This man was John Banner. That name never became famous in the North, but ask any of the old-timers if they ever heard of a fellow nicknamed "Carcajou".

Carcajou is French-Canadian for wolverine, and it is worthwhile knowing something about the animal before you try to comprehend the man. The wolverine is the largest weasel, as a matter of fact, but it looks like a little hump-backed caricature of a bear. Some of the Indians call it "skunk bear". It has short legs and a long, weasel body. It has claws with which it can chisel through yards of frozen ground to get at a buried cache that the keenest sense of smell in all the world has enabled it to locate. It has the biting power of a wolf and the tenacity of a bulldog. It is stronger, pound for pound, than any animal in the world. A one-hundred-and-twenty-pound timber wolf simply turns aside and gives up the trail when it sees the wolverine come padding toward it, for it knows that the smaller animal will not budge from the path and that it is better to tamper with dynamite than with the compressed ferocity of this beast. The strength of the wolverine is explained by the fact that there is not a straight line in it. Legs, back, neck, body, all are curves that loop into one

103

another and give continual reinforcement. But the strength of spirit is greater than the strength of flesh.

The Indians say that the soul of the carcajou is the soul of Satan. At any rate, it combines the terrible blood lust of the weasel with the patience of a grizzly bear. It is the only one of the weasel family distinguished for intelligence, and it seems as though the wits of the entire species are concentrated in that one small brain, for trappers will tell you that nothing that lives in the wilderness compares with the carcajou for diabolical cleverness. There are stories about old and cunning trappers with many years of experience who had been driven from fine trapping grounds by the ferocious cunning of the wolverine that will follow the trap lines, avoiding all poisoned bait, and ruin the pelts of the trapped creatures it does not devour. It has been known to work for long days, carefully prying and tugging, trying one leverage after another, until it has found a way into a ponderously built log cache. Thus men have died when, at the end of the long winter marches, they have found the cache gone.

This is not a full portrait of the carcajou. It is only a sketch, and, if you wish to get even an inkling of the true nature of the beast, you must go far North and abandon yourself for many a long winter evening to the talk of the French-Canadian trappers who will tell you tales in which the carcajou gradually ceases to be animal and passes into that legendary realm between flesh and fancy, where only the werewolf exists.

Bearing all of these things in mind, look now behind the doors of Steuermann's through the mist of steam and smoke at John Banner, who is to receive his new baptism of blood and to be renamed Carcajou before this day is an hour older. At first sight there is nothing unusual about him. He is simply a fellow of middle height, looking rather plump and, on the whole, lethargic. You will guess his weight at a hundred and sixty, and thereby you will make your first mistake, because there are twenty extra pounds under the loose clothes. Look again to note the depth and roundness of the barrel of the man. Gradually you see that here is a man composed of nothing but curves that loop and subtly reinforce one another. The shoulders slope into arms big at the top and tapering down to a perfectly round wrist. The hand that holds the glass of whiskey on the edge of the bar is daintily and delicately made. Perhaps the length of the thumb is rather unusual. Still, look as closely as you can, there is nothing very unusual about him, except that you begin to feel that perhaps what seems plumpness is not fat at all. At least, the line of the cheek bone and the jaw is clear cut and firm enough. Perhaps under the clothes the body of the man is like India rubber, firm and resilient.

So much for John Banner at this moment. More is to come. In the meantime, there were other people in that barroom worthy of attention. Just inside the door, pushing back the furred hood from his face, was Bill Roads, a huge, rawboned, powerful man. He looked over the crowd with the air of one who hopes to find a face. When his glance rested on the form of John Banner, it was plain that he had arrived at the object of his quest, his face contorted, and a light flared in his eyes. He started weaving through the crowd, with his gaze fixed upon the goal, and one hand dropped into the deep pocket of his coat.

Down the bar, not far from Banner, stood a pair of big French-Canadians, smiling men, contented with themselves. They had made one fortune inside, and they were going after another. Wise in the ways of the wilderness, their strength was more than doubled, because they were devoted friends, each ready to guard the back of the other against every danger, and ever on the watch to give needed help. Beyond the French-Canadians, there was an odd group of three, a group whose importance was to appear later. Jimmy Slade was there, and Charley Horn, their ruffian natures clearly appearing in their faces, and between them was that good old man, Tom Painter—Old Tom to most men. He was not so very old, either, not more, say, than fifty-nine or sixty, but men of that age are old for the far North. There was about his face an air of gentle resignation, as of one who has endured much pain and prepares to endure yet more before the end will come. The bartender, after filling a glass, pushed it across the bar and inside the grasp of the waiting hand of Old Tom. Then the veteran looked up with a smile, and the eyes were empty, totally darkened. Even a child could tell that he was blind.

Steuermann stared at him, hard. "Are you going inside, Old Tom?" he asked.

"Going back inside once more, the last time, Steuermann," said Old Tom.

"Along with these here friends of yours?" asked the bartender.

"You ain't met 'em yet, I guess," said Old Tom. "Here's Charley Horn on my right and Jim Slade on my left. Shake hands with Steuermann, boys, will you?"

They extended their hands with muttered words of greeting. Their eyes, keen and suspicious, probed at the mind of Steuermann, as though wondering how far he might suspect them of dark deeds. He, however, had looked at them before and did not feel that it was necessary to look again. Dark deeds were exactly what the pair seemed equipped for. Worse faces than these had been turned toward the Chilkoot. There was nothing strange about that. Only, why were they companions of a blind man? That was a question worth an answer!

"You'll find the trail sort of rough, won't you, Tom?" asked Steuermann.

"I can walk pretty good with a stick to feel the way," answered Old Tom. "Besides, we've got a good outfit, and I guess I'll have to ride a mighty big part of the way."

"A long way, eh?" asked Steuermann.

"All ways are long up this far North, ain't they?" answered Jimmy Slade, cutting in sharply.

"Oh, any way will be a pretty long way for me, Steuermann," said Old Tom.

The bartender just shrugged his shoulders. It had not been his intention to ask prying questions. It was merely that pity and interest bubbled up in him as he saw the helpless veteran and the two roughnecks who were his escort.

This conversation took place while big Bill Roads worked his way in from the door toward his man. He did not come up from the side, but from behind, where Banner stood at the bar with a glass of whiskey poised in his hand. He was close behind his quarry when the men on the right and left of him pressed suddenly back, for they saw that Roads had drawn a gun and at the same instant shouted: "Hands up, Banner, or take it in the back!"

Banner moved to throw up his hands, but as the right hand rose above his shoulder it flung the whiskey out of the glass straight behind him. Perhaps this was partly fortune; perhaps in greater part it was uncanny skill in locating the speaker by the mere sound of his voice. But certainly a few drops of the stinging liquor splashed into the eyes of Roads.

He fired twice, fanning the hammer with the thumb of his right hand, the two bullets smashing through the mirror behind the bar, the pride of Steuermann, and left two small holes surrounded by the white of powdered glass, from which the cracks extended outward in long, wavering lines. The second shot was the last that Roads could fire, for Banner was at him by that time.

He did not strike with his fists, but he caught hold of big Roads with his hands, and, as though the touch were molten lead, Roads yelled with pain and fear for help. Then he went down. There was something grisly about the sudden paralysis that seized on Roads. It was as though the spider had been stung by the poison of the smaller wasp, as if an electric shock had numbed all of the vital nerve centers. He still writhed and struggled, but blindly, helplessly, with rapidly decreasing strength.

Then the bystanders saw, with horror, what was happening, as Roads suddenly stopped struggling and began to scream. There were no words, no appeals for help, but simply terrible shrieking. Banner had his elbows on the shoulders of the fallen man and, with his hands interlocked under the chin of Roads, was forcing back his head farther and farther to break his neck.

II

"CORDED STRENGTH"

They lunged for Banner then. They laid on him powerful hands, only to find that their fingers, under his clothes, impinged on quivering masses of corded strength on which they could get no hold. The French-Canadians were among the first to try to pry the killer from his victim. One of them, after a mighty effort, muttered through his teeth to his friend: "Carcajou."

That was how the nickname originated—Carcajou. And the hoarse screams of the victim began to be throttled by the distance to which his head had been forced back. The windpipe was closing. The spinal column itself would snap and shatter presently.

Charley Horn was among those present, bending over the twisting, struggling men, his hands on his knees. He was laughing under his breath, a very horrible sound to those who heard it. But now he reached down and struck with the edge of his hand across the top of the neck of Banner. It was enough. For half a second the killer was paralyzed, and in that moment he was torn from the victim.

He stood back by the bar, looking down at big Roads. His face was utterly immobile, except that there was a slight cut in his upper lip, and the red tip of his tongue was touching the wound thoughtfully, tasting his own blood.

"What were you trying to do . . . murder that man?" shouted Steuermann, shaking his fist under the nose of Banner. "A carcajou is what you are! A regular murdering wolverine!"

Carcajou lifted his glance and stared at Steuermann. It was only a glance, but it made Steuermann snatch out a revolver from beneath the bar. Carcajou laid his left hand on the edge of the bar. "I'd put that gun down if I were you," he said.

It was the first time that he had spoken, and there was such a passionless calm in his voice that those who heard could not believe their ears. Steuermann was a brave man, as he had proved over and over again, but he put down the gun. People remembered that afterward, and not a man who was present blamed him for taking water at that particular moment, and from that particular man.

Carcajou left the saloon, stepping lightly, unconcernedly, through the crowd, asking the pardon of those he shouldered against, and always speaking in that same impassive voice that might have seemed perfectly gentle had not the others seen what he had done.

But now he was gone, and poor Bill Roads was stretched on a table near the stove, gasping for breath. They forgot that they had seen him try to shoot a man from behind. In fact, it did not seem to be a man, but a monster superhumanly evil. Besides, as they opened his coat to give him air, they saw the badge of a federal officer of the law. They poured a stiff drink of whiskey down his throat. His head was pillowed on a rolled-up coat.

"How is it?" asked Steuermann, who had taken charge.

"I don't know. My neck may be broken. I heard the bones snapping, I thought." He closed his eyes and gasped again. Then, his eyes still closed, he muttered: "I thought I had him at last. Ten thousand miles, and I thought that I had him at last."

One who had been a doctor in quieter days of his life took charge of the injured man, fingered the back of Roads's neck, moved his head up and down.

"That neck isn't broken," he said. "You'll be all right, but you need to be put to bed. You've had a shock, man, and that's why your temperature came up so fast. Get him into a bed quick, some of you boys."

"Get Banner, first," pleaded Bill Roads. "Get Banner, and let me go hang. I don't care what happens to me. I only care that he's caught."

"We'll attend to him later on," said Steuermann. "We ain't got time to gather him in just now. Take it easy, man. Take it easy. Don't go and burn yourself up. What kind of a crook is this here Banner, this here Carcajou?"

"Crook? He's more than a crook. He's a fiend. He's a jungle cat. He came out of the New York slums. There's nothing but Satan in him. Get him dead or alive. There's a reward. I don't want any share. There's ten thousand dollars."

Ten thousand dollars! It was a fortune. With it a man could go back to civilization without ever enduring the strain and daring the dangers of the terrible venture into the inside. He would have his stake ready-made. Yet not a man left the saloon on the blood trail.

To be sure, Horn looked at Jimmy Slade, but Slade muttered: "Ten thousand dollars ain't enough to buy the amount of prussic acid that you'd need to bump off that bird. Bullets, they wouldn't be no good. They'd just bounce off the surface, is all."

The blind man had asked no questions, but he waited with a troubled face, looking down always.

"Just a bird that hopped in here and done a gun play and got flopped on his back for his trouble," said Charley Horn. "That's all, Old Tom. There wa'n't no real trouble at all. Not the killing kind, but the gent that done the shooting pretty near got his neck broke." He chuckled a little. A hard man was Charley Horn, just a trifle harder than Jimmy Slade, although there was not much to choose between.

"Too bad, too bad," said Old Tom. "When folks get this far North they seem to think that they've left kindness and decency behind 'em . . . sometimes. And that's too bad, too."

His two evil-faced companions glanced askance at one another. Somebody was trying to say to Bill Roads: "What's this gent done? This Carcajou?"

"Banner? Carcajou? What does carcajou mean?"

"A weasel with the meanness of a weasel, the brain of a grizzly, and the most of a bear's strength, too."

"You've found the right name for him, then," said Roads. "But talking about him is no good. I'd have to spend days telling you what he's done. I'd have to tell you how I've done nothing but follow him for two years, and follow him I still will, working for the government or working for myself. I'll crawl on my hands around the whole world, but finally I'll split his skull with a bullet, or run a knife through his heart. He's got to die."

He was panting as he spoke these last words. Then a spasm of pain got him once more, and he groaned.

The others listened to him with a singular respect. A two-year-old blood trail is very interesting, indeed. Yet the thought of the ten thousand dollars' reward did not induce a single man there to leave the saloon and track down the enemy of society. The trouble was that they had seen too much and too intimately the dealings of John Banner in that same room. They did not want to find themselves flattened on the ground with the hands of the monster on their throats.

"It's a funny thing," said Steuermann, shaking his head, although "funny" was not really the word that he wanted. "It's a funny thing that he didn't take a shorter way of murdering you, man, when he had you spread out like that."

"What's killing more or less to him?" asked the officer of the law. "What does that matter to a demon like Banner? Not a thing! Killing, bit by bit, with his hands, that's what would please him. Three mortal times he could have killed me on this trail, and three times he's refused to shoot . . . he's tried to get at me with his hands every time."

They listened with horror. There was hardly a man in that room with delicate sensibilities, but what they heard was sufficient to make them sick. After that, if fifty thousand dollars had been offered instead of ten, it would not have been enough to get any man, or any four men, out of that room on the trail of Carcajou.

Steuermann found, at this point, a chance to draw Jimmy Slade to one side. Ordinarily he would not have dreamed of talking as he was about to talk now. But enough had happened to excite him highly, and his tongue broke loose from the usually severely imposed restraints.

"Slade," he said, "I've got to ask you a question. Where do you intend to go with Old Tom?"

Slade looked boldly and contemptuously into the eyes of the bartender. "Ask me again another way," he said. "I don't understand that kind of language."

Steuermann darkened and drew back a little. "All right," he said. "Only, brother, I wanna tell you one thing."

"Tell it soft and low, then," said Slade, growing uglier every moment.

"I'll tell you this. Old Tom ain't a stranger up here."

"No?"

"No, he's not a stranger. And if he goes in blind with you and your side-kicker, there's gonna be a whole lot of us anxious to see him come out again."

Slade stepped closer to the other. "Now, whatcha mean by

that?" he demanded savagely.

"You know what I mean," said Steuermann without flinching. "I've told you what I mean, and I guess you understand the language all right."

"Say it over once more, brother," said Slade through his teeth.

"I'll say it over," answered the bartender. "We'll be looking to see you and Horn come out with Old Tom still alongside of you."

"And where else would he be?" demanded Slade.

"Dead of frostbite, somewhere inside," said Steuermann, and turned back behind his bar.

III

"THE WAGER"

When the newly named Carcajou stepped outside the saloon, he stood for a moment and breathed in the air, pure, free from smoke—free, it also seemed to him, even from the language of man. Within the doors he could hear the murmur of voices that had been loosed the moment he left the room, but he regarded this not at all, except as a sign of his freedom. Mankind meant nothing to Carcajou, except insofar as the race furnished for him interesting enemies. Now and then the race was close, now and again the fight was hard, but the victory was always his. There might be, somewhere on the planet, men swifter, stronger, fiercer, more cunning than he, but he had never met such a one. Having gone unconquered all of his days, he expected to remain so to the end. As for friends, he never had known one, male or female, who valued him as much as they valued the price on his head. That price was of long standing, from the time he was fifteen, in fact. Doubtless the price would not have been placed had his age been known. At fifteen he had looked twenty, at least. At twenty-five he looked still hardly more than twenty. Ten years of breaking and evading the law had not aged him!

The reason that he paused now was not because he did not know where to go. It was simply that he was hesitating, wondering whether he really wished that famous man of the law, Bill Roads, dead or alive. He could have killed Roads easily enough. But if Roads were off the trail, what would remain to make things really interesting for him? Who would be able to make him sleep like a wolf, with one eye open? Who would be

115

able to make him keep constantly on the alert, waiting and peering about for danger?

Bill Roads was, on the whole, the most formidable enemy that he had ever known. Four times Roads had come in close contact with him. Four times he had defeated the enemy. This day he had wished to kill the man, but on the whole he was rather glad that he had not. One does not wish to subtract from life all of its spice! When he had reached this conclusion, he nodded slightly and set off down the street.

It was snowing, a fall of large, crisp flakes that came down in wavering strokes of dimness before his eyes. Where they touched his face, they did not seem very cold. There was a pleasant sound of them underfoot. The air was not yet iced. It was rather moist and still. Straight down the street he could see still the leaden waters of the sea.

On the whole he was content. Actual happiness he never knew, except when he was cracking a safe, say, or at grips with a foeman. But now he was fairly well pleased with himself. He had discovered that life in the States was growing a little too warm for him. He might, it was true, avoid the law for another few months, but he knew that there were too many posters about him here and there. Ten thousand dollars is a large enough sum of money to put brains in the most stupid and courage in the cowardly. It was not exactly that he was afraid to remain in the wide mileage of the States. It was simply that he considered it unwise to put his head in the lion's mouth. He had evaded destruction a hundred times, to be sure, but in the end the luck would turn against him and he would go down. It would be small comfort to him if he lay one day gasping on his back, grasping at the mud with his mighty hands, if he knew that the bullet that laid him low had been fired by a tyro who chance had favored. So he had determined to leave the country, and he had made his way toward the great white North.

He intended to go inland, and there he would be lost among the shifting crowds of miners for perhaps a year. When he came out again, no doubt the memory of him would be slightly dimmer in the minds of the police. After that, he could take a trip around the world and let his repute become still less familiar. When he returned to New York—well, then the old world would not know him, and he would begin the nefarious practices which he loved once more.

This was his general plan of campaign. This was his strategy. As for tactics, he was prepared to deal with each situation as it arose. He was not one to worry about the future. As he had dealt with Bill Roads in the saloon, so he had dealt with other enemies from time to time, and so he would deal with them again in the future! It must not be thought that he had a blind confidence in himself. He seriously had waited, all the days of his life, to find another man superior to himself in power, in speed and cruelly quick decision. He did not pray to encounter such a dreadful foe, but he yearned for the meeting as a child may yearn to have a younger brother born.

Striding down the street, he passed a gap between the buildings on his left and heard the shouting of a small crowd, the snarling of a dog, the curses of a man. It was not a pretty scene. A big crate had been opened in the space between the buildings, and a dog on a long chain had been let out of the crate. Just outside the length of chain stood a man with a club, and, as the dog rushed at him, he beat the beast to the ground again and again.

You'll never break that dog that way, said Carcajou to himself. He canted his head to the side as he stood and watched. Perhaps there was enough of the animal in him to make him sympathize with beasts very intimately. Now, at least, he thought that he understood in a flash the entire workings of the brain of the dog.

It was a monster Husky, its blood enriched with many crossings of the timber wolf, but of a size that the wolf never attains. What could the other strain or strains be? It was a frightful mongrel. That much was clear. It had the mousy, immense head of an Irish wolfhound. It had also the stature of that terrific beast. But there was the coat of a wolf, and the weight in the shoulders and in the quarters was more than an Irish wolfhound would ever be likely to show. He would not venture to guess lightly at the total burden of this frightful thing—two hundred pounds, perhaps, or even more.

As it lay flat on the ground, it seemed less. When it rose into the air at the dog breaker, it seemed as huge as a bear. Now the monster arose from the mud and snow, shook himself, and crouched, without charging. His head was bleeding. No matter whether he charged high or low, the club always met him, swinging in that expert hand. Always the exactly timed blow crashed down upon his head. So he waited, now, panting with fury rather than with effort, and, lolling out his long red tongue, he looked at the dog breaker with eyes redder still.

The latter shouted with angry triumph and shook his left fist, cursing. "Come on, you!" he yelled. "I've got plenty more of the same kind left!"

It was plain from the triumph in his tone that he had dreaded this encounter.

Carcajou stepped up and said: "You'll never break him that way."

The dog breaker moved back out of range of the monster and turned furiously on this mere human antagonist. The brute in him mantled in his face, and there was little but brute in his composition.

"You'll tell me how to break dogs, will you?"

"I could tell you a point or two," said Carcajou in that same tone of misleading gentleness. In fact, his voice was never raised. He never had shouted out loud in all his life, since a certain dreadful moment in his childhood.

"You could tell me a point or two, could you, you slab-faced piece of fish, you flounder-faced piece of putty, you!" shouted the dog breaker.

Carcajou stepped closer and with a swift, inescapable movement of his left hand caught the club arm of the other man above the wrist. The dog breaker looked down. The club fell from his paralyzed hand. The fury left his face. White wonder took its place.

"Well," he muttered. "What would you do with him?"

"That's a dog for a dog team, isn't it?" asked Carcajou.

"That ain't a dog. That is a dog team," said the breaker. "That's a man-killer, too."

"Oh, is he?" said Carcajou.

"He worse than killed Larry Patrick last week. Larry ain't gonna be no more than the sewed-up chunks of a man the rest of his days." Then he added: "What would you do with him, mister?"

"You've got to come to grips with him sooner or later. There's a brain behind those red eyes. You might teach him to be afraid of a club, but one day he'll catch you when you have no club in your hand."

"And then cut your throat, you mean?"

"Yes, unless he's been taught that your empty hands are better than his teeth."

"Empty hands?" repeated the dog breaker, and laughed.

Other people in the crowd joined in his derisive laughter.

"Back up, stranger," said one man, "and let this here show go on! Back up, will you?"

Carcajou looked on the unknown and smiled faintly.

There was a certain richness of harvest, he found, in this land of the great white North. Wherever one turned, there were reckless men and a harvest of great danger. Gun or knife or hand, or all three, were ever ready to break out into action. However, he merely said: "For a bet, I'd try my hand with that dog . . . my bare hands, I mean."

The stranger who had invited him to back up cried instantly: "I've got five pounds of gold dust in this poke. Is that enough to make a bet for you?"

"That's about fifteen or sixteen hundred dollars, isn't it?" said Carcajou. "All right! That will do."

Taking out a wallet, he began to count the sum requisite for the wager. The others fell silent.

IV

"THE TAMING"

"Unchain that dog," said Carcajou to the dog breaker.

"I'll have to knock him cold before I can unchain him," said the breaker. "Besides, I wouldn't unchain him. I wouldn't turn loose that big streak of murder inside the town. If you wanna give him room, just walk inside the circle he can run in, brother. That'll be about all."

"All right," said Carcajou.

He walked straight up to the dog. It was an amazing thing to those who watched it. There had been excitement enough every time the great brute charged the man with the club; it brought each heart up into the throat to see one with empty hands go straight up to the monster and lay a hand on that bleeding head.

The dog crouched, snarling, but the green and red gleaming was out of its eyes, or very dim, at least. Carcajou talked straight down at him, his voice calm and gentle, as always, and as always just a suggestion of iron clanking on iron somewhere in the sound. They heard what he said, and remembered it.

"You're not such a bad one. You only think you're bad," said Carcajou. "You've had a fool slamming you over the head. But you'd rather wag your tail and be friends, if you could find the right man. I'm going to be the right man for you, boy. You can trust me."

The dog snarled, but there was a whine mingling with the snarl. The breaker yelled suddenly in rage and surprise:

121

"He's a hypnotizer! That's what he is!"

At that shout, coming so suddenly, the great beast shot out his long neck and dragon's head to seize Carcajou by the arm. The fangs slashed through the sleeve, cut the skin, but that was all. Carcajou caught him by the throat and flung him to the ground. He looked a little, puny thing, struggling with the huge brute, and he was flung here and there by the mighty struggles of the dog. The claws of the beast tore the heavy furs of Carcajou to fragments and gouged his body. Blood dribbled on the snow, the blood of Carcajou. Then the dog made one great, last, convulsive motion and lay still, throttled to the verge of death, with his tongue hanging out of his mouth sidewise like a stream of purple-red blood.

The men who stood around had stopped shouting and jumping about in their excitement. They merely drew together and stared. With every fling from side to side of those dragon-like, gaping jaws, they expected to see the arms or the body of the man gnashed to the bone. But although the strength of the brute was like that of a horse, it was securely held.

Carcajou rose to his knees, patted the head of his victim, took a handful of snow and rubbed off the tongue, still hanging from the jaws, and patted the neck and back of the animal.

"What do you call the name of this little pet?" asked Carcajou of the dog breaker.

The latter answered in newly humble tones: "He ain't got any name. Slaughter would be about the right name for him, I reckon."

"Sure it would," said Carcajou.

He rose to his feet. Slaughter sprang up suddenly and stood on wavering legs, eyes still thrusting from his head, lungs heaving desperately. Carcajou laid his hand a second

122

time on the head of the great brute.

"Now we've been introduced, we can be good friends," said Carcajou.

"You better try sooner to be friendly with a pack of wild wolves," said the dog breaker. "That's what he is. A wild wolf is what he is, and he was runnin' wild when he was trapped."

"You mean," said Carcajou, "that he was running with a wolf pack?"

"Yes, and the leader of it," said the breaker.

"Then he's worth having," said Carcajou.

He reached out and took the canvas sack of gold dust from the hand of the silent, gloomy man who had made and lost the bet.

"What's the price you put on this dog?" asked Carcajou.

"On him? No price at all!" said the other. "I've worked ten days on him, beatin' him to a pulp every day, but I couldn't tame the beast. If you want him, you can have him for nothin'. Look out! He'll have your throat tore out."

Slaughter had crouched to spring, but Carcajou merely snapped his fingers.

"That's all right, brother," he said. "We're not going to have any trouble with one another. Steady, boy!"

Slaughter stood straight up and stared at this strange creature that spoke with the voice of a man but that had in his hands the iron grip of a bear's jaws. The dog stood quietly, waiting for the next move in the game, still murderous, still ready to battle to the death, but acknowledging the force of a mystery which could not be easily solved.

Carcajou stepped to the heavy crate in which the monster have been housed, broke out the iron bolt from the wood, and gathered the chain into his hand.

"We'll go downtown to get some new clothes, Slaughter," he said, and started off down the street.

Slaughter held back, planted his great feet against the snow, but Carcajou walked on, talking slow, taking slow, short steps, and the monster was dragged behind him.

"How long'll that go on before the dog jumps on his back and breaks his neck for him?" one of the men in the group of watchers said to the puzzled dog breaker.

"I dunno," said the dog breaker. "I talk about things that I know. I dunno nothing about gents like that one yonder. I never seen nothing like him before, and so I don't know." He shook his head. "Look at the strength of him," he pointed out. "That dog weighs two hundred pounds, and he's bracing every foot and leg of him to put on the brakes, but still Slaughter had to go along. I dunno. He held the neck of that brute like his hands were vises. I never seen nothing like it, and that's why I say that I don't know."

"Well, could that dog be made into something worthwhile in a dog team?" asked another man.

"You seen for yourself," said the dog breaker. "Slaughter *is* a dog team! He's sled dog and swing and leader all in one. But if you tried to make him part of a whole team, wouldn't he go and eat the other part?"

Only one man laughed. The others were too intently staring at the strange picture of the great dog as he gradually passed out of sight down the street through the white flurry of the snow.

V

"THE GIRL"

The law might be slightly benumbed in Dyea, but it was not altogether dead, and, therefore, Carcajou could not afford to linger in the town. Bill Roads would be out organizing a posse before long, for one thing. It was very strange that news, and Bill Roads with it, could move so fast. When he thought of this, Carcajou felt a thrusting up of admiration in his heart for Bill Roads. That man was a man, and no mistake about it!

There were some quick preparations to be made. He bought a new outfit of furs. Already he had acquired a sled, and the pack to go on it, with four excellent dogs. He needed merely to hitch up the dogs, put a thoroughly strong muzzle on his newly acquired monster, harness him in as sled dog, and strike out on the trail. He carried with him on this trip a burden of excess weight that few adventurers took with them. This consisted of an excellent Winchester rifle on the one hand, and under his coat a .45-caliber Colt revolver with the trigger filed off and the sights removed, also. He would rather have traveled without one leg than without that revolver.

He went up Dyea Creek on the run. There was no need of urging his dogs along. He had a good leader that knew its business in picking out the trail, and the three animals behind the leader were constantly trying to hump their way through their harness, because behind them pressed the gaunt giant, Slaughter, red-eyed, silent, but slavering with hatred and rage and pure physical hunger. He wanted, in fact, to get at those other beasts and destroy them. Very small, frightened, and frantic looked the four big Huskies as they tugged at their traces ahead of the dark beast. He looked to Carcajou more than ever like a vast, long-legged rat. He was the ugliest creature that the man had ever seen. There was something more than animal ugliness—there was a spiritual hideousness about the brute that appalled the mind. But the master was fairly pleased. He was more than ever pleased when it came to the terrible toil up the Chilkoot, where men labored inch by inch forward, groaning under their packs.

He put packs on each of the four dogs, another pack on his own shoulders, and what seemed to him a killing burden on the back of Slaughter. But Slaughter bore it lightly up the way! He had before him the currying tails and quarters of the other animals, and his greed to get at them whipped him forward. He chased the dogs and carried his own mighty load. He also dragged with him Carcajou himself, dangling at the end of a long chain.

Banner laughed a little, going up this famous slope at such a pace. In two trips he brought up the sled's load, and the sled itself. A man stopped him on the second trip.

"Is that a mad dog that you got there?" he asked.

"No, that's not a mad dog. He's only hungry," said Carcajou. "Like him?"

"He looks like the ghost or a dog's nightmare of everything that no dog, or wolf, either, would ever want to be. Tell me truthfully, is he any good?"

"He's as strong as any two others. You can see for yourself."

"Lemme tell you this, Cheechako," said the stranger. "You're a fool to take that big bundle of trouble into Alaska. There's enough trouble already inside. You don't have to take fire from the outside and bring it in! You'll burn before you been there very long."

It was rather strange advice, but it was the only word of counsel that Banner received all the way. Other men regarded him not at all, except as an obstacle before them to be cursed or a trail breaker to be accepted with a grunt of satisfaction. But all that mattered essentially to Carcajou Banner was that he was working his way inside.

When he got to Sheep Camp, he rested, as most other people were doing. It had been a strenuous time even for the limitless strength and the tireless nerve of Carcajou. For he was learning a great deal that he never had known before. He was working at the fine art of snowshoeing. He already knew how to handle skis very well from a certain strange and arduous winter of his youth, but he learned more and more about a similar craft now. He learned the knack of tree felling and how to build camp in the most expeditious and comfortable way. He learned that a carefully made camp and a good sleep were necessary even to him in this country.

The rigors of weather and the trail wiped out the large margin that he could usually allow. In a more southern climate he could disregard such trifles as temperature. But in the white North it was a different matter. He could do more than other men, but he had to be careful. A bullet will kill the loftiest giant, and the North will kill the mightiest man almost as quickly as it topples over the weakling, unless brains and forethought are used. But Carcajou had this advantage: that he learned not only as a thinking, reasoning creature, but also in an animal sense. When an old-timer pointed out the signs of coming storm in the horizon mist, Carcajou looked and listened and felt the lesson sink down into his innermost instinct. It was the same with signs on the trail. It was the same also with the handling of the dogs. By the look in their wind-reddened eyes he learned to guess what was in their minds, that is in all except Slaughter's.

That ugly monster was still a sled dog, pulling half the load, tireless as his new master, and hateful as a legion of demons. Every night came feeding time. Every night the muzzle had to be taken from the long head of the brute, and every time the muzzle was off, there was likely to be a fight between Slaughter and Carcajou. The man always won. He learned a wonderful adroitness in handling the spear-like thrust of those fangs, and yet he carried a dozen deep cuts even before he reached Sheep Camp. However, this constant battle pleased him.

Another thing pleased him when he arrived at the camp. This was to find that his reputation had preceded him. Reputation was the one thing he could not do without. Since he was fifteen, it had always been with him. Since the day of his first battle, admiration, dread, and an invincible loathing always had surrounded him. Just as the great timber wolves slink from the path of the wolverine, so men had shrunk from the way of John Banner. And now they were shrinking again, even these fearless adventurers in the Northland.

He had traveled fast from Dyea, but rumor had gone before him on invisible wings. What he had done in Steuermann's was known, and how he had mastered Slaughter with his bare hands was known, also, although both of these tales had been immensely embroidered and built upon. Any tale worth telling by an Arctic campfire is worth telling well. As for those who doubted, one glimpse of the dreadful figure of Slaughter convinced that Northern world. They saw the hero carrying with him down the trail the proofs of his heroism.

Thus in Sheep Camp Carcajou found that his fame was established even more firmly than it had been in the slums of New York and the underworld of half a dozen cities. There was the same admiration, dread, and loathing. He devoured this universal tribute with a savage and silent joy. He could not be loved, he knew. Therefore, he reveled in winning enormous hate!

Even the nickname had gone everywhere with him. That was best of all. Nobody knew him as John Banner. Therefore the law would not follow him so easily. It was always Carcajou now. Men who did not know the meaning of the word—and most of the men on the trail did not—nevertheless used it. It came to have a special meaning in their minds, more loathsome, more hated and feared than the animal to which it rightfully belonged.

At Sheep Camp Carcajou found the strange trio: the blind old man together with Charley Horn and Jimmy Slade. They had come in just before him, and he saw them unhitching a magnificent team of twelve dogs with two fine sleds behind the lot. It gave Carcajou a deep thrill of pleasure and suspicion to see the outfit. The whole atmosphere of it reeked with a suggestion of crime not very deeply hidden. There was some purpose in the minds of Slade and Horn that was not present in the mind of the blind man. What could that purpose be?

Well, whatever it was, it did not trouble Carcajou. All weakness he despised. There was no mercy in him. The world gave him hatred; he repaid the world with contempt. Still, it was interesting to observe the trio and ponder on the probabilities of the future. A calm, deep voice spoke within him and told him that Old Tom had not very long to live at the hands of this precious pair.

The arrival of Old Tom was a considerable sensation in Sheep Camp, but not more so than that created by another outfit of a dozen dogs and three people that came in still later. The dogs were as hand-picked as those of Slade and Horn. The drivers were Rush Taylor, a wiry half-breed, Bud Garret, a famous dog puncher in the North, and Anne Kendal, a twenty-year-old girl.

Carcajou went over and looked at the outfit, standing close and staring at it. Slaughter, leashed on a chain and unmuzzled, stood behind him. They had just had their daily battle, and Slaughter, well beaten, could be trusted for a time. It was pleasant to Carcajou to parade the big beast without a muzzle; it was pleasant to turn his back on the monster while the men held their breath. No doubt they hoped against hope to see the beast attack the man with murderous power. What they hoped mattered nothing to John Banner, so long as he had their respect and their attention.

So he stood close while other observers gave plenty of room to him and the four-legged thunderbolt chained to him. He looked with his calm, cold stare at the two men. It was a habit of Banner's to let his eyes rest for a long period directly on the face of anyone he chose to observe. Then, if they chose to resent his scrutiny, they could do so at their peril. That was all the better. In places where he was not known, he had worked up many a pleasant fight by no greater maneuver than this.

So now he stared, according to his old custom, at the men. They made a formidable pair. They were as brown as wind and sun could tan their leathery hides. The white man was almost as dark as the half-breed. They were both big. They moved alertly and quickly even at the end of a long day's march.

It was clear that they were well known. Other men in Sheep Camp hailed them by name, asked their destination, and, when no answer came, began admiring the string of dogs. But no one looked at the girl or spoke to her, and this was a great surprise to Carcajou. Certain ways of men in the North were still very new to him. But he knew little or nothing about women, north or south. They had not appeared in his life. They were unnecessary adjuncts. Now he looked over the girl with the same steady, grim eye he had used on the men.

She was almost as brown as her traveling companions, not beautiful, but handsome enough to give the illusion of beauty in this wilderness. It seemed that she was as much at home on the trail as either of her traveling mates. While they handled the camp apparatus, she went out and worked with the dogs, moving swiftly and fearlessly among the big Huskies. She had a certain touch and way with them that interested Banner.

Presently, standing with her hands on her hips, as though about to decide what she would do next, she encountered the eye of Carcajou, looked away, crossed her glance on his again, and suddenly let her eyes rest upon him.

That was very odd. Men had looked him straight in the eye from time to time in his life. Generally they had received enough attention later on to wish that they never had let an eye fall upon him. But never had anyone considered him with the same perfectly cold detachment that she showed.

Charley Horn came up to Rush Taylor, the half-breed, and said quietly, but with iron in his voice: "You're following my outfit, Taylor. What d'you mean by it?"

"I go where I please in this part of the world, Horn," said Rush Taylor steadily.

"Maybe you'll please yourself too much one of these days," answered Charley Horn threateningly.

Bud Garret stopped his work and stood straight and still, listening.

"I mean you, too, Garret," said Horn. "We ain't gonna stand being shadowed the way that you've started out to do!"

Garret merely shrugged his shoulders, but it was plain that he was ready for action of any sort. For a moment Horn's glance swung from one of them to the other, vengeance in his eye. Then he shrugged his shoulders and walked away.

The girl came straight to Carcajou.

"D'you think you know me, stranger?" she asked. "If you don't, my name's Anne Kendal. What's yours?"

He was both affronted and amazed. "I don't carry excess luggage in the way of names," he said. "Any old name will do for me."

"You were staring at me as though I wore stripes," said the girl. "What do you mean by that?"

"People that wear faces will have them looked at," said Carcajou, and sneered at her.

Her eyes pinched a little with scorn and dislike.

"I'll take care of this bird," said Bud Garret, approaching hastily with a dangerous look.

Carcajou took a quick breath of relief. Any man was welcome as an opposite in the place of this girl.

"Back up, Bud," she said. "I don't want trouble started on my account."

"He's been staring at all of us," said Garret. "I'll teach some manners to the half-wit!"

"Look out, Bud!" called some one sharply. "That's Carcajou!"

Bud Garret halted and suddenly grew pale. Then he stiffened his shoulders. "All right," he said. "It ain't the first murdering carrion-eater that I've handled in my time. I'll take him on!"

Carcajou did not answer threat with threat. Nothing about him moved except his lips. He wore a contented smile. He picked the place where he would strike home. That was all. But the girl stepped between them.

"This is my trouble," she said, "and I'll finish it." She faced Carcajou. "What have you got to say to me?" she asked.

Carcajou paused. There was nothing he wanted to say. There was only an emptiness in his mind. He could only sneer and keep it coldly sustained. But it was very hard, indeed. Suddenly he remembered what he had seen Charley Horn do, and, shrugging his shoulders, he turned away and moved off slowly.

He went back to his own tent and began his cookery. He had hardly started when a footfall came near him. Looking up, he saw a little gray-whiskered man well on in later middle age, who stared grimly down at him.

"Carcajou," said the older man, "I dunno where you was raised or what you got behind you. But up here this far North every girl is a lady until she's proved otherwise. After that she's a lady all over again. Don't you forget it, son, or you'll find more trouble than even your hands can put away."

VI

"A JOB"

The other moved away; Carcajou sat bewildered. He had been talked down to; he had been taught with a raised forefinger as though he were a child! Yet he did not feel like leaping up and starting trouble about this matter, because it occurred to him that there might be certain unwritten laws in this Northland about which he knew nothing. That little old chap would not have dared to speak as he had done unless he were aware that a vast weight of public opinion reinforced him.

It was a mystery to Carcajou, except that he was vaguely aware that there had been something admirable in the girl's behavior. She had courage, directness, everything that he expected to find only in brave, resourceful men of action. Yet he hated her with an emotion of sulky helplessness that he had not felt since his childhood. There was a tremor along his nerves and an aching in his heart. The world seemed a bitter place, and he wondered why he had come to this wild Northland to find refuge. Why should he not have gone, instead, to the Orient, where men are men and the women don't matter?

He gritted his teeth. American women were spoiled, he decided. Idle, uneducated, silly, proud, vain, useless creatures! Then he remembered how she had worked among those big, wolfish Huskies without fear, doing more than any man other than an expert dog puncher could have managed. No, all that he said to criticize American womanhood did not apply to her—only the pride, the self-confidence, the disdain of others. He looked back into his own heart. What were the qualities that endeared him most to himself? Why, they were pride, self-confidence, and disdain for the rest of the world! If he criticized her, he was criticizing himself. As he reached this point in his conclusions, he cursed between his teeth. The ache inside him grew worse, and there was a chill of fear along with it. He never had felt this way so long as he could remember. It was something like homesickness, a baffling disease of the mind.

A shadow sat down beside him. It was Charley Horn.

"Hello," said Carcajou, and then stared in his own blank, lion-like way. He remembered suddenly, as the other spoke pleasantly enough in return, that there were duties of hospitality that he never would have thought of in the old days, but they were sacred according to the unwritten law of this Northern land. Now he felt, whether he wanted to or not, he would have to pay attention to those traditional rules of the land of snow.

"Have some tea?" he asked. "There's another. . . ."

"No tea," said Charley Horn. "I dropped over here to talk business."

Carcajou nodded. He was not surprised to hear that Horn wanted to talk business. In fact, all of his dealings were with men of Horn's type.

"Business of what kind?" he asked.

"Day labor."

"Not interested."

"No?"

"No, not interested."

"I mean fifty dollars a day."

"What?" repeated Carcajou, lifting his brows. "Fifty a day?"

Horn grinned. "I wouldn't be offering your kind of a man pin money, would I?" he demanded, proud of the sensation that his offer had made.

Carcajou half closed his eyes. He knew perfectly well that Horn was a rascal, and that Jimmy Slade was another, but rascals were the only kind of men he was really familiar with. Again, the pair were up to some sort of sensational deviltry, and deviltry of that sort was what Carcajou liked. Usually he played a lone hand, but here in the North he was on ground so new that he would hardly know where to turn for employment. Finally, it would be amusing to learn that he had come this far into hiding at great expense, only to find that he had fallen upon his feet, and that other people intended to pay his expenses for him. This last item decided him.

"What's the job?" he asked.

"You'd consider it?"

"Yeah. I'll consider it."

"We've got a hard lot of work ahead of us. We're going down to Linderman and build a boat and cross the lakes. Then we hit the trail again. We want to build our boat fast, and we want to hit the trail fast."

"I'm no carpenter," said Carcajou.

"You can pull at your end of a saw, though," said the other. "I guess that you could do that as good as any three men boiled down and put into one skin."

"All right, go on," said Carcajou.

"That's all. We've got a good dog team. But we've got the blind old bat along with us, Old Tom, as they call him. He's got to be handled like so much dead weight of meat."

"How far do you let me in?" asked Carcajou.

The other hesitated, then lifted his eyes from the ground and stared straight at his companion. "We don't let you in at all. You're just a day laborer to us."

"Ah-hah!" said Carcajou. He also considered. For he was offended by this suggestion, and yet, along with his offense, he felt the great temptation of attacking a mystery, stepping deeply into it.

"It's this way. We want help along the trail up to a certain point," said the other. "After that, we wanna pay you off and say good bye. We pick the point when we pay you off. It may be thirty days. It may be twenty . . . it may be fifty. We don't know."

"Fifty a day, eh?"

"That's our rate of pay. We'll give you twenty days' pay in advance to keep you interested."

"Oh, that's all right," murmured Carcajou. "I guess that I can trust you fellows not to cheat me when the time comes for paying off."

"Yeah, you can trust us for that."

"You want me, and you want my dogs, too?"

"We want your dogs, except Slaughter. You can shoot that brute, far as we're concerned."

"He stays with me," said Carcajou.

"We can't take you on, then."

"All right, then, you can't take me on," said Carcajou, relaxing.

He glanced toward the great beast with redoubled hatred. Slaughter was separating him from an interesting adventure, but still he felt that there was more adventure in Slaughter than in the trio.

"Look," explained the other angrily, "the dog's no good. It'll tear somebody's throat out one day. You see if it don't. Whatcha want with that kind of a dog in your team, man?"

"Why, I like him," answered Carcajou.

"Blast it all, Carcajou, won't you come without him?"

"Not a step."

"We'll have to take him along, then, because we want you bad, and your sled and your team."

Carcajou said: "I'll tell you this . . . that dog will pull a whole sled's weight by himself. I won't let him do any killing in the team, if that's what you mean."

"All right," said Horn with a sigh. "We've got to have you, even if you've got Old Scratch himself along for a playmate."

"All right," said Carcajou. "When do you start?"

"In eight hours."

"I'll be ready. One thing more."

"Well?"

"Why are the others chasing you?"

Horn swore, but he added: "Questions are one thing that you forget to ask on this here trip."

Carcajou laughed softly. "All right," he said, "that goes with me, too. You let Slaughter go along and I keep my face shut!"

VII

"A MYSTERY"

All that Carcajou remembered of the start, later on, was a voice that struck with a strange loudness out of the dimness of Sheep Camp: "Now that they're together, you take and try to pick out a meaner three than them, will you? And may heaven help poor Old Tom."

It was never the habit of Banner to take notice of offenses until they were offered directly to his face, and, although this was almost under his nose, he was perfectly willing to allow the affront to pass.

On that occasion Jimmy Slade said: "I got a mind to look up the gents that are talking like that!"

"Why do that?" said Carcajou. "If we ever start in hunting for all the people that hate us, we'll have to kill most of the world, I guess."

Jimmy Slade looked at him with startled eyes, said nothing, and presently turned back to his work.

So they pulled out of Sheep Camp and started relaying the outfits to the summit. When that was finished, there was little trouble in getting over the nine miles to Lake Linderman, through a cañon bleak and barren, but frozen hard and offering good going for the sleds. From there on was the fine sledding of the lakes until they got to Tagish, where they would buy their boat, or build it, if necessary.

All of the first part of this trip was occupied with good hard work. While it lasted, Carcajou made his estimate of his two younger companions. They were both powerful men; they

139

carried the extra burden of guns, and they knew perfectly how to use them; they had been in the Northland before and were experienced in handling dogs and sleds and building camps. Their tempers were fairly bright. They never dodged labor and worked well together at every task. It was only now and then that the murderous evil of their natures broke out in a glance, a few caustic or bitterly sneering words, or some expulsion of sudden temper. On the whole, they controlled themselves well, like men who have a great task in hand and are willing to put up with all sorts of troubles, including the presence of one another, in order to accomplish the end in view. But the evil which he saw in them did not offend Carcajou. It merely made him feel more at home. It warmed his spirit. It was a touch of that familiar characteristic which he knew best in life among other men. Moreover, he liked the physical vigor that they showed on all occasions. There was only one thing that displeased him and that was their attitude toward Old Tom. When he was in hearing, they were likely to express their actual thoughts in winks, gestures, a sign language, while their spoken words remained polite and gentle. It was plain that they did not dare to let the old man guess what they really were.

As for Old Tom, he was too much of a problem really to interest Carcajou. He did not matter, and, therefore, he was dismissed. It was clear that through him the pair hoped to attain some great end, but what that end might be was a mystery to Carcajou. As far as he could see, Old Tom was simply an excerpt from a fairy story. He was always gentle, never raised his voice, never spoke in haste, never complained of cold or wind, insisted on getting out and running behind the sled, holding onto a line, whenever the footing was at all possible, managing himself wonderfully well on his feet for a man of his age, totally blind. Indeed, in every imaginable way he was as little trouble about the camp as a blind man could well be. But blind he was, and why should a blind man attempt to reach the frozen heart of Alaska? What could he possibly gain there? Gold? But he could not even see the wealth he might be dreaming of! A friend? But what friend would wish to have this helpless burden placed upon his shoulders in such a land? Some familiar place connected with his past life? But in the howling wilderness there was no familiarity worth finding.

No, Old Tom was a great problem for Carcajou, but since the fellow was old, blind, and therefore unimportant, he did not give any time to the solution of the difficulty. He used to feel that the most interesting moment of all was when, in an interval of quiet brooding beside the campfire at night, he saw the face of Old Tom harden suddenly and swiftly into lines that looked to Carcajou like an expression of the most savage cruelty. Age and pain and the cruel affliction of the loss of sight were enough to embitter the spirit of the veteran, but it was only now and again, at long intervals, that he saw a glimpse, as through a frosted window, of the tormented soul. The only incident of real importance on the way to Tagish was when Slaughter tore off his muzzle one day and killed three of the other dogs in the team in the few seconds before Carcajou got his hands on the beast. Carcajous's employers gave him black looks on this occasion, but they said nothing. There was another of the endless series of the battles between Carcajou and his dog, and the incident was closed.

When they got to Lake Tagish, Slaughter performed again, and this time with the most unexpected results. At Tagish they offered fantastic prices in their eagerness to get a ready-made boat, for it was feared that the thaw might come at any time. The frosty snow had disappeared from the face of the country; the limbs of the evergreens were no longer piled with white, and the river between the lakes was beginning to break up, the ice making noises that were anything from a cannon shot to a lion's roar. However, since the thaw was expected almost momentarily, no one was willing to sell a boat, completed or almost completed. Men who were that far into the interior of Alaska felt that golden fortune was just ahead of them. They were smelling and tasting the treasure, as it were. They felt that they would soon be at the heart of it.

So no one would sell, and the three had to set to work building. They had to build a scaffold, and on this they placed great green logs, from which ponderous planks were whipsawed, one man standing above and one man beneath. That is, this was the way that Horn and Slade labored, but Carcajou managed a saw all by himself, a little more clumsily because of the play that came in the saw blade after a wrong stroke, but when he had mastered this, he cut by himself more planks than the other two put together. Men used to come and watch him, the ceaseless pedal motion of his body from the hips causing them to shake their heads with admiration and wonder. If the thaw came soon, it was clear that the two partners would never forget this giant in their employ.

Three days after them the girl arrived with Rush Taylor and Bud Garret. All three set to work boat-building, but it was apparent that they would soon be distanced; all their work on the trail would be useless if they were trying to keep up with Horn and Slade, unless the thaw on the lakes delayed longer than was expected. Yet the thaw did not come.

It was the night of that day when they had commenced to build the boat out of their green planks that Slaughter broke loose again. He was chained to the trunk of a tree, but broke the chain, and the light *clanking* noise of the breaking link of the chain was enough to awaken his master. Carcajou got up at once. There was enough twilight for him to see the gaunt, powerful form of Slaughter standing over the place where blind Old Tom was lying. He could see the glint of the fangs of the brute, bared by the lifting of the upper lip, but Slaughter was making no attempt to tear the throat of the veteran. One hand of the old man was raised, without real strain or effort, and laid on the head of the dog, and under the quiet touch of that hand Slaughter stood still. It was an amazing sight.

Gun in hand, Carcajou waited, but he heard the voice of Old Tom speaking gently, and his bewilderment grew intense when he saw the great dog lie down beside the man. It staggered him utterly. He blinked and shook his head, told himself that he was a fool and seeing a dream, but there was the fact before him.

He strode to the spot.

"What are you doing to Slaughter?" he demanded harshly.

The shaggy head turned like a snake's to regard the master with hatred.

"Just talkin' to him, son," said Old Tom. "Ever try talkin' reason to dogs or men?"

Carcajou muttered a savage, nondescript answer and, seizing the brute by the neck, bore Slaughter off to the tree, where the broken chain was refastened. Then he went back to his own bunk and sat down in it.

Old Tom was propped up in his bunk, smoking. Carcajou had heard that blind men never smoke, but here was a proof to the contrary. More than once he had watched Old Tom working at his pipe with every sign of satisfaction, and here he was again, pulling calmly, serenely, no doubt, thinking over again the events of that evening and the way in which he had established his mastery over the huge mongrel. Carcajou slipped down into his sleeping bag with a gritting of his teeth. He looked up at the dim tops of the trees, all sharply pointing like spears that looked straight up to the sky. The sky itself was nearer, and the world beneath it more vast and confused and mysterious than the southern world that Carcajou knew, the world of cities.

He felt a sense of depression and helplessness, a childish sense of helplessness only to be equaled by what he had felt that day when he had faced Anne Kendal in Sheep Camp. But there was a different aftereffect this time. Before he had been amazed and down-hearted. Now he was swearing sternly to himself that he would penetrate the mystery and learn what it was all about. To him nothing was as strong as strength. He had lavished force in the training of Slaughter and made the dog more dangerous every day. How was it that a comparatively weak old man could subdue the brute with a quiet voice and the touch of his hand?

VIII

"THE THAW COMES"

The thaw held off, unexpectedly, so that the very day it came, Taylor, Garret, and the girl launched their boat. It floated at the most a quarter of a mile from the boat of Horn and Slade, and the latter fell into a frightful tantrum, when he saw the craft. But Horn merely said: "You can't make your luck over. And those birds, they ain't come to the real pinch yet."

He was handling his rifle in a significant way when he said this, and it was not hard for Carcajou to guess that they meant murder when that "pinch" came.

"Luck? They've got the luck of Frosty Smith," said Slade in answer.

"Who's Frosty Smith?" asked Carcajou.

They both looked at him askance.

"You never heard of Frosty?" asked Horn.

"No."

"Listen, Painter," said Slade to Old Tom. "Here's a gent that never heard of Frosty Smith!"

"All the better for him," said Old Tom with his usual calm.

"Frosty Smith," said Horn finally to Banner, "is the king of the thugs in Alaska. Is that right, Painter?"

Old Tom nodded. "Nobody knows how many men have died because of him," said the blind man. "Or how many millions he's stole that other folks dug out of the ground. They used to say down in Circle City that we all did the work and Frosty had all the profit."

145

That name was to stick in the mind of Carcajou, and to good purpose, at another time in his life. In the meantime, they were hoisting their square sail, consisting of odds and ends, and making good time across the lakes. The third day they lost sight of the craft of Garret and Taylor, but that did not mean very much. In the open water their clumsy craft could not expect to gain very much on even a dishpan. So they reached, in due time, the end of the lakes and Miles Cañon.

Horn was for letting the unloaded boat down the rough water with a rope and packing the stuff around to them later on, but Slade was made of sterner stuff. He pointed out that this was the chance for them to gain on the others! Horn consented. He would run the rapids, and Carcajou shrugged his shoulders. It was a point of honor with him that he should accept any venture that any other man dared.

They bound big sweeps fore and aft, extending them on outriggers, and cast off from the shore a hundred yards above the mouth of Miles Cañon. Below lay the more open water, but the frightful rocks of the Squaw and the thunder of the White Horse Rapids were between. They would soon be swept through to safety, or else they would split and be overwhelmed by the terrible current.

What Carcajou remembered of that passage through the white water was nothing except the grand, calm face of Old Tom as he sat quietly, with the shaggy head of Slaughter on his knees. They never needed to chain the dog when Old Tom was with him. Slaughter closed his eyes and shuddered from head to foot while the spray dashed over the craft and the waters howled like a thousand fiends in the hollow cañon, but the face of Old Tom was unmoved.

Carcajou, because he had the strength of more than one man in his hands, handled the forward oar, trying to keep the prow centered. But now and again, glancing back as they shot through a less dangerous stretch, he could see Old Tom smiling faintly, contentedly, with his head thrown back, and on his face the expression of one who listens to the most delightful music.

A dozen times Carcajou Banner knew that they were sliding from the piled-up waters in the center of the current, to be dashed to bits against the walls of the cañon, and a dozen times the rickety craft responded to desperate labor on the sweeps and continued safely on her way. These were miracles that were happening, and the miracles continued. They saw the end of Miles Cañon; they shot through the Squaw; they roared into the thunder of the White Horse, and so into the peace of the lower waters. They were safe.

As they unshipped the sweeps, the calm voice of Old Tom said: "Well done, lads! Well done! I've only been through twice before, but I've gotta say that going through with your eyes shut takes you a pile longer than going through with 'em open!" He laughed a little, still softly.

"We'll never see a girl and two birds like Horn and Slade run rapids like that," sneered Horn. "We can lay up to the bank and take things easy for a while, I got an idea."

They tied up to the bank and cooked and ate a meal. As they boarded the scow again and loosed her down the river, another boat shot from the spuming mouth of the White Horse. A faint cry reached them through the uproar of the waters, and, looking back as they made sail, Carcajou saw the craft of their trailers, with Rush Taylor laughing and waving at the bows.

Slade handled his rifle with a hungry look.

"Not here!" said Horn sharply. "We got too much light of day on us."

But it was plain that they both meant killing. That was

nothing to Carcajou. Death was a small thing in this world, as far as he was concerned. What mattered far more to him was such a thing as the expression on the face of the blind man, looking with unseeing eyes down the river. The white North had left his heart clean. That was certain. For the thousandth time Carcajou wondered at him. There was a mystery deeper than anything Old Tom could guide his two villainous companions to; there was a secret of the soul which he possessed that they never could learn. Not that Carcajou himself greatly cared to change—he merely wondered what the heart of this man could be like. In all the years of his life, he had told himself that one man is not much better than another. As for those who pretended to honesty and humane qualities, it was because they felt that hypocrisy paid them in the long run. Of that he was sure. He never had seen one person who would not take all possible advantages once he had the upper hand. Only in Old Tom he felt an imponderable element that dashed his surety. On those about to die, it was said that a peculiar grace descended, and there was something as profound as that on the brow of the veteran.

Horn and Slade were in close consultation by this time. They had failed once more to shake off the bulldog tenacity of those who pursued. Now they must attempt another shift as soon as they were securely out of sight of the others. With the first dimness of twilight they would try to run the boat ashore, unload it, cache a portion of the load, and sink the scow in the shallows. Then they would pack in as much as they conveniently could and make for their ultimate destination.

So for two days they struggled down the swift, yellow currents of the great Yukon, making sail where they could, laboring with the sweeps night and day, straining every nerve to get ahead. Not until the second day, however, did they manage to get well out of sight of the other craft. Then, as that brief night, which could hardly be called night but rather a prolonged dusk, began, they beached the scow, unloaded her at once, sunk her at the edge of the water, and hastily packed the goods inland. They dug a good deep trench and buried a quantity of provisions in it, covering it over with saplings crossed and re-crossed, so that even a bear would have had a great deal of trouble in opening up that cache.

What was left they packed on the backs of the dogs. There were fourteen of them now, including Slaughter, and they carried a stout burden, every one. Horn and Slade each took a heavy load; Carcajou, with equal ease, bore as much as both the others, and even Old Tom insisted on taking a burden of some forty pounds. With this he went along fairly easily. He was given a rope connected to the collar of Slaughter, and it was an amazing thing to see the dog lead the man. It might well be that Slaughter had in him an evil spirit, but Old Tom had managed to find the way to tame him. At any rate, there was never a moment when the beast was not ready to murder either dog or man in the rest of the party, but Old Tom he treated with more tenderness than a mother wolf would show to the youngest of her litter. When they came to an upward slope, he leaned forward and helped the veteran up. When they reached a deep rut in the ground, he paused until the staff of Old Tom touched him, and the man was warned to prepare for the obstacle in the way. Where a tree or a stump was ahead, he swung wide and steered Old Tom past the danger, and from morning to night Slaughter tended Tom Painter with unending devotion. It was not that he had learned how all at once, but during the three days they marched inland, steadily following the course of the Yukon but keeping it a mile or more to the right, he gradually picked up a hundred arts of conveying information to the blind and helpless old man.

149

Horn and Slade and Carcajou had fallen behind on that third day and were watching Old Tom striding freely before them, when they commented on the strangeness of that performance.

"Dogs are just like safes," said Charley Horn. "All you gotta know is the combination to the dumb fools."

Slade turned his head at that moment and suddenly exclaimed: "By the black heart of a witch, look yonder!"

Over a swale of ground behind them, striding through a thin growth of small timber, they saw a man, erect, with the bulk of a pack on his shoulders. Behind him came dogs, carrying packs, also, and last of all another man and what might have been a boy—only it was not a boy. With one accord all three of them knew that it was Anne Kendal with her two companions.

"Carry on," said Slade through his teeth. "They've found the trail again, and now the fools are gonna learn what else they've found. Charley, they gotta be turned back, and the only way of turning 'em is to use guns. Carry on now, but tonight we'll turn back and give 'em a surprise."

"All right," said Carcajou, "and I'll do the surprising. I've got a grudge against one of 'em. And the whole three I'd like to show how. . . ."

IX

"STRUNG UP"

What would he show them? He hardly knew, except that he felt
that he had been scorned by them all, and the proper answer for
scorn is blasting wrath and the irresistible strength of a right
hand. There were mysteries around him here in this Northland—the journey of Slade and Horn with the blind man they
hated and pretended to feel an affection for, the boldness of Bud
Garret in daring to affront him, the haughty bearing of the girl,
the unknown goal toward which all of these people were
striving. These made problems through which he could not
look, but of one thing he was sure. That night he would attend
to the affairs of at least one of those who traveled in pursuit.

His offer was readily accepted. Horn merely said: "We'll
want you along, all right, Carcajou. But we'll be there, too."

"I'll go alone or not at all," said Carcajou calmly.

"Leave him be, you fool," said Slade to his partner with ir-
ritation. "What d'you want more than a chance to sleep
sound and let somebody else do your work for you?"

Horn argued no longer.

When the twilight of the far North gathered, they increased their pace enough and marched long enough to leave
the enemy behind them. Then they made their camp. Carcajou ate a hearty supper, rolled himself in his blankets,
smoked a final cigarette, and went to sleep.

"You forgetting?" Horn muttered to him.

But Slade, more understanding, snapped impatiently:
"Leave him be! You gonna try to teach Carcajou better tricks

151

than what he knows already?"

Carcajou closed his eyes in sleep contentedly at this moment, and for three long hours he slumbered heavily. It was the time he had appointed for himself, and at the end of that time his eyes opened as though he had heard the ringing of an alarm bell. He did not need to yawn or shake himself into wakefulness. He was suddenly and completely alert, and, quickly dressing, he stood up in the icy chill of the night air.

It bit through his coat; it sank toward the bone like a cutting tooth, but he opened his lungs and inhaled a few deep breaths, and the strength of the cold fell away from him. A thin mist from the river had rolled over the land, rising to the top of the brush, but letting the trees stand up in little ragged islands here and there, with pools of paleness filling the hollows. It was a good night for such work as he had on hand, if only he could find the camp of the enemy.

He looked about him first and spotted Old Tom sleeping peacefully, his feet toward the embers of the almost dead fire, and the great dog Slaughter, curled into an immense circle beside him.

He stepped up to the pair and stood over them, while Slaughter raised his villainous head and favored him with a snarl. But it was a silent snarl, a mere voiceless convulsion of hatred, as though the savage brute did not wish to break in upon the slumber of the man he loved. Something of warmth touched the heart of Carcajou. Acts of thoughtful kindness were in his estimation the most absurd folly, and yet he found himself building up the fire again so that it could warm not those two rascals, Horn and Slade, but the old man whose face was so weary and so serene.

Then, as though ashamed of this act, as the flames began to catch in the wood and rise, crackling with dancing sparks, he strode hastily out from the camp and started on his journey. He had for weapons his Colt revolver, a good heavy hunting knife, and his hands. It should be enough in light like this, that made distant shooting impossible. But could he find the camp of the others?

It was amazingly simple. Not three miles back down the trail he heard a sudden clamor of dogs that led him better than a light, and then came a rush of savage Huskies about him. The biggest and strongest and bravest of the lot came first with enough of the wolf—or the watchdog—about it to take a running leap at his throat. More than one man has been killed by the rush of wolfish Huskies in a strange camp, but Carcajou laughed a little softly in the deep hollow of his throat, and picked the great dog like a ball out of the air.

He got in return a double slash that opened one sleeve of his coat from shoulder to elbow, and the other sleeve was torn straight across, just above the wrist. But that was the only damage done. He kneeled beside the struggling brute and throttled him quickly into submission, while the rest of the team dogs around him scattered back. Their howling and barking fell to a number of frightened, high-pitched yelps. They retreated into ghostly outlines in the distance.

Suddenly a voice not more than twenty feet from Carcajou said: "There's something out there!"

The voice of Bud Garret answered: "Yeah. Likely a wolf prowling. Look at them coward dogs come sneakin' back. The mongrels, they don't like the looks of a full-sized timber wolf. I tell you what I've seen . . . I've seen two real wolves chase a whole pack of sled dogs. Go back to sleep. I'm keeping watch."

"All right. You keep your eyes peeled, will you? Maybe I oughta be standing watch myself all this time."

"We argued that out. You've done your half of the shift. It'll be real daylight before long, and this mist'll clear. But I guess they won't try nothing on us tonight. Even three like them need time to get up their nerve for murder."

"Carcajou, he needs no time. He's always ready to kill," said the half-breed.

The talking ended, and Carcajou smiled to himself with a heart filled with delight. This, to him, was as great a tribute as he could expect. It showed that men feared him even in this wild Northland, and what more did he ask from the world than fear? As for what Old Tom got from Slaughter, well, that was another matter, a mystery which no ordinary man could hope to penetrate.

So he waited there on his knees for a full hour. Another man would have turned numb, and every nerve would have failed in the extreme cold and in that cramped position, but Carcajou had the patience of a beast of prey, which must have patience if it is to live in the wilderness. He would let that camp settle down completely before he moved again. In the meantime, the dog in his hands did not move. It was not dead, but it squatted on the ground with eyes closed and with ears pressed back against its neck in a frenzy of icy terror.

At last Carcajou stood up, released the dog, and moved on. He glanced behind him and saw that the Husky had not stirred, but lay where he had put it, as though shot through the brain. That sight pleased him, also. Even dumb beasts could feel that there was a deadly terror in him—in his touch a fatal and cold magic.

He got down on the ground now. He saw before him two or three red eyes, the glow of a dying fire. Then there was the shadow of a man sitting near the coals of the fire, a black silhouette cutting through the night mist and facing directly toward the hunter. Carcajou moved inch by inch to the left, inch by inch until he had come through the half of a circle. He lay, finally, between the sentinel and the fire behind him. Not a sound did he make, and not a warning yip came from the dog team. Perhaps they had scattered too far and heard nothing.

He could see the girl in her sleeping bag on one side of the fire. He could see the half-breed on the other side. Then he rose behind Garret and gave him the blow that he himself had received in Steuermann's. He knew it perfectly. It was delivered with the edge of the palm, and it fell across the top of the neck and over the two big cords that run up to the skull. The head of Garret jerked back. He slumped sideways from the stump that he was sitting on. In one arm Carcajou received the falling rifle. In the other hand he received the body of the man, lifted him, and stepped slowly, soundlessly, into the mist.

The trees thickened and blackened before him. He paused as his burden began to stir and mutter. So Carcajou put him face down on the ground, gagged him, and lashed his hands behind his back. He had plenty of cord for the purpose. It had been in his mind from the first.

Then he selected two trees a proper distance apart. He freed one of the man's hands and tied it well up the trunk of one of the saplings. Toward the other he stretched the right arm of Garret, and then drew the cord very tight. Before he had ended, Garret was strung in the air with his weight on his tensely drawn arms and with his toes barely touching the ground.

At present this was nothing, but after a time the weight of his body would wear out the strength of the arm and shoulder muscles. Then the full strain would come upon the tendons, and these, in turn, would begin to stretch. The real agony started at that moment. It would not take long. An hour or so of this would leave a man perfectly capable of walking, but his arms would not be fit for real service for a month.

Then Carcajou stepped close and said at the ear of Garret: "I was a murdering carrion-eater the other day to you, Garret, and now I've walked back here through the night to tell you that it's a bad business to call names. Don't call names, Garret. Kill your man if you have to, but don't call him names. You can stay here a while and think it over."

Then he turned and went off quietly through the night. The pleasure of his adventure filled him to the throat with joy. He wanted to burst into song.

X

"THE BLIND LEADER"

When he got back to camp, the noise of dogs again showing him the way, he slipped back into his bed, and there he was found by the others when they awakened in the morning.

Horn said dubiously: "Well? What happened? Have a good sleep all night?"

"All except a funny dream," said Carcajou.

"What kind?"

"A kind that would make you laugh," said Carcajou. "I dreamed that I went back about three miles and found their camp, and Bud Garret was standing watch, or sitting watch, rather. And I dreamed that I got hold of him and snaked him away and said to myself that one helpless man would be a lot worse for the others to handle than a dead man. So I tied him between two trees with a gag between his teeth. I tied him so that his toes just touched the ground and the whole of his weight was pulling on his shoulders. By the time they find him, I've got an idea that he'll not be able to use his arms for a month or so . . . if he hasn't strangled to death trying to work against the gag and screams for help."

He chuckled as he said this. The other two grinned sympathetically.

"Got any sign that you really went into that camp and did all this?" asked Horn.

Carcajou looked narrowly, earnestly at Horn, without making a sound in reply. But here Slade averted trouble, perhaps, by snatching up a rifle. "This here gun wasn't in our

157

camp yesterday!" he exclaimed. "Look here, Carcajou! Did you bring away Garret's gun, along with him? A man in one hand and his gun in the other?"

Carcajou seemed to have lost interest in the conversation, but at this point Old Tom broke in: "D'you mean to tell me, Carcajou, that you tied up a man where he'll be tortured like that for hours, maybe?"

The voice of Carcajou was a mutter that sounded like a low growl. "How else would I do up a gent like Garret?" he asked. "Want me to ask him politely to turn back from our trail? Or would you like to have me kill him straight off, instead? I wouldn't have minded doing that, but one helpless man will tie up his partner as well. That was my idea."

Old Tom stood up straight and struck the ground with his staff. His empty eyes were turned under a depth of darkened brows toward Carcajou. "According to my lights," he said, "nobody but a mean hound and a low hound would do a thing like that."

Carcajou rose from his food with his face perfectly calm, except for the slight lifting of his upper lip. Opposite him, and in front of Old Tom, rose the monster, Slaughter, and stood with a frozen smile facing his real master. But suddenly it dawned upon Carcajou that ownership in the eyes of the law is a very small thing compared with ownership of honest and sincere affection.

Slade cut in at this point. "Carcajou is a rough man, Tom. You know that by this time. But he's all right. We had to turn 'em back, didn't we? They were gonna trail us right to the . . . spot, weren't they?"

The face of Old Tom was still stormy with wrath, but, fighting fiercely with himself, he controlled his speech. "We're far North . . . it's a hard country," was all he muttered, "and I'd rather lose all the gold in the world than put another man through torture before his time."

"Looks to me . . . ," began Slade angrily.

Horn exclaimed: "Jimmy, shut your mouth!"

He made a significant gesture toward Old Tom as he spoke. Slade controlled himself in turn. But all three were now glaring at Old Tom with a savage concentration. The same emotions that Carcajou felt, he could see clearly mirrored in the faces of his two employers. That did not altogether please him. They were a low cut, he knew, and it was far better to be like Old Tom than to be like either of the younger men.

It was a very sudden check, an odd shock to Carcajou, and it kept him in brooding silence for hours. It was not the first time that he had received a shock to the soul from the words and the behavior of Old Tom. It was not the first time that something in the dignity of the man overcame him with awe first, and with shame and hate later. He merely said that day: "I've loaned you my dog these days, and you pay me back as a dog would. You can get on without Slaughter from now on!"

So with his own hands he took Slaughter on the lead.

It was not a very convenient arrangement. It simply meant that either Slade or Horn had to walk in front of Old Tom that day, with a cord tied from the belt and running back to the hand of the veteran. But neither Slade nor Horn seemed to feel it strange that Carcajou had acted as he did. Neither of them appeared to bear the slightest resentment, and Slade actually said to Carcajou: "I don't blame you. We hate the old fool as much as you do, and after he's brought us to. . . . Well, listen to me, Carcajou. Me and Charley have been talking things over. If you've turned back the girl and her friends, it's a load off our minds. I'll tell you what . . . we ain't chasing this far North after any rainbow, brother. We're lookin' for the pot of gold. I guess you figgered that out a long time ago. And we want you to get a slice of the profits. Suppose we split the thing five ways. You get one way, me and Horn get the other four, because we had the idea first. Does that sound to you?"

Carcajou only answered: "I've got three wishes."

"What are they?" asked Slade.

"The first one is that Old Tom were just half his real age. The second is that he had his sight back. The third is that he should be forty pounds more of muscle."

Slade grinned brightly.

"I know," he said. "You'd like to go at his throat, then? It's all right, son. Maybe you'll be even with him a long time before you think. Brother, me and Charley have pretty near choked over the old hound and his church talk."

They traveled on slowly that day, and yet there was never a sign of pursuit. Even when the air cleared of all mist and they reached a comparatively high knoll from which they could survey a great sweep of country, there was no trace of the train of pack dogs and people that had followed them the day before. The joy of Slade and Horn was great indeed! But Carcajou could feel no pleasure in the praises they heaped on him.

Watching Old Tom as that pioneer stumbled and staggered on his way, guided infinitely less by his human leader than by the dog on preceding days, a cold wave of shame swept over Carcajou. Shame had been a stranger to him before his journey to the Northland. Shame was a thing that one felt, according to his code, after one had shown the white feather, or had been outwitted or tricked or beaten by sheer force by other men. Shame was the emotion of the weakling, insufficient for the task in hand, and Carcajou never had been insufficient for the task in hand. But now he felt himself hemmed in and baffled and beaten in a strange way. He would have given more not to have taken the giant dog from Old Tom than to have undone any other act of his life. There were, indeed, few things that he would have wished to undo in his long career of successful crime. But this was different. As he watched the dog, constantly straining to get to the man he loved, it seemed to Carcajou, for the first time in his existence, that some all-seeing eyes must be fixed down upon the scene in judgment. What that judgment would be he could guess with much wretchedness.

They came to a creek, at midday, running down to the Yukon between steep, high banks.

"This ought to be the place," said Slade. "We've come about the right distance down the Yukon, Tom, according to your way of reckoning."

Old Tom stood on the edge of the bank and turned his empty eyes from side to side. With haunted faces, Horn and Slade watched him. It was clear to Carcajou that much hung upon this moment. Since he had been made a partner in their venture, he should have felt some excitement, also. Strangely enough, that was not the case. With a sort of melancholy disgust, he eyed the straight shoulders and the fine head of the old man.

"How does it come into the Yukon? About south, southwest?" asked Old Tom.

"Just that!" said Slade eagerly.

"Is there a low bank on the north side, covered all over with brush and a few small trees?"

"No," groaned the other two in unison.

"A bank like that could be washed away any season, if a flood came down," said Old Tom. "Any fringing of trees on top of the bank across there?"

"Yes. There's a scattering of trees."

"I think that it's the place," said Old Tom. "Is there a big double bend of the bank off here to my left?"

"Yes, two big bends."

"It's the creek," said Old Tom. "It's Thunder Creek! And we're only a half day's march from the mine . . . ah, you told me not to use that word. I'm sorry!"

"That's all right," said Slade. "Carcajou's in the partnership now."

"Carcajou?" exclaimed Old Tom.

He said no more, but the expression of his face was enough to fill the heart of Carcajou with a hot wave of wrath, and then an icy shock of this new shame went through him. He was beaten and depressed, but now his attention was taken up entirely by what followed. Old Tom had turned about and was saying: "I remember that the wind that day was just east of south, and, when I was lost in that fog, coming down the bank of the Yukon, I had to feel my way along till I got here to the mouth of Thunder Creek. When I got here, I felt that I could hit out the direction pretty well. I figgered that it would take me about four hours of steady marching. The fog was so thick, blowing down the wind, that I couldn't see two yards ahead of me. But I had to get back to the mine. I was nearly starved. You remember, it'd been two days since I'd eaten? And marching along all of that time! Well, I knew that wind prevailed out of the south, or a point east of south. I got the feel of it on my face and my hand and marched for four hours. I crossed about half a dozen creeks, got through a tangle of trees, and at the end of the four hours I started to cut in circles." He paused and shook his head.

"Go on!" urged Slade eagerly.

"Why," said Old Tom, "just as I was about to cut for sign in circles that fog lifted a mite, and the willows around me had a kind of familiar look. And all at once I understood. I'd been lucky enough to walk plumb onto the old mine! But I've told you boys this before."

"I could hear it a million times more," said Slade. "Now,

you think that you could walk blind to that same spot?"

"If somebody can give me south by east, a point or two, I'll try to make it. Mind you, the map ain't as clear in my mind now as it used to be. I guess I'm stepping a little shorter, too, since I've lost my eyes. Suppose we make it five hours of marching and then stop and look around? But if we don't come out close on the spot, you'll have to start searching that swamp from head to heels, and that's no joke, I reckon. If I can't bring you right on the place, maybe you'll never find it in a life of searching. But I've warned you before. There's a hundred of those creeks, and every one of 'em the same, and every one of 'em with the landmarks washin' out and fillin' in every year, y'understand? It's a regular labyrinth. You'll see, pretty soon! Head on, then, and give me the direction, and I'll try to measure out the right distance once more. Oh, for some luck! The folks back home certainly need it!"

XI

"THE BACK TRAIL"

Money for its own sake was a small thing to Carcajou, and yet he could not help being stirred by the possibilities that might be ahead. As they trekked across the rolling miles in the hours that followed, he found occasion to say to Slade: "If the split is in five parts, one for me and four for you and Horn, where does Old Tom come in?"

"Why should he come in anywhere?" snapped Slade with an oath. "Ain't he old enough to die?"

He sneered as he said it, his eyes flashing, and John Banner looked straight before him, seeing the future and amazed because he did not relish it. It seemed to him as though a mist lay over his spirit, through which he saw all things dimly. He felt that he could not criticize Horn and Slade without criticizing himself, and he had never learned to sit in judgment upon himself.

They came, now, to a district shrouded in dark trees, all small and rarely growing closely together, but with heavy brush between. As they climbed a knoll, they could look forward upon the gleaming face of a swamp that was cut by the waters of scores of twisting creeks. It was such a tangle that even a compass seemed of little use in guiding one across.

But Old Tom was going confidently on, feeling his way a little with his staff, when Slade looked back and exclaimed: "There! By all the demons below!"

Looking back, the other two saw four Huskies come through a thicket not half a mile from them, and after the

Huskies a small stripling, carrying a pack. It was the girl, then?

The brain of Carcajou spun into a dark mist. He had the explanation easily at hand. The disabling of Garret had been enough to make the half-breed see that this trail was no longer practicable. Even Garret and Taylor together might have a hard enough time in facing the dangers before them, but those dangers were impossible for a man to combat single-handed. So Taylor had turned back, taking his companion with him, but the girl, dauntlessly, had gone forward. For there she was, trudging steadily on toward trouble.

"Go back and turn her around and start her toward the Yukon!" said Horn to Carcajou. "Throw her into Thunder Creek and let it carry her into the Yukon, for all that we care!"

"I'll handle her," said Carcajou.

He turned and hurried back with long, swift strides. The affront that she had put upon him long before still rankled in his very flesh like a poisoned barb, and it seemed to him a pleasant thing to stand before her on this day as master. The others disappeared behind him into the brush; he went rapidly on, down a small hollow, and over the next swale he stepped fairly out before her.

She stopped, closed her eyes, drew away from him, and then pulled herself together with a mighty effort. The four dogs crowded about her feet, snarling at the intruder, and Carcajou laughed with a sound like an animal's snarl.

"What were you gonna get out of this?" he asked. "Walking straight ahead, what were you going to get out of this? Tell me that, Miss Kendal?"

He heard the catch of her breath. She was looking at him as at a nightmare. "I kept on because I'd gone too far to turn back," she said. "That's why I kept on trailing you."

"You can turn around and follow your own trail back into

the Yukon, then," he said.

She made no answer to this, but eyed him gravely.

He waved his hands. One of the dogs jumped far to the side and yelped.

"Start going!" commanded Carcajou.

Still she did not move.

He laughed brutally, saying: "I gotta force you, do I?"

Her eyes were as steady as they had been back there at Sheep Camp, where there had been plenty of people around to support her, and at this he chiefly wondered, seeing the dismal emptiness of the landscape about them and hearing the growling of the currents in Thunder Creek, not far away. He walked up close and towered over her.

"Start moving!" he repeated.

Nothing that he had ever seen in his life amazed him like what he saw now—for she was actually smiling up at him, although rather faintly.

"You can't do it," she said.

"I can't do it?" echoed Carcajou, still more astonished.

"You could torture Garret till he was half mad," she said, "but you can't touch me."

"Oh, I can't, eh?" muttered Carcajou. "You tell me why, will you?"

"People are made that way," said the girl. "A man who can take another man as you took big Bud Garret couldn't lay a hand on a woman."

He stared at her. It never had occurred to him that Garret was particularly big. A six-footer, to be sure, and with plenty of shoulders about him, but that was all. Bigger men than Garret, by far, had been as fragile reeds in his hands long before this.

"You're trying to now, but you can't," said Anne Kendal confidently.

"Why, you talk like a fool!" he broke out, and strove to rouse his anger at her assurance, but anger was a cold, dead thing in him.

"I may be a fool, but you're not the demon people make you out," said this strangest of women, nodding at him. "I guessed it the first time I saw you and heard your name. You're more man than carcajou. I'd be a thousand times more afraid if Horn or Slade stood in your boots just now."

"There's a short cut to the Yukon, and that's Thunder Creek that's muttering over there," he said.

"Meaning that you could carry me over there and throw me in?"

"Well?" he said.

She put her hands side-by-side and turned them palms up and looked down at them. "I suppose you could," she said. "But you won't."

"I've taken a job on my hands," he said. "D'you think that I'll come short of it because of you? What started you on this crazy trail, anyway? Your partners have turned back. If they're beaten, you're beaten."

"They're beaten, but I'm not beaten," she insisted.

"Talk some more," said Carcajou. "Because I'm interested. I like to hear you. Talk some more, and tell me how you can carry on without a man to help you."

"Perhaps I'm not without a man," said the girl.

"No?" He swept the horizon with his eye. "Where's any man?" asked Carcajou.

"In your own boots," she amazed him by answering.

"In my boots?" said Carcajou with a snarl.

"That's what I mean," she replied.

"I'm listening," he said. "There's a joke behind all this, I suppose. What's your idea?"

"My idea is that murdering hounds like Slade and Horn

167

couldn't buy as much of a man as you are."

"They couldn't?"

"No, nor a scoundrel and hypocrite like Old Tom."

He started. "He's not a scoundrel, and he's not a hypocrite," said Carcajou.

It was surprising to him that he felt sure of what he was saying as of nothing else in the world—the virtues of Old Tom, who he detested so!

"He's both things," said the girl. "You're merely pretending that you don't know it."

"I'd like to hear your proof about Old Tom before you start on the back trail along with me," he said.

"What sort of proof do you want?" she asked. "When a man lets down his partner and breaks his word, isn't that enough?"

Carcajou shook his head. "Old Tom never did that, never could do that," he said.

"I *know* he did," said the girl.

"How do you know?"

"The partner he let down was the husband of my sister."

"Then he lied," said Carcajou brutally.

"Dead men don't lie," answered the girl. "He was dying when I heard him say it for the last time."

XII

"AN INDIAN TALE"

It is true that death seems to brush away falsehood. Carcajou sobered, listened and looked, hard and deep, into her eyes. Suddenly it seemed to him that in this world of lies it would be almost as hard to doubt her as to doubt Old Tom himself. Yet a lie must have existed somewhere between the two of them. His eyes turned small with suspicious doubt.

"Well, go on and tell your yarn," he said.

"Jimmy Dinsmore was my brother-in-law," said the girl. "He came up into Alaska four years ago for the first time. Then he went away and came back two years ago. He'd made a good stake the first time. He wanted to make a bigger one, because there were a wife and two children to be supported. So he came back last year. When he came home, he had a hundred pounds in gold dust. That's over thirty thousand dollars, you know. But he talked as though that were nothing, as though he had millions in his pocket to spend, if he cared to, and the story he told was this. He'd heard an Indian tale about following down the Yukon and up Thunder Creek, a little tributary of the big stream. He went on this particular trail, and there he struck a huge marsh. While he prospected in it here and there, he ran out of provisions and he could get at no game. He was close to starving when he happened to run across the camp of an old sourdough who had heard that same Indian legend and had beaten him to the spot. The Indian yarn was true. Jimmy Dinsmore saw the sourdough wash three hundred dollars out of one pan!"

169

"Hold on," muttered Carcajou. "Three hundred dollars out of one pan?"

"Yes. Just that! Oh, you could trust Jimmy if you'd known him. He was the soul of honor. He stayed with that prospector for a few days, and the old man took care of him. Jimmy was half dead, and he gave him food and treated him like a father. He was absolutely square with him. Then one day the sourdough tried a shot at some birds near the diggings, and the shotgun exploded." She raised her hand to her face, which had twisted with pain. "He wasn't killed," she said. "But both eyes were put out."

"Old Tom?" exclaimed Carcajou, immensely interested.

"Old Tom," she said.

He shrugged his shoulders. "This doesn't prove that Old Tom was a hound," he said.

"Not yet. You'll hear," said the girl. "The next thing was to get him out of Alaska, or far enough south to find a good doctor. It was the worst season of the year, but they had plenty of good dogs and enough provisions to make the try, so they pulled out. It was a terrible march going out, but Jimmy was an iron man. He had to handle himself, and he had to handle Old Tom as well. It was a frightful trip. They had two dogs left when they mushed the last mile down to the sea. They got a boat and went to Seattle. Jimmy took Old Tom to a doctor, and the doctor said that nothing could be done. It was a hopeless case. There and then Old Tom swore that he would reward Jimmy for sticking by him on the long trek out. He said that he would give Jimmy a half interest in the mine and let him go back and clean out the placer. It was a rich find. There was no doubt of that. One man could wash out a fortune in a single summer! Jimmy was for turning about and going back straight into Alaska, but about that time he got a telegram from my sister in Portland, Oregon, telling him that their little boy was terribly ill. So down he came with a rush. Old Tom was to make out the legal papers and send them after him, giving him his share of the mine. Then, on the way down, in a steam-heated train, he caught a cold that turned into pneumonia. He was a mighty sick man when he arrived. I know, because I met him at the train."

Carcajou, focusing his eyes beneath a frown, continued to stare at her. "Go on!" he commanded harshly.

"I got him home," said Anne Kendal. "The next day he was delirious. The day after, he seemed a lot better. He told us all about Old Tom, and we began to watch the mails for the letter that was to come from Jimmy's partner. But the letter didn't come. Two weeks later Jimmy was well enough to sit up. The next day he had a relapse, and died in less than a week. And there was never a sign of a letter from Old Tom. I knew then that Jimmy was being cheated. He had saved the life of that old sourdough, I knew . . . and I knew, also, that half of the mine was no more than his by right. So, finally, with everything going worse and worse at my sister's home, I went to Seattle to look up Old Tom. It wasn't easy to trace him. But finally I located him, trailed him, and found him walking up a gangplank on board a boat bound for Juneau. Well, I followed him. He had two men with him that looked like criminals. They were your friends, Horn and Slade. If you call them your friends! I took the next boat for Juneau, found the three getting an outfit there for the inside, and I decided that I would do the same thing. I had enough money to stake one try. Everybody recommended Garret. Through him I got Taylor, the better man of the pair. They bought the dogs and the outfit, and we loaded onto the same boat that carried the others to Dyea. Since then we've hardly had them out of sight. If there had been only the two of them, I would have won, too. But they came across you. That was their good luck. They persuaded you to join them. Otherwise, right now I'd have Taylor and Garret beside me, and their guns would clear the road if the road needed clearing. That's the story. I've finished."

He cleared his throat and said: "Either you're a liar, or your brother-in-law lied to you, or else Old Tom is the greatest faker in the history of the world."

"What d'you believe?" asked the girl.

He closed his eyes and thought. It was hard to doubt her and her straight-glancing eyes. But it was still harder to doubt the man who had conquered Slaughter with a touch of his hand. "Old Tom is not a faker," he said finally, shaking his head.

"Good for you," murmured the girl.

He was surprised to see her eyes shining.

"You like him, and you stick up for him," she explained. "There's nothing better than that. I knew you were the right stuff, even if they call you Carcajou. I know you'll do right by me."

"What would doing right by you mean?" he asked.

"Let me stand in front of Old Tom and tell my story, and see if even a blind face can keep from admitting the truth!" she exclaimed.

Carcajou started. It seemed, at first glance, a quick and too simple a defeat for him. On the other hand, he was tempted by the thought of seeing the two of them face to face, the girl and Old Tom, both, apparently, so dauntlessly devoted to the truth. The thought made him smile. He had always felt that honesty is only a mask that some people are able to wear more effectively than others. He was sure of it now, in looking forward to that encounter. Either the girl lied, or Old Tom was a consummate cheat. To be sure, he had half the value of an incalculably rich mine to influence him. But the girl had the same idea to influence her. Should he believe the man or the woman? He hesitated and shrugged his shoulders.

When he looked at her again, he saw that she was smiling, and she explained: "I wanted to see you blasted off the face of the earth when we found poor Bud Garret tied between the trees this morning. Then I started hating Bud when he begged Rush Taylor to turn back with him and not to go on when there was such a thing as Carcajou ahead of them. But now it seems to me as though the whole thing were planned out for me by a good jinni, because I can see Carcajou will give poor Molly better justice than both Garret and Taylor put together."

"And who's Molly?" snapped Carcajou.

"Why, Molly's my sister," said the girl with an air of surprise.

Carcajou frowned. It was all too simple and virtuous. "Nothing for you to gain yourself in making this long march?" he asked.

"Except to see Molly well fixed. No."

"Bah!" grunted Carcajou in disgust.

She shrugged her shoulders, and then looked straight back into his face.

"You're smiling at me. You're mocking me right now," he said angrily.

"I'm smiling," she said, "because I know that you'll help. Brave men are never wrong. They're always on the right side."

He glanced back through the annals of his life—with its scent of gunsmoke in the nostrils and the sickening odor of red blood spilling all the way across a table. Brave men are always on the right side? Well, he could have told her a few little incidents in which they had been on the side of death and destruction for its own savage sake! But he merely said: "You think that I'll go with you on that trail and catch up with 'em?"

She nodded.

He drew in a quick breath. He wanted to swear, but his tongue was tied. "If I put you in front of Old Tom," he said, "will you promise to tell the same story that you've told me?"

"Promise? I'll swear!" she exclaimed. "Do you think that I've made it up? Oh, if there were light in his eyes, I'd make him blench!"

He looked around him at the gloomy rolling landscape. Even where there were trees, there was little green along the boughs, as though life feared to show itself openly to so cold a world. Then he shrugged his powerful shoulders again.

"Come on with me," he said. "I may be a fool, but I want to see which of two honest people is the liar!"

XIII

"GOLD DUST"

It was not hard, of course, to trail Old Tom and the other two men. If there had been any difficulty, it was removed by a sudden outcry not far ahead, a wild and wailing sound that, nevertheless, was not one of lament, but rather of maddening joy.

"They've found the place," said the girl. "Although how a blind man could lead them. . . ."

"I've heard of things like that," said Carcajou. "And blind men able to find things in houses they haven't been in for half a lifetime, too," he added.

They hurried on. To the voices of the men was added the howling of the dogs, and the pack of Huskies of Anne Kendal began to yelp as though they were on a wet blood trail. Presently they broke out from the trees into pandemonium. It was only a small clearing that extended from the edge of the creek over a low hummock, with the remains of a shelter hut on the top of it. Over that hill the dogs were racing or rolling to get off their packs, some of them leaping up and down or sitting to point their noses at the sky, some bristling their neck fur and howling with a melancholy abandon. Their frenzy was nothing compared with that of Slade and Horn. Staggering drunkenly back and forth, they shrieked and howled. It was as inarticulate as the yelling of the dogs. They clapped one another on the back. They laughed till they cried. They flung up one hand and brandished clutching fingers as though they were trying to tear the blue out of the sky. But each kept one hand close to his breast, palm up, and from time to time they stared down at the contents of that hand.

Carcajou, approaching the clearing, had stepped out a little ahead of the girl. When the pair saw him, they did not pause to ask how he had managed with the girl. They simply rushed at him, babbling madness and joy. They thrust out their hands, and he saw the gleam of yellow dust in the hollows of their hands.

Horn raised his own few grains of treasure and flung them far, drunkenly laughing. "You dunno what it means, Carcajou!" he yelled. "It means that the yarn was true. The stuff is here. Whoever in the world seen a lay like this? Gold that ain't behind a steel door with a combination lock, but gold that's salted away through the ground like so much grit. Look, man! Look, look!"

He dragged Carcajou to the edge of the running water, tore up a bit of the peaty soil, put it to the hand of the other, and forced him to hold the clod in the running water. As the ground disintegrated, the yellow stain of it floating down the current, there remained in the hand of Carcajou two or three pinches of bright, glittering gold dust. He had handled plenty of money before, in large sums, too, but never had it had such an effect upon him. Money was a social product, along with jails and the other tools of the law. Money was a thing to be desired, but for which one had to pay either with labor or with crime, or with both. But this was different. Here was gold that the bare hands could take from the earth; here was gold growing, as it were, out of the headwaters of the river of happiness and prosperity.

Then a strange aftermath of emotion overwhelmed Carcajou, and he looked up with sullenly savage eyes, like a dog that had found food and is ready to defend it from the rest of the pack. They had offered him one-fifth share in this, had they? And he had accomplished the great feat that baffled the others—turning back Garret and Rush Taylor? He would see these partners of his in perdition if he did not get a larger share!

Ordinarily Horn forced himself to a decent attitude toward Old Tom. Now, however, he lunged for the old sourdough, shook him by the arm with a mighty grasp, and into his hand pressed the particles of gold he was holding.

"You don't need your dog-gone' eyes now!" shouted Horn. "There's something that you can buy new eyes with. There's something that will buy you everything you want most in the world. Except youth, Painter. It won't buy you that! You're that much closer to the infernal regions, but you can brighten up the rest of the way downhill."

Old Tom lifted his face and the dark hollows of his eyes turned up like the glance of a statue, in vain. There was trouble in him, not pleasure. "When I hear you yammerin' like this, Charley," he said, "I don't hardly recognize your voice. It's like a wild howlin'. It's like murder. I've heard men yell before they started to shoot. They sounded the way you sound now. I remember that it made me pretty giddy and sick, too, when I found that stuff. I got more'n four hundred dollars in one pan. I got more than a pound of gold in one pan! Not average, mind you, of course, but in one pan I picked up more than a pound. That's worth a day's work, lads, I guess?"

He laughed a little as he said this, but he was not overwhelmed by his emotions. Instead, he was as calm as could be and at ease. He merely smiled at the frantic excitement of the other men, which had driven even the dogs into a frenzy.

A thunderclap came in the brain of Carcajou as he asked himself what Old Tom had that was worth so much that he could actually despise a vast fortune in new gold? No, Painter did not despise the money. He had worked hard years before getting to it. But it was an end subordinate to other ends more important in the life of the sourdough. What ends might those be?

Carcajou shook his head and sighed a little. He let the gold dust spill out of his hand. He almost forgot the water behind him, the world about him, for the sake of staring at the illumined face of the blind man. For there was a secret, Carcajou knew, worth far more than gold or diamonds.

A yell came from Horn: "Look! There she is! Carcajou, I thought you was gonna either turn her back or throw her into Thunder Creek!"

She was coming slowly down the slope from the edge of the woods toward the rushing water.

"Carcajou, what's the meaning of this?" roared Slade in turn. "I'll handle her!"

"Hold on, boys! Hold on!" exclaimed Old Tom, fumbling vainly in the air before him, as though trying to find the cause of the trouble. "What's wrong? If it's a girl, don't yell at her like that!"

"Back up from her, Jimmy," said Carcajou to Slade.

He had only delayed long enough to watch her manner of encountering a man like Slade when the latter was simply an hysterical animal. Now he saw, and he was filled with admiration. She was not afraid, it seemed. She merely stood still and faced the rush of Slade.

"Come back here, Slade!" shouted Carcajou.

Slade yelled over his shoulder: "I'll come back when I've taught her the way to start back for . . . !"

He grabbed her by both arms. His head was wavering from side to side in the excess of beastly joy and triumph.

"You'd foller us, would you?" shouted Slade. "I'll teach you to foller. I'm gonna make you turn back, Annie, my dear, and if. . . ."

Carcajou took him by the nape of the neck and squeezed. It was not a pleasant trick. Nerves were crushed against strong tendons, and tendons against the neck bone. Once, when he was a boy, a grown man with a powerful grip had done the same thing to Carcajou, and he had practiced all his life to gain a grip so strong that it would cause white, shooting flames of agony to dart up through the brain and cause a paralysis downward through the body when he tried the same maneuver.

Jimmy Slade gurgled in his throat and fell on his knees, with both hands raised to thrust away the remorseless pressure of that strong hand. Carcajou sneered down at him with a brutal complacency.

"Don't go grabbing people, Slade," he said. "Because this is how it feels sometimes." He released Slade. Then he said to the girl: "Now you explain what you meant by calling Old Tom a traitor and a crook that didn't keep his word, will you?"

Savagely she faced the old sourdough, and Old Tom was now coming slowly toward them, fumbling with his staff and resting his left hand on the lofty, powerful shoulders of Slaughter, for the dog had been given back into his hand when he started up Thunder Creek to find the mine if possible. A very odd picture he made as he came with trouble expressed on his face.

The girl said: "If you're Tom Painter, you've done everything I say. You've cheated a man who might have let you rot in the snows right here!"

"Cheated?" said Old Tom in distress. "Cheated, did you say, ma'am?"

His eager humility did something queer to the heart of Carcajou. He pinched his lips together and stood there, searching their faces, looking from the face of the girl to Old

Tom. One of them lied, of course. Both of them seemed perfectly brave and fearless in their integrity, but the very point of their debate proved that one of them had lied and was still lying. Which could it be?

Charley Horn rushed up, shouting loudly: "Don't talk to her, Tom. Don't say a word to her. Don't believe her. She's crazy. She's a crook!"

But Slade chimed in: "Aw, let them have their confab, anyway. What difference does that make to us?" But he added: "Unless *he* turns crooked on us, and tries to help 'em out!"

"He's not a fool," said Horn.

"Who are you?" Old Tom was asking the girl.

"I'm the sister of Jimmy Dinsmore's wife."

"By thunder!" cried Old Tom, and came toward her, stretching out his hand. "Are you really?"

"You detestable hypocrite, keep away from me!" she screamed, and he stopped, stunned by what he had heard.

XIV

"CLEARED UP"

"If you're Jimmy Dinsmore's sister-in-law," said Old Tom, "you've got no right to speak mean to me, I guess."

"No?" she asked, savage with anger.

"If Jimmy were here . . . ," began Old Tom.

"You know well that he can't be here!" she interrupted. "You know well that he's dead and in his grave."

Old Tom caught his long staff with both hands and leaned upon it. "Jimmy Dinsmore dead?"

"Ah," cried the girl, "he loved you! He was never finished talking about you and the fortune that you were going to make with him. And you left him to die, his wife and youngsters stripped of everything, except a little saved from what he brought home. Why did you do it?"

"Why did I do it?" exclaimed Old Tom. "Are you Anne Kendal that he was always telling me about?"

"That's my name. Poor Jimmy."

"I wrote to Jimmy . . . I wired to Jimmy. Why didn't he ever send me an answer? Did he die then right after he got back, my poor partner?"

"What address did he give you?" asked the girl, her voice sharpened by hostility.

"He gave me number seven fourteen North Shore Drive."

"That's the right address," said Anne Kendal.

"But wasn't he there to get the letters or nothing?"

"I was there," said Anne Kendal, "either my sister or myself. Never a word came from you. Why do you pretend?

181

Why don't you admit that your greed made you go back on him?"

He sighed, murmuring: "Poor Jimmy Dinsmore . . . dead. Poor old Jimmy." Then he added: "How am I cheating Jimmy?"

"By throwing him off and running away to locate the mine with other men!" she challenged.

Still Carcajou looked eagerly back and forth from one of them to the other. Before long now the truth would come out in its ugly nakedness, and one of them would go down—Old Tom, no doubt, unless all the fire of this girl was the merest pretense. A savage excitement possessed Carcajou. It was better to him than watching a fight to the death between two fierce men. Whatever the result, it would prove to him that one of them was a scoundrel. Of the two only honest people in the world, only one would remain. The rest, all the rest, were wretches like himself, criminal wretches, too, if they simply had the strength to turn desire and conviction into acts. They were all like Carcajou—all the rest! That was the grimness of his satisfaction as he watched this debate. From one face to the other, the mask was now about to be stripped.

Old Tom had paused to consider her last remark. The length of the pause convinced Carcajou that the blind man was the villain. Men do not have to pause so long, he said to himself, when they have free consciences and open hearts.

"Jimmy Dinsmore," said the sourdough, "was the last man I ever knew with my eyes as well as my ears. I depended on eyes, Anne Kendal, after all those years of prospecting. Slade and Horn had stuck by me through thick and thin, but you tell me why I would throw over Jimmy Dinsmore and give a half share to these two, will you, if I could have got in touch with him?"

"Nothing but diabolical spite!" said the angry girl.

"Were you in town all last year?" he asked her suddenly.

"Yes, all the time."

"If you didn't get any letters, any telegrams . . . and that I don't understand . . . how come, then, that my advertising in every morning and evening newspaper didn't get to your eye? Big, black-letter print, asking for information about Jimmy Dinsmore, describing him, and offering a reward?"

"How can you say such things?" asked the girl, more and more indignant. "A thousand people knew Jimmy. One advertisement would have been enough!"

"Charley," said the old man, shaking his bewildered head, "you know how many letters I dictated to you, how many telegrams you wrote out for me, and wasn't the bill for the advertising more'n fifteen hundred dollars?"

Charley Horn scowled at the face of the blind man, his upper lip curling. He answered nothing at all.

"You can give 'em your word that I've told the truth, Charley, eh, boy?" said Old Tom.

Carcajou, catching a new idea at last, whirled sharply around and glared at Horn.

Then Jimmy Slade cut in: "Why, you old fool, you were sold out from the start. D'you think that we weren't playing you for a long chance? Why else would we've trailed up here with you? You simply led us to the right spot, but dog-gone' little good you'll ever get out of it, you half-wit."

Old Tom freshened his grip on the staff on which he was leaning. The great dog, Slaughter, looked suddenly up and licked those weather-browned hands. Understanding rushed on Carcajou, on the girl, on Old Tom, in a single instant.

Then Anne Kendal said: "I see what happened, Old Tom. When Jimmy Dinsmore lay there dying, groaning, cursing his luck because he had to leave his wife and the youngsters behind him unprovided for . . . all that while, all those terrible days, he might have been at ease. Is that it? But this . . . this Charley Horn was lying to you all the while?"

"Charley, the chills that I've had up my spine about you now and then, they were the truth, weren't they?" asked Old Tom.

"You've talked enough," said Charley Horn. He turned to Banner. "Now, Carcajou," he said, "you and Slade and me had better step aside and talk this here thing over. We've got a pair of 'em on our hands. There might have been only one, if you'd done your job and turned the girl back. It was a fool thing to let her come through. Now there's two of them that've got to be handled. We'll have a sit and talk it over."

"We don't need to talk," said Carcajou.

"You got a bright idea already?" asked Slade eagerly. He ran his eyes curiously over their hired man, as though finding and admiring infinite possibilities.

Carcajou took from his pouch a thin, sausage-shaped canvas bag, filled with the gold dust that was his advance pay, and threw it at the feet of Slade. "I've made up my mind," he said. "There's your share in me. You can have it back. I stand with the girl and Old Tom. I've done my share of hard things, and crooked things, old son, but it seems to me that I'm stopping short of the pair of you."

Horn gasped. "Hey, Carcajou, you're crazy. You dunno what a placer like this means. Millions, likely, millions, man. D'you hear me?"

"Why, sure," said Carcajou, "I hear you well enough. I've heard dogs bark before. I've heard them growl, too." He made a gesture, while they gaped at him in astonishment. His gesture indicated the girl, who was standing petrified with amazement at the side of Old Tom, her two hands affectionately clasped about his arm. "They're honest, Slade. It's the first straight up-and-up pair that I ever drew at one deal in my whole life, and I'm not going to play out your hand with them."

"It ain't really possible," said Slade.

"He thinks that he can slide us out of the picture, the fool!" shouted Horn. "He thinks that, and then he'll try to pass them out of the picture after us, and have the whole ca-boodle for himself. But the fool don't think that we. . . ."

He went for his gun as he spoke. It was not clear of leather before his hand stopped, and he stared bitterly at the blue-black length of the Colt that glistened from the fingers of Car-cajou. The latter held the gun carelessly, a little above the height of his hip, and thrusting forward half the length of his arm. His thumb had raised the hammer of the weapon and held it with familiar ease. He made no effort to glance down the sights. By touch and the instinct of long practice he would do his shooting, if shooting there had to be.

Both Slade and Horn stood frozen before him. "Old Tom, I've got 'em on the draw," said Carcajou. "I've got 'em stopped. Now you tell me what to do with 'em, will you?"

Old Tom broke in: "Carcajou, I've been thinkin' that you was a pretty mean, rough customer. But I dunno but I'm the greatest fool in the world when it comes to readin' character ever since I gone and lost my eyesight. What to do with Charley and Jim Slade? Dog-gone it, Carcajou, I don't know. If they're what they seem to be, if we turn 'em loose, they'll try to knife us from the bush. If we don't turn 'em loose, we've got to watch and guard 'em here, and that would be a pretty hard job, Carcajou. I dunno what to say."

"Disarm them," said the girl, "and then let 'em go. If they try to come back, we have enough dogs about to spot 'em."

"Take their guns, then," said Carcajou briefly to the girl. "Take their guns and let 'em go. I might have known that would be your way with the pair of 'em. But they were aiming straight at murder, and I'd give them what they wanted to give Old Tom . . . a bullet through the brain. But go get their guns while I cover 'em. You fan them, will you?" He added sharply: "Turn around, the pair of you, and keep your hands up. Keep trying to touch the sky, will you?"

One revolver apiece was all that she took from them.

"Keep your hands up and now start for that brush!" said Carcajou. "Faster, faster!"

He began to shoot rapidly. The bullets struck the ground at their heels, driving stinging volleys of grit against their legs. Suddenly, capering, bounding, they rushed with a loud yelling into the shadowy bushes and disappeared.

XV

"THE COMEBACK"

Seven days followed before the end, and they meant, to Carcajou, seven steps toward a strange heaven. He learned a number of things with mysterious speed. In the first place, in a single moment, by one act, he had destroyed the suspicion and disgust with which Old Tom and the girl had looked upon him. In the second place, once they accepted him, they opened their hearts and minds to him. That was the way to the new heaven for Carcajou. He had not known before what it was to talk freely with another human being. There were always doubt and hesitation. Contact with other people had been always war, a war of wits, craft, or savage strength. He had won many a battle, and now he hardly knew how to adapt himself to the society of people who accepted his naked word as through it were gospel. He responded as one entranced.

They worked hard and through long hours. The plan was to gather what they could in a month, and then take the out trail. Now that they had the bearings of the mine accurately taken, they could send in a crowd of hired laborers. So Carcajou was always toiling. The girl did the cooking. In between meals she came down and helped in the washing of the dirt. They began to take out three, four, five thousand dollars a day. Wealth of incredible proportions began to loom before their eyes.

They had to labor, moreover, with all of their attention alert. It was true that Slade and Horn had been driven off, but they were not very far from the Yukon, and boats were many on the great river at this season. It would be strange if they could not get new weapons and perhaps return with reinforcements.

That was still in the minds of all three of them when they sat down outside the shelter hut for the second meal of that seventh day. They finished eating, and sat about drinking cups of steaming, strong coffee. Slaughter, lying across the feet of the blind man, was sleeping, and suddenly Carcajou leaned and laid his hand on the dog's head.

Slaughter wakened like the wild thing that he was. A twist of that snaky head and he had the forearm of Carcajou in his jaws. One crunch of his teeth would ruin that arm forever. The girl sat frozen. Old Tom, unaware of anything, was continuing calmly in a yarn of the early days. So Carcajou waited, looking steadily into the eyes of the dog.

Little by little the green gleaming disappeared from the eyes of Slaughter. At last he relaxed his grip. Head high, ready for a spring, he silently showed his long white fangs to the man. But Carcajou reached out again and laid his hand once more on the ugly head. The head sank down. Carcajou patted it gently, drew back his hand, and for a long moment he and Slaughter stared at one another.

The story of Old Tom halted suddenly. "Ah, something's happening," he said. "I kind of feel it in the air."

"John and Slaughter have made up," said the girl. "He let Slaughter take his arm in his teeth. Why, John, that's pretty brave. Look there! Slaughter's wagging his tail a bit."

"You trust a dog or a man . . . it seems to do something to 'em," muttered Carcajou. He stood up. "I've got to be getting back to work."

"Wait a minute," answered Old Tom. "I've been talking things over with Anne, here. We both think, and we both know that you ought to have a share in this mine. A fair share.

Does a third sound right to you, Carcajou?"

"I don't like that name," said the girl.

"Nor me, neither," said Old Tom. "Does a third of the thing seem right to you, John?"

John Banner shrugged his thick shoulders. There was a puzzled look in his face. "I was working for Horn and Slade for fifty dollars a day," he said. "That's plenty for me. I didn't come inside to try to find gold. I came to keep low for a while. That was all. I'll take wages, not a share in the gold we wash."

Old Tom cried out in husky protest. "You're washing forty days' wages every day!" he said. "We can't cheat you, son."

"We'd have nothing, nothing at all," said the girl. "Except for John Banner, we'd both be dead, I suppose."

"You'll take a third. You oughta have a half," said Old Tom.

Dimly, like the voice of a stranger speaking far off, Carcajou heard himself saying: "I stick by what I've said. I don't want a dead man's share of this, or yours, Tom, or yours, Anne. I'm a day laborer, that's all."

He had turned from the shack down the slope toward the creek when a scattering sound and a clamor of dogs broke out in the brush. As he stopped, staring, Anne Kendal said: "They're after a rabbit again."

"No, they're scared of something," interpreted Old Tom.

Then there rang out from the bushes the unforgettable voice of Bill Roads, that patient hound of the law, yelling exultantly: "Shove up your hands, Carcajou, because I've got you covered over the heart! Shove 'em up!"

What Carcajou might have done would have been hard to tell, for on the heel of the call of Bill Roads a rifle rang in the ambush, and Carcajou felt a hammer blow on his left leg. It turned numb, and he slumped heavily to the ground. He had drawn his revolver in falling, but it spilled from his hand as he tried to break the shock of the fall with his arms. It rolled half a dozen feet away down the slope.

"Don't do that!" shouted the voice of Roads. "You hound, that's murder. That ain't the law."

The voice of Horn answered: "You take chances with him and you're a fool. I wish I'd got him through the heart, but I got buck fever and shot too low, I guess."

They came hurrying from the shrubbery; Roads first, with Horn and Slade behind him, rifles in their hands. Old Tom, feeling before him, found the fallen man and gripped him. "Are you hurt bad, son?" he asked the wounded man.

"I'm only scratched," said Carcajou calmly. "But if I had . . . Anne, throw me a gun and I'll show 'em. . . ."

Anne Kendal, he saw, had snatched up a rifle and stood on guard.

"Stop where you are!" she called to the trio.

"Look out, Roads!" exclaimed Slade. "She's as sandy as they make 'em, and she can shoot."

"Lady," said Bill Roads, "I've brought the law with me."

He showed her the badge inside the flap of his coat. The strength for resistance wilted out of the erect body of the girl. Roads came striding up to her.

"It's straight law," he told her. "Don't you doubt me. This bird goes back with me to look a jury in the eye. That's where he goes. At last! Three years' work wound up!" He dropped to one knee beside Carcajou. "Where did you get it?" he asked.

"Through the leg," said Carcajou without emotion. "It'd be all right in a few days. It didn't get the bone, I'm sure."

"Good for you," said Roads. "It was a long trail, Banner. But it was worth it! You don't mind if I fan you?"

He was searching the fallen man as he spoke.

"There's nothing else on me. Not even a penknife," said Carcajou.

"Are you trying to let him bleed to death?" exclaimed Anne Kendal.

"Bleed to death?" said Roads happily. "I tell you, no one bullet could make a hole big enough to let out the life of this man, lady. We'll tie him up, though."

He rolled the trouser leg as he spoke and exposed the wound, wonderfully small where the bullet had entered, but with blood streaming from the back of the leg where the bullet had torn its way out of the flesh.

"Get some hot water. Some of that coffee would be better still," said Bill Roads. "We'll wash the blood away and pack a bandage around it. I've got bandages in my shoulder pack. I never take Banner's trail without a first-aid kit along. But it's last aid that I've been nearer needing a pile of times!" He talked cheerfully in this manner as he went about the bandaging of the wound, with the girl helping skillfully.

Horn and Slade were equally exultant for different reasons. Horn had found the canvas sack in which the washed dust had been stored. He weighed the ponderous burden with his hand and shouted with glee. "They been doing our work for us, Slade!" he cried. "We just been having a little vacation while they worked for us!"

"You fool," said Slade to Carcajou, "did you think that we wouldn't come back? But it was luck that ran us into Bill Roads, I got to admit. Still we'd've been back, anyway. It ain't the gold, only. It's your scalp that we wanted mostly, you sneaking traitor."

Old Tom said: "If one of you is a policeman, which is it?"

He was standing, grasping his staff with both hands, leaning upon it, a favorite attitude of his, as though he were braced to receive a shock from any direction.

"I've got the warrant and all," answered Bill Roads. "You're Old Tom, I guess? You've got a reputation up here, Tom. How d'you come to be trying to beat Horn and Slade out of their mine?"

"Their mine?" exclaimed Old Tom. "Who said that it was their mine?"

"He can lie, too, old and blind as he is. He can see his way to the telling of a pretty good lie," said Slade. "Don't be wasting your time on the old fool, Roads."

The bandaging was finished. Roads stood up. He shrugged his shoulders. "What do I care about the infernal mine?" he said. He pointed to the prostrate form of Carcajou. "There's my gold mine," he said, "and my diamond mine, too!"

XVI

"JOURNEY'S END"

"That's right, Roads, but you're going to get a slice out of this from us, too," said Slade. "You just herd the girl and the old man off along with Carcajou. Just clean 'em off the claim for us, and. . . ."

At that moment Anne Kendal spoke up: "He's honest, John? Is this man honest?"

Carcajou nodded. "Bill Roads is one of the honest men, I guess, or an honest bloodhound. Call him whichever you please. But he will shoot at a man from behind. That's his style."

"It was a bad play I made there in Steuermann's," admitted Roads. "I'm sorry about that, and I got what was coming to me for it. I went sort of crazy, I think, when I saw you at last, after the long hunt, Banner. Something went crash in my head. I wanted to see you dead, that was all."

"You intend to take us away from the claim and then turn it over to Horn and Slade?" the girl asked Roads.

"That's what I intend to do," said Bill Roads. "They've helped me to turn the best trick. . . ."

"Will you listen to our side of the story?" she asked.

"Hey, Bill, don't be a fool," said Charley Horn. "She's the slickest little liar that ever stepped in a shoe!"

Bill Roads frowned. "Down in Texas," he said, "we don't call any woman a liar. Go on, lady, and let's hear what you have to say."

It did not take long. She told the entire story in a hundred words, hardly more. But truth weighted every phrase that she uttered. She reached the death of Dinsmore, the attempts of Old Tom to locate his young partner, how those attempts had been blocked by the knavery of Horn.

Then Bill Roads broke in: "Horn, this sounds pretty straight and pretty black to me."

"Look, Bill," said Charley Horn. "You ain't simple enough to believe what a girl says . . . this far North, are you?"

Laying a friendly hand on the shoulder of Bill Roads, he patted that shoulder familiarly and laughed a little. Therein he made a vital error, because the laughter had no ring of conviction in it. Bill Roads stepped back from under the caressing hand and shook his head.

"This here," he pronounced, "is no case that I can settle out of hand. No, sir, it's gotta be done according to a court of law. You can arrange for a hearing when you get back outside. Maybe the best thing is for the whole lot of you to come back outside with me, and then the law'll say what's what. Old Tom, here, has a pretty good name. I've heard a hundred men talk about him, and never an accusatory word."

"Wait a minute, Bill," pleaded Slade, "you mean that you're gonna make us waste our time? Is that what you mean? Make us mush all the way back to get the cursed law to . . . ?"

"Don't curse the law, brother," said Bill Roads, growing colder and colder. "Maybe you're all right, you two. But if Horn double-crossed a blind man, while another man was dying, then Horn oughta be burned alive, and maybe you alongside of him. That's what it looks like to me."

While Roads was speaking to Slade, the latter gave one hard, bright look to Horn, and the latter stepped instantly behind the man of the law. Now, with a very faint and cruel smile pulling at the corners of his mouth, Slade raised his pistol.

"Take it, you!" gasped Horn, crashing the barrel of his revolver against the skull of Bill Roads.

The man of the law made one stumbling step forward, stretching a hand toward the ground to save himself from the inevitable fall, with the other hand tugging at his revolver. But blackness was in his brain, and, as the revolver came forth, it fell to the ground, with its owner beside it. Not uselessly did it fall, however, for Carcajou, giving his body a sudden pivotal movement, came up on his good knee and one hand. His other hand held the Colt.

It was a twin brother of the gun he himself had lost the moment before. There were no sights. They had been filed away like the trigger. There would be only five shots in that gun. No one would have a cartridge under the hammer that was controlled by such a delicate spring as this that operated in the old-fashioned, single-action Colt. To the grasp of Carcajou, nothing could have been more welcome. He was ready to shoot as Slade yelled: "Behind you, Charley! For God's sake, Carcajou!"

Slade's own gun was out. Charley Horn raised his revolver and spun toward Carcajou, shooting as he turned. One bullet struck the ground and knocked a handful of turf into the face of Carcajou, but the latter was not perturbed. Without haste and without delay, he fired. Charley Horn promptly turned his back, raised his face toward the sky, to which he seemed babbling a wordless complaint. Then he fell on his back, dead.

His partner, Slade, had seen that bullet strike. He had heard the dull, heavy, pounding stroke of it as it went home, and the spirit went out of him. He had an idea of what Carcajou could do with a gun. He had seen him shoot birds out of trees. The heart of Jimmy Slade collapsed. The big Colt in his own hand became a mere encumbrance. He cast it far from him. He screamed as he turned and fled, and threw out his arms as if to grasp at safety.

Carcajou raised his gun.

"No, no, John!" cried the girl.

He looked across at her. The evil went out of his heart, and he dropped his hand. Jimmy Slade disappeared into the brush.

They were left alone, suddenly, with the senseless body of Roads on the ground, and the groaning, curious voice of Old Tom murmuring: "What's happened? Somebody tell me! Anne, John, somebody tell me!"

Carcajou barely heard the question. What mattered was the shining eyes of the girl, as she answered: "John has saved us all again. That's all. It's the same old story, with one dead man added. I don't think that Roads is badly hurt."

Roads, in fact, was on his feet in five minutes. For another five he sat staring about him, before he spoke.

"You could have tagged me while I was down and out, Banner," he remarked.

"That's all right, Roads," Carcajou said. "They don't play the old game that way up here, this far North."

"I'm gonna take a walk and think things over," muttered the man of the law.

He picked himself up and strode off into the brush, his head bent forward, his whole attitude one of thought.

"He won't come back," said the girl, looking toward Carcajou.

"He won't come back," agreed Old Tom. "That leaves a blind man, a wounded man, and a girl. Can we beat the game?"

"We can beat the game," said Carcajou. "I'll be on my feet again in a couple of weeks."

"Ah, man," muttered Old Tom. "How can we reward you?"

"There's only one reward that I'm going to try for," said Carcajou, staring.

Anne Kendal met the glance steadily, unabashed, unblushing, and she smiled her answer.

"Only," said Carcajou, "I'd still need a lot of teaching, and a lot of remaking, and all I know is that I want to learn. Slaughter and I can learn at the same time."

"You know, John," said the girl, "this far North the days are pretty long. We could learn a great deal together."

She stopped. A harsh, metallic calling came faintly to them out of the air, and, looking up, Carcajou saw a scattering wedge of wild geese flying toward the north. Let them go, he felt, for he, John Banner, had reached the bourn of all his journeying.

Voyageur of the Wasteland
Frederick L. Nebel

Frederick L(ewis) Nebel (1903–1967) was born at Staten Island, New York. He completed grammar school but quit high school after one day. He believed in self-education and by fifteen was reading Arthur Schopenhauer and working as a car checker on the New York wharf. At the age of seventeen he went to live in the Canadian north woods, working on his great-uncle's homestead as a farm hand. He fell in love with this wild country and became a self-taught expert in Canadian history, absorbing as well its lore and legends. He returned to New York in the early 1920s and got a job as a brakeman on passenger trains. When he wasn't working, he was writing. "Stuart of the City Patrol" appeared in *North-West Stories* (12/25) and was followed by numerous other North-Western stories for this magazine, including the three-part serial, "Defiance Valley," in March and April, 1926. He sold his first crime story to *The Black Mask* and by the time he sold his second story to this magazine, Captain Joseph T. Shaw was its editor and for the next decade Nebel was a regular and prolific contributor. Raoul Whitfield and Dashiell Hammett, who also were *Black Mask* writers, became close friends. In my *Dark Cinema* (Greenwood, 1984), I said of Nebel's crime fiction that he "never approached Hammett's bleakness nor his sense of the omnipresence of moral corruption. . . ." The hope embodied in the Western story obviously had too great a personal appeal for Nebel, and it is probably why he continued as a contributor to *North-West Stories* long after its name was changed to *North-West Romances* and even when he was no longer interested in writing any crime fiction for pulp magazines. This story first appeared in *North-West Romances* (Summer, 1938).

I

Ed Stryker drew up before his spruce-log trapping shack as the swift Labrador night was closing in. He unstrapped his oval-shaped rackets, pushed open the door, and booted it shut behind him. Little icicles hung at the corners of his wide mouth and frozen ridges of rheum were under his eyes. It was November and the long cold had come to stay.

"Hello there, Keepee, old scout!" he called to a tall Indian who stood by the sheet-iron stove, mixing fresh bannocks.

Keepee, which is Cree for "make haste", said, without looking up: " 'Lo."

Stryker, a whale of a man, shrugged out of his deerskin *koolutik* and hung it on a peg near the stove. They were not Labrador men, these two; their native habitat was many miles westward, beyond Hudson Bay, way over in the Saskatchewan River country. But furs run mighty fast along the Koksoak and the Barren Lands produce no finer black foxes. Stryker, an old Hudson's Bay Company "freeman", had seen wealth in the Labrador while still with the company, and, when he resigned, he had persuaded Keepee, an old friend, to join him and try their luck here.

"Say, Keepee," he remarked, "there's a blackie snooping around that deadfall you made. Bet we'll nab him before the week's out. Three prime marten today and a beauty silver. Some running, eh?"

"Um."

Stryker bathed his face with snow while the Indian set out the supper. The cabin was small, barely clearing Stryker's head. It was thatched with earth and moss, which subsequently had been treated with water, so that a layer of ice covered it and checked the bitter winds that were always howling down from Ungava Bay.

Stryker was just about to sit down to a steaming meal when the door whipped open and a fur-swathed man pitched forward to the floor, clawing at the boards. Keepee closed the door. Stryker bent down and turned the man over, and gave a little gasp when he saw the stranger was white. There are not many white men in the Labrador wilds.

"That brandy!" snapped Stryker, at the same time tearing open the man's furs.

Keepee brought a black bottle from the larder and put it to the man's lips. Stryker went outside and came back with an armful of snow, bathed the man's feet and hands and face. The nose was in critical condition, and he pressed it in his cold hand instead of using snow, for at a certain state of frostbite snow will tear the skin. The man began to mutter unintelligible things. He stirred; his hands writhed. His red-rimmed eyes opened and in them was an appeal that beckoned Stryker to lean closer.

"Letter . . . pocket . . . Kuglictuk . . . go . . . life depends . . . name o' God. . . ."

A rattle choked the words in his throat. His eyes glared for a moment, then became glazed and expressionless. A sigh fluttered from his blackened lips. Then he lay very still.

Stryker rose, a little awed, then bowed his head for a brief moment. After which he bent down again and rummaged in the dead man's pockets. He found a little notebook, a sort of diary, bearing the name, **Harry P. Kavanagh**. He scanned the entries made under various dates, from which he learned that a certain sloop had put out from Fort Churchill in hopes of making Whale River Post before the freeze up. Things had gone wrong. The sloop had been wrecked by floe ice. The writer claimed to be the only survivor. He didn't know the country. He was without food.

"I guess that about tells the story," muttered Stryker grimly. "Now he said something about a letter and a life and for me to go some place. Let's see. Oh, yes! Kuglictuk, he said. That's a river."

After further searching he found an envelope bearing one word—**Jack**. He paused before breaking the seal, then finally tore it open and read:

Dear Jack:

Everything is all right. The beast disappeared into the Barrens almost a year ago, and no one has seen him since. I am counting the days till I see you. Harry was always a good boy, and he volunteered to go and find you, and both our hearts are broken while you are away. . . .

There were two pages of maternal sentiment, written in fine script, and signed: **Mother**.

Stryker folded them after two perusals and sat down to think. There were two roads open to him. He could disregard the letter, continue with his trap lines, and bury the late Harry P. Kavanagh when the spring thaw came. On the other hand, he could take his dog team, mush to Fort Chimo, and then start east for the white, barren tundra that lies between there and the Kuglictuk River. If he chose the latter, he would face death and starvation, and after it was all over he would return to the Saskatchewan with empty pockets. A man named Jack was apparently in hiding. It is bad for a white man to stay in the Labrador alone. Ed Stryker was of the brotherhood of the wilds. So he said to Keepee: "Old scout, I'm pulling out tomorrow. Got a little job. You go right ahead with the trapping and make yourself rich. I may get back to nab a few more furs and I may not. When you got all the furs you want, leg it to Chimo and I'll meet you there when it's over. I'll have to take the team, but I'll leave most of the provisions with you and stock up at the post. You can have my traps, too. I don't know what this letter's all about, but this chum who just died tried to tell me to carry on, and I'm obliging him."

Keepee, having finished his meal despite the newly dead, mumbled: "Want me to help? Me go damn' quick, betcha."

"No, Keepee. I know you're a good sort. But this is a whim of mine. I brought you over here and I want to see you get something out of it. Maybe I'll try next year, maybe, as I said, I'll get back in time to run the traps again. Anyhow, I'm going, for some chum's struck a streak of bad luck and I'm going to lend a hand."

Keepee understood his white companion and he pressed the subject no further.

In the morning, when it was still dark, they drove the six wolf-dogs out of the lean-to in the rear and then brought out the twelve-foot *komatik,* a sturdy Eskimo sled that Stryker had purchased at Fort Chimo. Quickly it was loaded with grub, blankets, and sealskin robes, and some blackies that Stryker intended to sell at the post. Then they shook hands, the white man and the red, and their hearts were in their palms.

" 'Luck, Ed," murmured the Indian, then waved his hand skyward. "*Kisse-manito* . . . watchum."

"Thanks, Keepee. I'll see you later at Chimo."

"At Chimo. Good."

The thirty-five-foot walrus-hide whip snaked out and ended with a sharp report, and the big wolf-dogs lunged ahead, passed through a growth of stunted larch and tamarack and then struck the Koksoak River, heading north.

II

They found it good going down the Koksoak. The dogs were in fine fettle, and Stryker reeled off fifty miles the first day. At dusk of the second, when a cold moon hung over the frozen world, Stryker trotted into Fort Chimo at the head of his outfit and went directly to the H.B.C. store.

Flemming, the acting factor, looked up from a copy of *Pilgrim's Progress* and said: "Hello, Stryker. What brings you up here already? Thought you were holed up for the winter."

They shook hands.

"Strange things happen." Stryker laughed. "Chap blew into my shack and cashed in. Had a letter on him. Asked me to find somebody named Jack."

Briefly he related the whole affair, showed Flemming the letter, and asked for a guide.

"A guide?" echoed the factor. "I wish I could, but every Indian and Eskimo are off to the traps. Seems you've struck bad luck to begin with. Why not take a run over to Revillon's?"

"Hmm. Might as well try. Thanks. See you again."

Monsieur De Loge, the agent at the Revillon Frères Post, was a genial man. He said after Stryker had given him the details: "Ah, *m'sieu,* I should lak' to help you ver' much, but you will see by glancing about dat no one ees here. It ees a bad time, dis, to secure guides. De traps, you know. Meantime, howevaire, you will be my guest? De table is ready."

After a splendid meal with *monsieur le facteur,* Stryker went out to a clump of scrub spruce and fed his dogs. He had suspected all along that a guide would be unavailable, and now

205

that the fact was thrust upon him he was a little undecided just what to do. He knew very little about the Ungava, and for a stranger to get stranded in the white peril of snow and ice and low temperatures is suicide.

He went back to the French post. A lone Eskimo had just arrived from the east and on his *komatik* was a dog that had been unable to stand the toil of trail and trace. The Eskimo's dark face glistened with a layer of ice and his sealskin *netsek* was caked with hoar frost.

De Loge greeted him.

"Ah, Chevik, a bad trail, *oui?*"

Chevik grunted and threw open his skins.

"Chevik, my frien'," proceeded De Loge. "*M'sieu* Stryker, here, desires a guide to de Kuglictuk. It ees a mission of great importance. *M'sieu* desire to find someone by de name of Jack, who is white."

Chevik's eyes narrowed. He shot a quick look at Stryker, then at De Loge. Then he stuffed his pipe and moved away toward the stove.

"Say, Chevik, what do you say about that?" called Stryker. "Good pay, Chevik."

Chevik, holding a match to his pipe, looked up and straight into Stryker's eyes. Stryker saw hatred in that gaze. The whole face, with its pulpy mouth, its slanting forehead, and flat nose, emanated danger. With a faint sneer, Chevik continued to light his pipe, then drew his skins about him and went outside.

"Now what do you know about that?" exclaimed Stryker softly.

De Loge said: "He would be a good guide, too. Speaks ver' good English, unlak' most de Eskimo. A great fighter, *m'sieu*, and marvelous wit' de knife. Hence his name, Chevik, which means knife. Ah . . . he dislikes you, howevaire."

"That's putting it mild." Stryker laughed. "He *hates* me. Why, I don't know."

Flemming managed to find sleeping quarters for him that night in a cabin that was also shared by one of the assistants. He was worn out from the day's hard traveling and he turned in early. But he lay awake a long time, figuring things out, and before he finally closed his eyes he had decided that, guide or no guide, he would leave next day for the Kuglictuk.

He awoke some minutes later to find a dark, fur-swathed form standing in the doorway. For a moment the stranger did not move, but Stryker felt that a pair of eyes was regarding him, despite the thick gloom. Cautiously he slipped his hand toward the stool beside his bed, where lay his belt and revolver.

Then the stranger moved. Instinctively Stryker dodged to one side. A knife whizzed across the room, grazed his cheek, and stuck in the wall behind his head. With that he dived for his revolver, but the door slammed shut and the stranger was gone. Gun in hand, Stryker jumped to the door, hurled it open, and swung his gun low for immediate action. But only a sharp wind and the cold night sky greeted him, and farther away the yellow square of light that marked the H.B.C. store. He thought of dressing and going over to tell Flemming and his assistant, but changed his mind.

In the morning he said nothing about the attack. He went over to see the agent at Revillon's and discovered that Chevik had departed more than two hours before. Stryker was almost positive that it was Chevik who had thrown the knife and he felt that he would cross Chevik's trail before long.

When he announced his intention of proceeding alone, Flemming threw up his hands. De Loge, a bit of a humorist, wanted to know what kind of flowers should be put on the grave. But between them they mapped out a course and gave him hints on the country, for they were wise in the ways of the Labrador.

Daylight was almost complete when, his *komatik* loaded with a month's provisions, Stryker pulled out of Fort Chimo. As he put the Koksoak farther and farther behind him, the timber died away, until finally nothing but bare, ragged hills swept away toward the horizon and the frosty air hung like gauze all about him. It was the land of *Torngak,* the Death Spirit of the Eskimos, but Stryker was entering it unafraid.

That night he took some wood from his *komatik,* built a little fire, ate bannock, pork, and beans cooked in seal oil. He cut blocks of snow and raised a snow wall against the wind. He went to sleep huddled in his blankets and robes. Some time after midnight he was startled awake by a big form that was bending over him. With a sharp oath he tried to heave himself up, but a mittened hand smashed him between the eyes, and things spun around and then went black.

When he awoke, he was sitting against his *komatik*. On the other side of the fire sat Chevik, regarding him impassively with a rifle resting across his knee.

"Don't move," grunted the Eskimo who was smoking a pipe.

Stryker began cramming tobacco into his own pipe. "What's the idea of the big grudge you've got against me, Chevik? I'd like to be your friend."

Chevik sneered. "Me your en'my. Me kill you, you don't go back Chimo."

"You will, eh? Well, let me tell you something, Chevik. I'm bound for the Kuglictuk. See? I'm turning back for no damned Eskimo, either. The factor at Chimo knows I'm over this way, and De Loge saw that look you gave me. If I don't get back, he'll tell the Mounties, and he'll tell 'em about you."

Chevik frowned darkly and nursed his pipe. "Me kill," he muttered thickly.

Stryker got up. Chevik rose, also, his rifle leveled, his eyes beady. They locked gazes. Then Stryker, shrugging his shoulders, bent down by the fire, looking for a fagot with which to light his own pipe—or so it seemed. He pulled out a flaming stick of tamarack, held it to his pipe, then with a rapid movement flipped it up so that it struck Chevik across the forehead.

Snarling, the Eskimo hurtled backward. At the same time his rifle boomed and the shot *buzzed* over Stryker's head. But Stryker cleared the fire in a mighty leap and bore Chevik down upon the snow. The Eskimo lost his rifle in the mix-up and met Stryker with his short, powerful arms. Still locked, they struggled to their feet, reeling, staggering about the fire, while the wolf-dogs looked on with eager eyes. They understood.

In a break Chevik whipped out a short, broad knife, crouched, then dived at Stryker with animal-like ferocity. It was a downward thrust, and it carried all the Eskimo's weight behind it, so that, when he missed, he toppled over and buried the knife hilt-deep in the frozen snow. With a mad little laugh Stryker was upon him and lifted him up with such force that he ripped away the stout hide collar. His next blow caught Chevik on the Adam's apple, and he jackknifed to the snow and writhed, struggling for his breath.

When he tottered to his feet, Stryker had a gun on him. "Where's your outfit?" he snapped.

Chevik nodded toward the gloom suddenly.

"Lead me to it," said Stryker.

Chevik started off and half an hour later brought up before his campfire. Stryker bound him hand and foot, piled more wood on the fire, then said: "It'll take you about five hours to work loose. The fire'll burn till then. After this, don't go fooling around with strangers. Good night."

209

III

At noon of the following day Stryker crossed the Whale River a hundred miles south of Whale River Post, one of the loneliest stations in all the Ungava. Chevik had not yet put in an appearance, although this did not cause Stryker to relax his vigilance, which he maintained night and day for the next two days. After passing the Whale and then the Mukalik, he headed northeast and at last came to the headwaters of the Kuglictuk. Flemming and De Loge had given him good instructions and he knew that without the map they had supplied he would never have reached the river. Desolation was all about him, stark, naked hills, fading into the cold film that always hangs over the Labrador, with here and there a wind-blown tree and the frozen waterway winding silently to the distant Ungava Bay.

"It's a hell of a country for a man to live in," he said aloud. "I wonder what the devil drove that Jack fellow up this way."

He made a fire and put up his small Eskimo *tupik,* banking it with blocks of ice. Later a high wind worked across the tundra and snow began to drive down, pattering on the tent like buckshot. The dogs crouched down on the lee side of the shelter. The wind became a howling maëlstrom, hurling the snow madly before it, so that in a short time the fire was beaten out and Stryker huddled deeply in his robes.

He drowsed despite the bedlam. He was sound asleep when a man cautiously pulled aside the flap of his tent and looked in, then, satisfied that Stryker was sleeping, bent down and tapped him on the head with the butt of his rifle.

Stryker jerked awake. "Chevik . . . damn you!" he burst out.

210

The Eskimo chuckled. "Me come. Me kill. Not with knife. Not with gun. Me let *Torngak* kill. Take dogs, grub, gun. You starve, freeze."

"You dirty. . . ."

His words were cut short by another blow on the head, so hard he passed out completely. Chevik chuckled again, then began to tear down the *tupik*. Then he piled it on the sled along with the robes, lined up the dogs, and drove off into the white cloud of the blizzard.

When Stryker came to, his face was covered with snow. His shelter was gone. Only one 4-point blanket remained with him and the awful cold was gnawing into his bones. He struggled to his feet, drawing the blanket about him, cursing deeply in his throat. Everything was gone, even his axe, with which he might have built a snow wall. No food, no rifle, no robes—nothing.

"God," he whispered.

He kept up a brisk pace to prevent his blood from freezing. He kept it up when the storm died and the dim dawn broke, bleak and cold, with all around him swells of virgin snow— and nothing more. He figured he was about fifty miles from the mouth of the Kuglictuk. If he followed it to the sea and then struck west, he might by chance strike Whale River Post, which was almost another fifty miles away. But then his snowshoes were gone! How can a man trek through the Labrador without them?

He cursed the Labrador and every Eskimo in it. And he cursed himself for having penetrated it. He had a little tobacco and a dozen matches. He made a fire and had for breakfast one pipeful of tobacco.

Sinking knee-deep in the fresh snow, he began to follow the river northward. Perhaps that mysterious Jack was holed up somewhere along it. Perhaps he would meet a friendly Indian or Eskimo.

Three hours later, as he topped a barren ridge, he saw far ahead several wisps of smoke rising. His heart missed several beats, and he gave a glad little cry. He summoned every bit of strength he possessed, until he rounded a bend in the river and saw on the west bank a settlement of three shacks and several *tupiks*. He summoned his last burst of strength, tottered up to the largest of the cabins, pushed open the door, and rocked in.

Smoke hung heavily in the low room. There was a sheet-iron stove in the center, and sitting about this were three men. Two were French *voyageurs,* and the saucy clothes they wore suggested the country west of Hudson Bay. The third man was big and thick-chested, freshly shaven, with a hard jaw and a hard, cold eye.

"Hello!" called Stryker. "I'm a stranger over this way. Had a team but some blasted Eskimo banged me over the head and ran off with everything I had."

The *voyageurs* looked at each other sharply. The big man spat deftly out of the side of his mouth and said: "Don't say! This is no tourist country anyhow, stranger. What brings you up this way?"

"Do I look like a tourist?" shot back Stryker crisply.

"Well, I didn't mean it that way." He winked at one of his companions. Then: "Sit down. What's the news?"

At that moment the door opened and a young woman entered clad in sealskins. Stryker eyed her for a long minute, marveled at the beauty of her dark eyes.

The big man interrupted. "My name's Delevan. What did you say about that Eskimo?"

"Oh, yes," said Stryker, and gave his own name. The woman passed to the rear of the room. Stryker went on: "Well, as I said, the fellow robbed me. Didn't like me since he saw me at Fort Chimo. I'm over here looking for someone whose front name is Jack."

The girl gave a little cry. Delevan fixed her with a threatening look. She turned away, trembling, and disappeared behind a curtain that separated part of the cabin.

"Yes, Jack's the name," continued Stryker. "I was running a trap line over on the Koksoak when a chap blew into my shack, gave me a letter, mentioned this river, and then died. The name on the letter is Jack. That's all."

"Let's have it," said Delevan.

"I'm sorry, chum, but it's only for Jack."

Delevan glowered. "Oh, you don't say? All right, then. Well, there's no Jack around this camp, so you might as well move on. Who'd you say was the man died?"

"I didn't say, but it was a chap named Kavanagh."

"Kavanagh!" Delevan half rose from the chair, his eyes wide.

A choked sob issued from behind the curtain. Delevan snapped to his feet and went behind. Stryker could not hear what he said, but he noted the low, menacing tone of his voice. Then Delevan came out again, his face a little flushed.

"Stranger, there's a cabin next door you can share with Paul and Rex, here. Show him, Rex," he said to one of the Frenchmen.

A little perplexed at the way things were going, Stryker followed Rex to the little shack. It had but one room; robes on the floor served for bunks.

"You expect to go on soon, *m'sieu?*" purred Rex, his dark eyes sparkling.

"As soon as I get a guide. I'd like to run up against that Eskimo that swiped my outfit. Crack team that was. I'd break his greasy neck."

Rex chuckled liquidly. "Good luck to you, *m'sieu,*" he said, and sauntered out.

Stryker did not fail to get the sinister note in his voice.

IV

Rex and Paul came into the cabin later, and the latter made supper. Stryker, sitting beside the little stove, told himself that both of them bore the earmarks of the devil. Rex was always chuckling, and Paul, as though understanding the meaning, would wink back and then favor Stryker with a wide, ingratiating smile. Stryker was charged with a desire to get up and knock the fellow for a row of stumps. He bided his time, however, for he felt that he was on a warm trail, that Delevan and his henchmen knew something about Jack, and that the girl would be prevented from telling what she knew.

He tried to stay awake that night. He lay on one side of the stove, while Rex and Paul lay on the other side, and he damned the luck that had left him without a gun. But try as he would, his eyes refused to stay open. He fell into sound slumber.

Later on, he awoke with a start and tried to cry out, but found a dirty piece of hide across his mouth. Then a bag was pulled over his head and tied about his neck. Hoarse whispers floated to him. Rough hands picked him up, and then he felt the bitter cold against his body and he knew he had been carried from the cabin.

Five minutes later his captors halted. More whispers . . . a brief, rasping argument . . . silence. He knew that something terrible was going to happen. He struggled frantically. Then he felt himself released. A moment later an icy shock went through his body and his blood seemed to congeal instantly.

He was in the cold waters of the Kuglictuk!

He struck out. His feet touched the river bottom, and he guessed that the water was no more than eight feet deep. He

215

sprang up in an attempt to grasp the edge of the hole through which he had been dropped. His head bumped against the ice. He tried again, and this time his frozen hands caught onto the rim of the hole, but his fast-dying strength was not sufficient to haul his body clear. With a groan he started to sink again.

Then, magically, he felt himself being drawn up. His body was too numb to sense contact, but he knew that he was clear of the water, that someone was carrying him across the ice. Already his clothing was frozen stiff as a board.

He heard a door slam. He felt a new warmth. Then his clothes were being torn off. Brandy was thrown down his throat. Deft hands were massaging and slapping his purple flesh. He could see nothing. He was in a semi-stupor, and he could only hear. By-and-by he began to feel.

Warm, soft Hudson's Bay Company blankets were wrapped around him. He was lying on a pile of robes. His eyes opened, but he saw through a haze. The red stove looked like a big evil eye. Several short, squat figures hovered near him. Another shot of brandy was poured between his lips. Things cleared. He was in a cabin. A round, swarthy face was near his own.

"Better?" a voice inquired.

He squinted, and, as his vision became perfect, he gave a little start. The man bending over him, administering to him, was Chevik.

"You!" he choked.

The Eskimo raised a hand in warning. "No noise. You better soon."

An hour later Stryker sat up. His vitality was remarkable, and anyhow a bath in frozen water is not so bad as it often is supposed, provided expert attention is given immediately. He looked around for Chevik. The Eskimo was gone, but an-

216

other squatted stolidly by the stove.

"Chevik?" asked Stryker.

The Eskimo made signs that Stryker took as indicating that Chevik had gone out and would return shortly. He rose to search for the letter and the notebook that had been in an inner pocket. His clothes, hanging by the stove, were still wet, and both letter and book had been removed.

"Delevan's work," he muttered bitterly.

The door whipped open. Chevik waddled in, regarded Stryker studiously for a moment, then went to the rear of the shack and came back with dry clothes.

"Put on," he said shortly. "And quickly."

"Say, did Delevan and his gang heave me in the river?" Stryker asked.

Chevik nodded.

Stryker proceeded: "Tell me what it's all about, will you? First you try to kill me, then Delevan tries his luck, and then you come along and save me. Damn it, what makes me so blasted important anyhow? And where does the lady fit in?"

Chevik pointed to the fresh clothes. "Put on . . . damn' quick." He went to the door and looked out, then closed it quietly. "Damn' quick!" he repeated.

While he dressed, Chevik went out. Ten minutes later he reëntered, only to pause in the doorway and jerk his thumb over his shoulder. Stryker followed him outside. His old dog team was there, and he saw that his *komatik* had been replenished with provisions. Chevik handed him the walrus-hide whip.

"Go north," he said. "Turn west mouth river, reach Whale River. Go!"

"What's the idea?"

"Go. Delevan kill."

"Who sent you?"

"White woman."

Stryker thought over this. "What is she here?"

"Delevan's wife."

Stryker spat sharply. "But that letter. Delevan stole a letter from me. I want it."

"Go!"

"Damned if I will! Who the hell does Delevan think he is? I'm going to get that letter. Where's my rifle?"

Chevik pointed to the *komatik*. Stryker snatched up his rifle. Chevik grasped his arm.

"White woman say go. Delevan kill."

Stryker tore the Eskimo's hand away. "No, Chevik, old chum. I'm indebted to you for saving my life. But I'm looking for somebody, and I've got a hunch this is the end of the trail. I'm going over there to Delevan's cabin and talk turkey to that bum. Hands off, Chevik!"

V

Chevik's cabin was only a quarter of a mile from the one in which Stryker first had met Delevan. When he left the Eskimo, he trotted briskly along on the hard surface of the snow, topped a rise, and then swung down toward the river where he could see the lighted cabins. He drew up before the large cabin and put his ear to the door. He heard a loud guffaw, then the unmistakable, fiendish chuckle of Rex. He held his rifle tightly, then banged open the door, entered, and kicked it shut with his heel.

Delevan and his two henchmen were sitting at the table with a bottle of whiskey between them. Delevan was the first to look up. His face froze. Rex almost toppled over. Paul clenched the glass of whiskey that he was about to raise to his lips. The room was deathly still.

"Not a move!" snapped Stryker. "You, Delevan, out with that letter and book you swiped. Quick! Don't look at me like a damned fool! Show some life!" His voice rang with command.

Delevan, his mouth twitching, fumbled in his shirt pocket and brought out the letter, and then the notebook. The two Frenchmen had overcome their momentary paralysis and were now eyeing Stryker craftily. Tension was high in the low room.

Stryker said: "Get up, the three of you. Put your guns on the table and line up against the wall."

Delevan, now sullen with rage, obeyed reluctantly. Rex and Paul followed their chief's example. As they backed against the wall, Rex's hand rested lightly on his right hip.

"You, Rex, take that knife out of your sash!" lashed out

219

Stryker. "Something tells me you're not going to live long. Out with it!"

With a sneer the Frenchman pulled a knife from his sash and threw it upon the table. As Stryker stepped forward to gather up the letter and book, the curtains in the rear parted and the mystery woman stepped out. There was a big revolver in her hand.

"Back!" she warned Stryker coolly.

With a nasty laugh Delevan, thinking he had the better of the break, lunged toward the table for his knife.

"You, too . . . back . . . all of you," said the woman.

Delevan snarled: "You bitch!"

Stryker said: "What the devil?"

"Back!" warned Delevan's wife.

Perplexed, angry, yet marveling at the girl's cool nerve, Stryker held his peace. She picked up the letter and the book, then smiled across at Stryker.

"You'd better keep your gun on these fellows," she told him.

"But those . . . they're mine, madam."

Without another word she disappeared behind the curtains. A moment later she came out dressed for the trail. For a brief instant Stryker was undecided whether to detain her or keep his gun on the other three. But that brief instant, the split-second relaxation, gave Rex time to dive for the table, snatch up his revolver, and drop behind it. The next moment his gun blazed. Simultaneously Delevan and Paul jumped for their weapons. The girl was tugging at Stryker's arm.

"Come! Out!" she screamed.

"I'll not let these dirty. . . ."

"Fool! Come!"

She half-dragged him through the door and began to run off toward Chevik's cabin, yelling for Stryker to follow her.

He was taking her advice a little against his will, for he felt that he had more than one score to settle with Delevan and the two Frenchmen, his blood was up, and he was ripe for anything short of murder.

"I wish you'd let me . . . ," he started to say.

"Never mind. It's only started," panted the girl. "You'll get all the fight you want."

Delevan and his henchmen were already on their trail. Half a dozen Eskimos came tumbling out of the smaller shacks and took up the pursuit, and the frosty night was shattered with rifle fire and mad oaths.

Stryker and the girl reached the cabin and burst in. Chevik and the other Eskimo were sitting by the stove, half asleep. The door was bolted.

The girl said: "Chevik, Tuktoluk, quick! Big fight!"

The Eskimos grunted, yawned, and picked up their rifles. The girl took a handful of shells from her pocket and placed them on the table. Stryker loaded his rifle to capacity. The grimy oil lamp was extinguished, and the heavy table was braced against the door.

The pursuers arrived, and Delevan's voice boomed: "Open that damned door! Open, d'you hear?"

"Go 'way, you make me laugh!" shot back Stryker.

"I do, eh? All right, you pup, you'll laugh the other way when I'm finished with you."

"That's cheap talk, Delevan. Let's see what you can do."

Delevan swore and fired, but the door was of stout spruce and merely absorbed the lead. Then the attackers hurled themselves against it *en masse,* and it shivered but gave no hint of breaking down.

"I want my wife!" bawled Delevan furiously.

"You don't say," replied the girl. "Try and get me, then." She was as cool as ice.

221

There was a lull. Then there were sounds on the low roof, the crunch of many feet, and after that came the ring of an axe. Stryker stood so close to the girl he could look into her eyes.

"They're going to chop through," he muttered.

"Yes," she said, and let her hand fall upon his arm.

He thrilled. "But we'll win through," he grated out.

"Yes . . . we will," she said.

The axe was still pounding away. The roof was straining and snapping. Then the axe stopped, and several men began to jump up and down. The roof strained more and more until finally the middle of it caved in and a deluge of snow and men crashed to the floor. Chevik caught Paul neatly across the back of the neck with a wielded gun and reduced their number by one. But more dropped through and guns and knives were swung with murderous ferocity.

Stryker, having killed one of these attacking Eskimos, swung open the door and led the fight out into the open with the girl beside him. Chevik, his face bleeding, rolled out after them, and close on his heels came Tuktoluk, shooting backward as he ran. Delevan's gang, falling over one another, burst out in hot pursuit, their guns flaming, with Delevan himself, a gun in each hand and red murder in his eyes, at the fore.

Stryker reached the settlement of three cabins and drew the girl down with him beside the nearest. Chevik and Tuktoluk rocked up behind him and threw themselves onto the snow. The attackers came up over the ridge, and, as they swung down toward the cabins, Stryker bowled over one of them with two fast shots. Chevik wounded another but did not put him completely out of the fight.

The attackers drew up and dropped onto the snow, taking pot shots at the cabins. The Northern Lights grew brighter, flinging their ghostly banners across the white tundra. The attackers, realizing they were too much in the open, retreated and worked away toward the river, but Tuktoluk dropped one of them and the girl's shot made another stagger until a companion helped him along.

VI

"About six left," observed Stryker. The girl started to say something, but at that moment a gun was poked into the air, and from it fluttered a piece of white cloth.

"Come on up, only one, and have your say!"

It was Rex who came forward over the little ridge that concealed the others, holding the flag of truce before him.

"Well?" snapped Stryker.

"*M'sieu,*" began the man, "we have no desire to murder you. *M'sieu* Delevan says to let his wife go and call t'ings off. It ees bad policy, *m'sieu,* to steal another man's wife."

Stryker looked at the girl. "Did you hear that? I'm here to help you out. I'm not interfering, but Delevan tried to murder me, and it seems he's none too good to you. I'll fight this thing out as you say. If you go over to him or not, he's got to settle with me for other things." He paused. He was not a man to mince words. That is why he asked: "Do you love him?"

She shuddered. "No. But I'd better. . . ."

"That's all. You were going to say you'd better go over to save me." To Rex he said: "Tell Delevan to go to the devil."

The Frenchman did not move. He regarded Stryker with a strange twinkle in his eyes.

Then something happened. There was a rush from the rear. At the same time Rex swung his gun butt to hip. Stryker, sensing immediately that the others had crept around while Rex was offering a truce, swung his rifle in a short arc and broke the Frenchman's jaw.

He whirled around and found the girl in his arms. She

whispered: "There's one bullet in my gun. I'll keep it for myself."

Scarcely without knowing what he did, he kissed her, then pushed her behind him and fired his gun pointblank at an Eskimo that was just about to brain him. He went down with a scream. Chevik and Tuktoluk were at close quarters with four others, and Delevan was lunging wolfishly toward Stryker.

Stryker, his rifle empty, advanced to meet him. They both swung at the same time. The rifles crashed in mid-career, broke, and the two men grappled. Delevan broke away and came back with a mighty fist that grazed Stryker's jaw and turned him completely around. Following up, Delevan caught him behind the ear with a short but terrific jab that sent him head first into the snow. But Stryker was a hard man and quick for his size. He was up and at Delevan, and everything he had was behind his blows.

It was furious, the way they mixed it, and before many minutes both were spitting blood and their hide mittens were soggy with it.

Tuktoluk went down with a smashed skull even as Chevik broke one opponent's neck. The other three piled on him, and, fighting to the last, he went down. As one of the Eskimos raised his knife to stab him, the girl, with a little cry, swung her revolver about and fired her last shot—the shot she was going to save for herself. The Eskimo dropped across the groaning Chevik.

The other two rushed at the girl and overpowered her, then began to carry her off, each striving to tear her from the other. With a mad snarl one let her go, whipped up his knife, and buried it in the other's back. Then, cackling, he picked her up and disappeared behind one of the cabins. A little later he mushed out behind a *komatik* and a four-dog team, and the girl was strapped to the *komatik.*

Stryker and Delevan, struggling to the death, did not see this. Now they were down on the snow, locked in each other's arms, kicking, biting, cursing, with one and then the other on top. They carried the fight over the little ridge and right down to the river. Then they were up again and out on the frozen waterway, slugging, taking and giving, streaming blood.

"Delevan," ground out Stryker, "this is the last fight you'll ever do. I'm going to pound you to death."

Delevan spat out a tooth. "D'you think so? G'on, you pup . . . the wolves'll get you before morning."

They closed and rocked farther out on the river. They neared a hole cut in the ice that apparently had been used for fishing. Delevan had Stryker by the nose and was trying to twist it off, and with the intense pain the latter's knees buckled as he tried to tear away. Then they went down in a heap, with Stryker underneath. Frantically Delevan pulled a long, slim knife from inside his sealskin coat and raised it high above his head.

Chevik was tottering and reeling down toward the waterway. He saw Delevan draw his knife. Chevik, the cleverest Eskimo with a knife in all the Labrador, hesitated for a moment. He fingered his own knife gingerly, gauged the distance with a calculating eye, and threw it. It sang eerily through the air, striking Delevan point first in the side of the neck. His throat rattled. He heaved to one side, lost his balance, and plunged through the hole in the ice into the bitter waters of the Kuglictuk.

Panting, Stryker struggled up and lunged toward the shore. He fell upon Chevik, grasped his hand, and pressed it till the Eskimo winced.

"Thanks, Chevik! God . . . thanks, old chum!" Then: "Where's the white woman?"

"Gone. I see go. Man take."

The two badly mutilated men stumbled to Chevik's cabin, lashed up the dogs, and followed the trail made by the abductor.

VII

The dawn broke, gray and leaden, above the winter-locked Labrador. Stryker was running up beside his lead dog. Chevik was trotting behind the *komatik* and cracking the whip. Men and dogs were covered with hoar frost.

Rounding a bend in the river, Stryker raised his hand, and Chevik called the dogs to a halt. Up ahead, on the west bank, was the smoke of a campfire, and Stryker could make out two figures beside it.

"It's them," he said.

He rummaged in his equipage and found a revolver, then continued at breakneck speed. Immediately there was a stir in the camp. One of the figures bundled the other upon the *komatik,* swung out the dogs, and began to drive madly northward.

But Stryker was a powerful runner, and in a short time he was within pistol shot of the kidnapper. He fired. Missed. The other, without stopping, turned and returned fire. The shot went wild. Stryker stopped, took careful aim, and shot again. This time the man stumbled, tried to grasp the gee bar of his *komatik,* missed, and sprawled headlong on the snow.

He was dead when Stryker came up. A hundred feet farther on, the team had stopped. He found the girl trying to struggle free of her thongs. When she saw him, she stopped struggling and lapsed into a coma.

Chevik made a fire. Strong tea revived the girl, and, when she came to, she found herself in Stryker's arms. She did not resist.

"Thank God you came," she said with a shudder. "That beast of an Eskimo. . . ."

"Yes, I understand." Stryker nodded. "I may as well tell you now that the whole gang is cleaned out, including your husband. He was about to stick a knife in me when Chevik, here, pitched his own knife and hit the bull's eye. Delevan is now at the bottom of the river. This Eskimo here was the last of the pack."

"Good Chevik," she murmured. Then: "My husband dead? It might sound cruel, but I'm glad. And . . . and thanks for bringing that letter. Poor Harry, he had to die."

Stryker looked puzzled. "Letter? Harry?"

"Yes. You see, I am Jack. Funny name for a girl, isn't it?"

Stryker was stunned. "You . . . Jack?"

"Yes. Harry Kavanagh was my brother. It's hard to say why I ever married Pete Delevan. It happened two years ago. But I haven't lived with him for one day. He was a beast. My folks didn't believe in divorce, so what could I do? I told him to stay away from me, but he wouldn't. Delevan hounded me wherever I went. My father used to run a trading post in the Labrador, and, when he gave it up and came home, he brought his servant, Chevik, with him. It was Chevik who helped me get away. He knew the Labrador well, and I asked him if he would bring me here and help me to hide. He did. He's faithful, Chevik is. He'd never seen Delevan, so when you asked him to guide you over this way, he suspected you were the man. He told me of that meeting at Fort Chimo, how he had left you to starve and all that. Then when I told him that while he was at Chimo, Delevan had tracked me with the aid of the two French guides, he was very sorry. Delevan had whiskey and with it he bribed most of the Eskimos, but Chevik and his brother Tuktoluk remained loyal, although they gave Delevan to believe otherwise. When you came in and told Delevan what you were after, he threatened to kill you if I revealed my identity. I figured he would try to kill you anyway, so I set Chevik to watch him. And Chevik saved you from drowning. I . . . I guess I've caused you an awful lot of trouble, Mister Stryker."

"Mister? My front name's Ed."

"Well, Ed, then." She smiled up into his bruised face.

"No trouble at all, Jack," he lied nobly. "Just a little excitement."

VIII

One day, as the sun was making its brief appearance above the southern bulge of the earth, *Monsieur* De Loge, of Revillons, went over to pay a visit to his rival and friend, Donald Flemming, acting factor of the H.B.C. post at Fort Chimo. He said: "*M'sieu*, I wonder if dat daredevil, *M'sieu* Stryker, has found himself a grave out dere near de Kuglictuk, or if he ees safe."

"It's hard to say, De Loge," returned Flemming. "He's an old-timer on the trail, you know, and maybe he's pulled through. Let's hope so anyway. But between you and me, I'd be damned if I'd take that trip for some mysterious person named Jack."

"It ees youth, I s'pose, *m'sieu*. Youth ees afraid of nodding."

The conversation was interrupted by a commotion just outside the door. There was a boisterous laugh, the snarl of a dog, and then the sound of a woman's voice.

The door swung open. De Loge stared, speechless. Flemming dropped his pipe. Ed Stryker, his face and *koolutik* sparkling with frost, rocked in with his arm around a very charming young lady.

"Hello, De Loge . . . Flemming!" called Stryker. "How's everything?"

De Loge jumped to his feet and wrung Stryker's hand, and Flemming, his face beaming now, was close behind. Then they looked at the girl.

"This is Jack." Stryker laughed.

After that the factors argued at length as to who should act as host to Ed Stryker and the girl he had brought out of the wilds. They compromised. Stryker went with De Loge. Jack stayed with Flemming.

But first Stryker asked: "Listen, Flemming. *Pst!* Is the missionary at the post?"

Jack blushed. Stryker felt a little uneasy. Chevik shoved his head in the door and blinked. And the two factors looked at each other knowingly.

The Craft of Ka-Yip
Dan Cushman

Dan Cushman (1909-2001) was born in Osceola, Michigan, and grew up on the Cree Indian reservation in Montana. In the early 1940s his novelette-length stories began appearing regularly in such Fiction House magazines as *North-West Romances* and *Frontier Stories*. The character Comanche John, a Montana road agent featured in numerous rollicking magazine adventures, is the protagonist in Cushman's first novel, *Montana, Here I Be* (Macmillan, 1950), and in two later novels. *Stay Away, Joe* (Viking, 1953), an amusing novel about the mixture, and occasional collision, of Indian culture and Anglo-American culture among the *Métis* (French Indians) living on a reservation in Montana became a bestseller and remains a classic to this day, greatly loved especially by Indian peoples for its truthfulness and humor. Yet, while humor became Cushman's hallmark in later novels, he also produced significant historical fiction like *The Silver Mountain* (Appleton-Century, 1957), concerned with the mining and politics of silver in Montana in the 1890s. This novel won a Spur Award from the Western Writers of America. His fiction remains notable for its breadth, ranging all the way from a story of the cattle frontier in *Tall Wyoming* (Dell, 1957) to a poignant and memorable portrait of small-town life in Michigan just before the Great War in *The Grand and the Glo-*

rious (McGraw-Hill, 1963). Two of his more recent novels, published as Five Star Westerns, have been North-Westerns: *In Alaska with Shipwreck Kelly* (1995) and *Valley of the Thousand Smokes* (1996). "The Craft of Ka-Yip" was originally published in *North-West Romances* (Fall, 1945).

Ka-yip's years were many as the leaves of the chokecherry tree. His skin was browned the color of an old moccasin sole and dehydrated until its wrinkles were infinite and patternless like the skin of a withered potato. Ka-yip sat in the door of his buffalo-skin teepee just behind the woodchopper's shanty and let the morning sunshine sink into his brittle old bones. From time to time he bent forward to inspect a row of cigar butts that were drying on a flat slab of sandstone.

The cigar butts were part of Ka-yip's harvest from the barroom floor of the *Southern Pride*, a Missouri River steamboat that had stopped at the wood lot of his white son-in-law's the day before. They were of many lengths, thicknesses, and colors. There was a thick one that had been less than a third smoked; another, a panatela, had been trod on and shredded by some careless feet; others had been smoked down to their final inch and hence were seasoned a good, rich black. Part of the longest butt was quite dry, so Ka-yip ground it to a leafy pulp between his hard old palms, mixed it with a shred of red willow bark, and loaded the redstone bowl of his pipe.

Ka-yip smoked these long ones first, next those of medium length, and so on down, hoarding the richest and shortest ones throughout the day. Then, as dusk settled over the swift Missouri and its barren bluffs of whitish clay, Ka-yip would savor the good smoke of the shortest and strongest butt of all while he thought deeply of life and its mysteries. Generally, as he sat there in the long twilight, his friend, Wappa-moo, the little gray field mouse, would come for a few last nibbles of food and listen to the wisdom that is the harvest of man's years.

"Behold this cigar butt of the white man," Ka-yip had said the night before, tapping his pipe bowl. "When I picked it up, it was heavy with goodness, and now, dried by the sun, it smokes rich and strong. You would think the white man would treasure such a butt as this, but, no. He throws it away!"

At this, Wappa-moo had stopped nibbling for a while and looked up, his little beady eyes shining with comprehension.

"Indeed, Wappa-moo, are not these white men a race of lunatics? These cigars they make at great expense. I have heard it said that the cost of a box of them is as the cost of one cayuse. It would be great wealth to own a dozen of those boxes. And the white men bring them far, carrying them inside a glass case on the boat driven by the great fire. Yet, after all this, they cast away the best part for another to enjoy, like the foolish squaw who took the tail of the buffalo and left the tongue for the magpies."

Before Ka-yip had finished his first morning pipe, there came the jabber of voices and wail of papoose from inside the log house. In a few minutes the stovepipe gave forth smoke, there was an odor of frying food, and soon afterward his daughter, Nis-wah, a name that the white man had shortened to "Agnes", came out with a pan of salt pork and doughgods for breakfast.

Ka-yip ate slowly, pulverizing the crisp fat pork between his gums. The doughgods—unleavened flapjacks—were soft and easy to eat. Part of one doughgod he laid aside for the breakfast of his friend, Wappa-moo.

Rupe, Ka-yip's white son-in-law, came from the back door, stretching himself and fingering doughgod from his red whiskers. He was a gangling man of forty or so, long-necked,

235

with a pointed Adam's apple and a complexion which tended to freckle and turn rusty in the sun.

" 'Mornin', Yip," yawned Rupe. "How's the cigar butts holdin' out?"

Rupe always asked that, following up with a snicker that hinted there was something humorous about good, mellowed cigar butts and as though smoking them were beneath his white-man's pride. Ka-yip deeply resented this tone of his son-in-law's, and he also resented being called "Yip". (His name was not Ka-yip even, but Ka-yip-wa-wata-waw-ses-sik which, in the Cree dialect, meant literally "the wise eye", although through usage much more—"the eye of the wise eagle" perhaps, or "the eye and the mind of bravery and wisdom".) It was far too proud a name to be shortened to a mere "Yip" to please the white man's impatient tongue.

Still, deep as was his resentment, Ka-yip gave no sign. He bowed slightly as was the custom of his tribe and gestured to the cigar butts. "See, *ne koosis*, my son. I have only these."

Rupe yawned again "The *Great West* should be in tomorrow. Maybe you can pick up a few there."

Rupe hitched the bay mare to the Red River cart, tossed in his axe and Henry rifle, and set off toward a grove of big cottonwoods up the coulée. As the Red River cart was made exclusively of two materials, wood and rawhide, the anguish of its axles could be heard long after it had turned a bend and rolled from sight. Wappa-moo, who feared Rupe and the noisy cart, now scurried up through the dry buffalo grass. Ka-yip nodded good morning and commenced rolling up the little ball of doughgod for his little friend's breakfast.

"Behold him, Wappa-moo! Behold my son-in-law, my daughter's husband, that chopper of wood! My family were hunters, and warriors, and mighty stealers of horses, Wappa-moo. Neither my father nor my father's father ever chopped wood for the fire. They would rather lie scalped by Gros Ventres than be seen doing squaw's work. When he came to my lodge, Wappa-moo, and asked for my daughter, I thought him a great hunter . . . a long knife. I thought he was great among his people. But what was he? He was a chopper of wood, an *iskao* weakling."

While Ka-yip sat there, bent forward, savoring his disgrace, his daughter who the white man called "Agnes" went to the river for a bucket of water. On her way back she paused to look toward the northeast, shading her eyes against the early sun. Ka-yip looked, also. A line of horsemen was approaching across the bench land that sloped down from the low summits of the Bear Paw Mountains.

Ka-yip counted to his last finger. Ten riders. Ten—not since the Blackfoot war party burned the cabin and woodpiles two years before had he seen so many raiders all at once. But these were not Blackfeet. They did not ride long-legged in their saddles, bounding stiff-spined with each jog of the horses—they rode high, taking the jolts with limber knees and sway of hips.

"Behold, Wappa-moo! The white men come, riding like so much boneless meat on their cayuses." Ka-yip made a gesture of misgiving. "It is not well when the white men come in tens without pack horses. It was always such white men without pack horses who took the squaws from our teepees and lifted the hair of our warriors."

Ka-yip puffed his pipe while the riders moved across the bench and descended the trail that crawled like a twisting bull snake down the little badlands hills that separated bench from river. They were white men, as Ka-yip had guessed, a hard, bewhiskered lot, traveling light, save for armament that was unusually heavy and included rifles, pistols, and sawed-off shotguns. In the lead was a long man of hawk-like nose and eye. Seeing Ka-yip, the hawk-like one rode up, lifting his hand, palm first, in a signal of friendship.

"How!" he said.

"How!" answered Ka-yip.

"This is Alkali Coulée landing, ain't it?"

Ka-yip was inscrutable. "No savvy."

The man gestured toward the coulée. "Alkali. Steamboat stop. Heap savvy?"

"No savvy."

A pig-eyed man with a large nose and great, rounded shoulders came forward then to look at Ka-yip and grunt contemptuously: "Hell, Skinner, what's the use of tryin' to talk to an Injun?"

Skinner paid no attention. He tried sign language, gesturing at the dock and forming the figure of a diamond with his two hands. "Diamond B boat stop, savvy?"

Ka-yip watched patiently, but, when Skinner was done, he rocked from side to side and repeated: "No savvy."

The pig-eyed man hee-hawed and beat dust from the leg of his homespun pants. "You sure got aplenty out of him, Skinner." Then in a voice intended for the others to hear: "Any fool would know this was the right place."

Skinner overheard the remark. "Bignose, you're too damned smart. You never been here before. None of us have. If this happens to be the wrong place, that Diamond B boat will wheel right by."

"Don't let me bother you. Go right on, seein' you and gran'pap are gettin' on so well."

Skinner was now more determined than ever to get some information from Ka-yip. He swung down and drew a diagram in the dust, but when he was through, Ka-yip rocked from side to side with sad negation.

"No savvy."

"*Ave-ax el-ax,*" said Skinner, reaching far back in his memory for the words. "*Qhay-ax we-at-ack?*"

"*Kitta meyo kes-i-kaw,*" responded Ka-yip.

It was plain that this answer in Cree meant as little to Skinner as his question in Chinook had meant to Ka-yip.

"There's your answer," snickered Bignose, showing a row of decayed teeth.

Suddenly enraged, Skinner drew his heavy cap-and-ball pistol and waggled it under Ka-yip's nose. Ka-yip puffed at his cold pipe and stared unblinkingly at the bluffs beyond the river. "Is this Alkali Coulée?" Skinner asked again.

"No savvy."

Skinner was tempted to pull the trigger, but instead he thrust his foot against Ka-yip's chest with a force that sent him rolling backward, almost into the teepee fire. Ka-yip did not change expression. Slowly, as though his joints were hinges that needed oiling, he resumed his old position and stared out across the river. Skinner thrust the pistol back in its scabbard and looked around at the cabin, the dock, the long woodpiles.

"Where the hell's the wood hawk?" he asked of nobody in particular.

"No savvy," moaned Ka-yip.

"He didn't understand that, neither." Bignose smirked and several of the men laughed.

Skinner spun around. "You don't care much for the way I'm runnin' this, do you, Bignose?"

Bignose was uncomfortable. He showed that in the shiftiness which appeared in his little eyes, but he had a standing to maintain, so he repeated his sarcastic laugh.

"Think you could do it better?" Skinner drew out the words slowly.

A small, gray-whiskered man now spurred his horse between them.

"If you want Old Dad's judgment, you'll hold your temper," he drawled. "We'll need all the men we got before this little piece of business is done. A steamboat is some bigger job than a stagecoach when it comes to liftin' the heavy color."

Bignose and Skinner looked at each other over the neck of Old Dad's horse, but the tension was broken and everyone breathed more easily. They drifted away from the teepee, finally dividing into two groups—Bignose and three others rode up the coulée to find Rupe, while Skinner and the rest loitered around the cabin and the steamboat dock.

They soon brought Rupe back, riding bareback on the old bay horse. His eyeballs had a protruding, frightened look, and he kept gulping as though something had become lodged beneath his Adam's apple.

Now that it was again peaceful near the teepee, Wappa-moo returned for more doughgod.

"Behold these strangers!" said Ka-yip. "They have come here to lie in wait for the boat of the great fire so they can stealum yellow dust that is worth more than horses to the white men. If they do this, Wappa-moo, the boats will be frightened from the wood yard of my son-in-law, for it is said at the lodge fires of my people that the fox which escaped the snare does not travel the same trail again." Ka-yip considered deeply this ancient wisdom. "This is not good, for, if the boats stop coming, there will be no more cigar butts."

Ka-yip wanted to speak of the matter with Rupe, but Rupe did not come near the teepee—he was busy trotting around, doing the bidding of the strangers. Several times Ka-yip signaled, one finger held aloft, but Rupe pretended not to see. It was mid-afternoon before he came close enough for Ka-yip to stop him.

"Those white brothers of yours, *ne koosis,* my son . . . they are bad men. *Meyo-meyo,* heap savvy? It is not good that you stand by while they stealum yellow dust worth more than horses. That is not brave, *ne koosis,* and I know you are a brave man."

"Quiet down!" Rupe growled from the side of his mouth, apprehensive of the two men who sat at the back door of the cabin, feasting on dried apples.

"You have wisdom, *ne koosis.* Tell Ka-yip, your father, how you will stop these white men from stealum yellow dust."

"You must think I'm a damned fool. I wouldn't run up against a gang like that for my own money, let alone some heavy color belongin' to a Benton or Saint Louis millionaire."

The bend slowly left Ka-yip's back. "These are not the words of my son! No, this is some stranger I hear speaking!"

"The hell it is!"

"Then you are not a chief?"

"Chief be blowed! I'd ruther be a live woodchopper than Stonewall Jackson in his seven-by-three."

Ka-yip weaved from side to side and moaned.

"You wouldn't be so brave if it was up to you," muttered Rupe defensively.

Ka-yip lifted one forefinger. "*Wache!* I was great brave when the lodges of my people were many like the mounds of the prairie dog town. Once, with only my knife, I rode into a village of Sioux, those eaters of roasted snakes, and stealum five horses. Alone, I did this, *ne koosis,* for I was brave. . . ."

Rupe snorted. "You weren't so brave when the Blackfeet raided a couple summers back. You hightailed it plenty quick that time."

"Rupe!" shouted Bignose. "Get us some more tobacky."

Rupe hopped up obediently, and hurried inside the house

for his tin bucket of natural-leaf chewing tobacco. Ka-yip sat watching him while the insult burned into his brain.

"Did you hear what he said, Wappa-moo? He said I ran from the Blackfeet. He said I was not brave. Well, I will show this son-in-law of mine . . . this chopper of wood. I will show him the craft and bravery of the warrior. I will keep watch on these white men. I will trick them so the boats will still come bearing their cigar butts. He will not dare laugh at me tomorrow, Wappa-moo."

Ka-yip sat there, hunched over, seeming to sleep while his shadow grew longer across the ground, and he watched each move, listened to each word of the white strangers.

"Behold these white men, Wappa-moo! Are they not a race of lunatics? They come a long distance to rob the boat of the great fire . . . and of what? I will tell you! To rob it of the yellow metal too soft for knife blade or arrowhead, or anything except the rings on a squaw's finger. These whites! What would they do without their guns that shoot far? They do not have the Cree's bravery or wisdom. No! I would ask nothing easier than to trick them. Once, long ago, a black robe came to our village and told us about these white men. He said that once, far across the great water, there lived the greatest of all white chiefs, a Manatouwa, who pretended to be poor and went around without eagle feathers in an old capote. Now this white chief did great magic so as to make all the medicine men jealous, and what did they do? They cried out with many lies until the other white men seized the great chief. 'Who are you?' they asked. '*Wache!*' he answered. '*Wache! Keche Ookemawit!* Behold! I am a king!' 'Oh, ha!' laughed these foolish white men, 'see who is here in his old capote and worn-out moccasins saying he is a king! He is a madman, let us nail him to a great tree!' And this they did, these white men. But would he have been treated thus among my people? No, Wappa-moo! We would have honored him, and given him a dry teepee, and feasted him on young boiled dog as we do all madmen. Yet even today these white men look for their great chief to return, but will he come to them? No, he will not. He will come to the Crees who will treat him better." Ka-yip shook his bony old shoulders in a hacking chuckle "Ah, Wappa-moo, I ask nothing easier than to fool such white men."

The bandits remained split into two groups—the followers of Bignose and the followers of Skinner, with Old Dad wandering back and forth, attempting to keep the peace. Skinner and his men sat around the woodpiles, on the dock, while the Bignose faction preferred the cabin. Several times Bignose felt of some object inside his shirt, and once, when there was no one around, he drew out a tiny, buckskin bag and peeped inside.

"Did you see him, Wappa-moo?" asked Ka-yip. "Did you see that Bignose peeping into the little sack he keeps tied around his neck? It must be great medicine that he hides it beneath his capote away from even the eyes of his friend. I would give much to know what is in that bag, Wappa-moo."

Ka-yip plotted. He plotted with cunning greater than the lynx cat while the sun swung in its southern arc and slid behind the horizon. Twilight was settling when he signaled with upraised finger to Bignose.

"*Wuniska oogemah!*" he called.

"What in hell do you want?" Bignose asked.

Ka-yip signaled again, so he walked grudgingly over to the teepee.

Ka-yip looked all around, then he asked in a guarded monotone: "Heap savvy whiskey?"

"Me savvy, but if I had any, I'd drink it myself."

"Me . . . Ka-yip . . . know where plenty whiskey, savvy?"

"Where is it?" asked Bignose with sudden enthusiasm.

Ka-yip assumed a crafty attitude. "Me tell . . . you give
. . ."—he gestured with his fingers, one, two, three—"*nestoo
mawutche.*"

"Three what?"

"You give . . . three dollar."

"You'll get no three dollars from me, you flea-bitten old
rag bag. Tell me where it is or I'll wring your neck."

Ka-yip pretended to have great fear. His eyes rolled and he
moaned as he rocked from side to side. "No savvy."

"Where's that likker?"

Ka-yip pointed a trembling finger toward the root cellar.
"*Akota watchee.*"

"In the root cellar?"

Ka-yip nodded. He spread a ragged fragment of blanket
on the ground and peeped under it. "*Akota watchee!*" he repeated.

Bignose hopped up and set off for the root cellar with long
strides. He flung open its pole door and leaped into the hole
to reappear a moment later with an earthenware jug in each
hand.

"Hey, boys!" he bellowed. "Look here what that damned
wood hawk had hid on us! Likker . . . gallons of it!"

No bugle ever assembled troops quicker than that cry of
"likker" brought the bandits. The jugs commenced passing
from hand to hand, and in a short time no hatred, suspicion,
or rivalry was left in them. Old Dad was so happy he sang,
while others formed sets for an impromptu quadrille. Ka-yip
chuckled as he smoked one of the rich, short butts in his
redstone pipe.

When darkness settled, the men touched a match to one of
Rupe's woodpiles and hilariously kept working on the jugs.
Ka-yip covered his teepee fire with dry sod so the coals would

hold throughout the night and retired to the heap of buffalo robes that was his bed. He did not lie down. He sat quietly, cross-legged, in the dark, watching the white men through the flap of the teepee.

The woodpile was long, so half the night was over by the time it burned from one end to the other. By that time most of the men were sprawled in various attitudes of alcoholic coma, but three still held on—Bignose, Old Dad, and a man called Dakotah.

Old Dad still sang, lifting his quavering monotone in a popular ditty of the day:

> **Oh, what was your name in the States?**
> **Was it Johnson or Thompson or Bates?**
> **Did you murder your wife**
> **And run for your life?**
> **Say, what was your name in the States?**

The sentiment of this song was so overpowering that Old Dad dropped his grizzled head in his hands and wept. Bignose and Dakotah were jangling about the Wingate expedition of 1862 against the Cheyennes. Old Dad wept himself to sleep. Bignose and Dakotah got through the name-calling stage of their dispute without resorting to firearms, and soon they, also, fell asleep.

The coals crackled and died down beneath a thick coating of ash. A night breeze sprang up and fluttered the wind sail of the teepee. Ka-yip crept outside and circled the sleeping white men. He found Bignose sprawled out with his feet almost in the warm ashes. Silently as a night hunting weasel Ka-yip crouched and unbuttoned the front of Bignose's shirt, revealing the little buckskin bag nestled in the hair of his chest. Ka-yip was in no hurry to take it. He drew his knife and stropped the blade a few times on his moccasin, then, with two deft movements, he cut the thongs.

He faded back to the shadow of a nearby woodpile, opened the bag, and peeped inside. It contained about twenty bright, many-sided stones of the kind he had seen set in the rings of men and women on the steamboats. Some of them were colorless like ice, while others gleamed red as crystallized blood in the starlight.

Ka-yip took the largest of the stones, a bluish-white one about two-thirds the size of his little fingernail, and hid it under the slab of rock at the door of his teepee. The rest he carried over to where Skinner was snoring near the back door of the cabin and rolled them loosely in the top fold of his buckskin legging. This done, Ka-yip crept back inside his teepee, curled up on his pallet of buffalo skins, and seemed to sleep.

The last coals of the woodpile died out. The night breeze, sucking down the deep cut of the river, chilled some of the sleepers until they got up and found blankets. Bignose, Skinner, and most of the others slept on while the dawn came up over the Bear Paw Mountains and drove the mist from the river.

At this hour, when the first rays of sun shone yellow through the seams of his teepee, it was Ka-yip's custom to arise and smoke his first pipeful, but this morning he stayed inside. He watched Bignose get up, make a wry face at the flavor of his tongue, and stagger down to the river for a drink. He came back and hefted the jugs until he found one that contained a heel of liquor. A few swallows of this seemed to be what he needed. With the liquor warming his inside, Bignose made his habitual movement of feeling inside his shirt. He dropped the jug and searched frantically, but was rewarded with nothing except the length of buckskin. He stared at this for a second, and then raised a bellow like a wounded bull buffalo.

"Who stole my buckskin bag?" he roared.

Dakotah sat up and stared blearily. Chiefly because he was the nearest, Bignose reached down, grabbed him by the collar, and shook him like a bulldog shaking a poodle. Dakotah tried to draw his pistol, but Bignose slammed him to the ground so hard it was knocked from his hand.

"Give me that bag you stole!" shouted Bignose.

"I don't know what you're talkin' about," protested Dakotah.

Bignose had his pistol out now, waving at the men who had gathered around. His eyes came to rest on Skinner.

"So you're the one that lifted it!"

"Now, Bignose!" It was Old Dad, still playing his rôle of peacemaker. "Any man in camp might have lifted your nuggets or whatever it was. Put up your gun and let's talk peaceful."

Grudgingly Bignose put up his gun, but he didn't take his eyes off Skinner. Nothing was said for a while. Rupe came from the cabin, wondering what the excitement was about. Ka-yip shuffled from the teepee and sat down in his accustomed spot by the door flap. The bandits, sensing that the incident was not closed, silently split into the same groups as the day before, three going with Bignose, four with Skinner, leaving Old Dad in the middle.

"Listen, boys," Old Dad pleaded, "this here is bad medicine. No use splittin' up in two camps this way. There's no tellin' who might have got away with it."

Bignose was implacable. "Skinner took it! He. . . ."

"I never took a thing," growled Skinner.

Dakotah snarled: "What you got tied up in this, Welch?"

Old Dad waved them back. "Now hold on. We got no reason to suspect. . . ."

But even as he spoke, Bignose lunged forward, his eyes on the ground by Skinner's foot. A diamond flashed there in the early sun. He snatched it up. Skinner backed away, shaking more jewels from the cuff of his legging with every step. Bignose seemed about to pick up these, too, then he reconsidered and leaped back, his hand streaking for his pistol.

It was war. The morning air rocked with the almost instantaneous explosions of a half dozen guns. Skinner went down from a bullet in the hip, but he rolled to his side and aimed a shot that drove Bignose back on his heels. He fired again, and Bignose toppled. But Skinner's triumph was short, for one of Bignose's followers took aim and downed him for good. Old Dad fled to the protection of a woodpile, but by the time he reached it the battle was over.

Bignose and his followers were wiped out. Skinner and one of his men also lay quiet under the blue-white drift of powder smoke. Another man sat holding a shattered arm and cursing the pain. Rupe had fled behind the cabin, but Ka-yip, inscrutable as always, puffed his morning pipe.

"That settles it," announced Old Dad. "Four men can't rob a steamboat."

Within the hour the surviving bandits saddled and rode away. Ka-yip and Rupe watched them climb the winding trail toward the bench.

"I knew they'd get to fightin' amongst themselves," Rupe swaggered. "That's why I didn't try to keep 'em from robbin' the boat."

Ka-yip did not speak. Instead, he reached beneath the slab of sandstone and drew out a gem that flashed blue fire in the sunlight.

Rupe gasped. "Where'd you get that diamond?"

"From the Bignose I took it."

"You mean you stole them rocks off Bignose and cached 'em on Skinner?"

Ka-yip nodded.

"You old fool!" Rupe stamped around and shook his reddish hair indignantly. "Why didn't you keep the rocks and let them fellows rob the boat, or shoot themselves, or whatever they wanted? Them rocks would have put me on easy street. I'd never have had to chop another stick in my life!"

He ranted for a minute or two, and stamped angrily off for the cabin. After a while Wappa-moo scurried up through the grass.

"Good morning, Wappa-moo, my little friend," said Ka-yip. "Did you hear what he would have had me do . . . that chopper of wood? He would have had me take a handful of pretty beads in place of a lifetime of good, strong cigar butts."

Maintien le droit
Tim Champlin

Tim Champlin is the *nom de plume* of John Michael Champlin. He was born in Fargo, North Dakota in 1937, and graduated from Middle Tennessee State University, subsequently earning a master's degree from Peabody College in Nashville, Tennessee in 1964. He began his career as an author of Western stories with *Summer of the Sioux* (Ballantine, 1982). This became the first in a series of novels about the adventures of Matt Tierney who begins his professional career as a reporter for the Chicago *Times-Herald*, covering an expeditionary force venturing into the Big Horn country and the Yellowstone. His second series character is Jay McGraw, who is plunged into outlawry at the beginning of *Colt Lightning* (Ballantine, 1989), but who soon finds himself working as an agent for Wells Fargo & Company. More recently Champlin has departed from series characters to concentrate on historical fiction, such as *The Last Campaign* (Five Star Westerns, 1996), concerned with the final pursuit of Geronimo in the Southwest, *Swift Thunder* (Five Star Westerns, 1998), a story that takes place during the days of the Pony Express, and *By Flare of Northern Lights* (2001), a novel of the Alaskan gold rush. In all of Champlin's stories there are always unconventional ingredients, striking historical details, vivid characterizations of the multitude of ethnic and cultural

251

diversity found on the frontier, narratives that are rich and original and surprising. *"Maintien le droit"* first appeared in the anthology, *Tin Star* (Berkley, 2000), edited by Robert J. Randisi.

Constable Derek Barker threw back the bearskin cover and sprang from the bunk, clad only in wool socks and long johns. He caught his breath as the heavy cold in the one-room log cabin shocked him like a plunge into an icy stream. Clenching his teeth and shivering violently, he opened the cast-iron door of the squat stove and thrust a handful of long splinters into the banked coals. In the several seconds it took for them to blaze up, he glanced at the dull gray light filtering through the small window. Frost an inch thick covered the glass pane from top to bottom. But he didn't need to see the spirit thermometer hanging under the eave just outside to know that it showed a reading of minus thirty or lower.

"Probably at least ten below in here," he muttered aloud.

The thin splinters flared up, and he quickly added three hunks of split, dried oak from the wood box. He briefly considered jumping back into the warmth of the feather tick and bearskin, but forced the temptation aside and grabbed his clothes hanging from a nearby chair. He knew he would never toughen himself to the cold if he continued to give in to his whining flesh. He pulled on his breeches and long boots, then the red tunic and, until the fire drove the cold into the corners, his long sheepskin coat and his peaked, straight-brimmed Stetson. Then he proceeded to add more wood to the stove and fix breakfast, setting some pre-sliced strips of venison in a frying pan on the stove lid to thaw, along with a blackened coffee pot filled with solid ice.

The other man assigned to this outpost, Sergeant Cecil McKee, was an early riser and would have had all this done, but he was gone on patrol downriver and not expected back until sometime tomorrow night. Just yesterday, Barker had turned the page on the wall calendar to April, 1899 and he reflected that he was close to surviving his second winter in the Yukon with nothing worse than a mild case of cabin fever— no scurvy, no frostbite, no broken bones, no lacerations from ricocheting axes or the slashing fangs of his half-wild sled dogs, no madness brought on by the isolation of weeks of darkness on this frozen tip of the planet. It was more than could be said of most men who chose to winter in the sub-Arctic. He smiled grimly to himself, knowing that the flood of prospectors, along with foreign settlers and tradesmen expected members of the North-West Mounted Police to be bigger than life, to have the solutions to all problems, and to be even-handed dispensers of justice. It was as if the red uniform endowed them with some special powers.

He stepped outside into the biting cold and, taking the short axe from the woodpile, chopped some hunks of frozen fish from the cache beside the cabin and threw one piece to each of the sled dogs that were sheltering in a lean-to behind the cabin. Then he scooped a bucket of clean snow and added some chunks of icicles from the low roof to thaw for water.

As he went about his routine chores, he pictured the sun passing a little higher across the sky each day. In its strengthening rays, icicles were beginning to form on the south-facing side of their cabin. The spring breakup was still several weeks away and winter had not yet shown any real signs of relaxing its iron grip, but Barker knew he had weathered the worst of it. As he chewed his beans and venison, he thought again of requesting a transfer to Regina Barracks or Fort Macleod, or one of the more southern posts. They still had bitter winters, but those forts would seem almost tropical by comparison to the lonely outpost he and McKee shared on the Stewart

River. They'd been on detached duty for two years, responsible for patrolling hundreds of square miles. At age thirty-one, he was a ten-year veteran of the North-West Mounted Police. But, for many months, he'd ridden nothing but sleds or canoes. At the forts to the south, he would lose his independence and be subject to much external discipline, routine mounted drill, and would be dealing with persistent whiskey traders and horse thieves who were as hard to stamp out as ticks in summer.

The rush to the gold fields had forestalled the dissolution of the force by the Canadian Parliament, and now it was rumored the law would be amended to allow men to retire from the Mounted Police with a pension after twenty years' service or on disability. Should he try to wait it out? Or should he resign while he was still young enough to find another occupation? He had no other skills or interests. Sighing deeply, he drained his cup of tepid tea. For better or worse, he was astride this horse and determined to ride until he was thrown.

He finished eating and donned his coat again, then his fur hat, before going outside to split more firewood for the voracious stove. As he opened the door, he heard the unmistakable sound of a whip cracking and the distant yell of a human voice. He knew that hail. It was Julien Beaudoin, the half-breed mail carrier approaching from upriver. Until this winter, when Beaudoin had been hired to haul the mail, he and McKee had performed this additional duty—for no extra pay. He had to admit the half-breed kept to a much better schedule, even in the most extreme weather.

Barker stepped outside as Beaudoin swung his dog team in toward the cabin. Barker caught a glimpse of white teeth flashing in a dark face. "Constable!" Beaudoin's face was nearly hidden in the fur hood and the wreath of steamy breath.

"Julien!" Barker raised a mittened hand. "Come inside for a cup of hot tea."

The half-breed grinned his appreciation, and threw a loop of rope around the wood-splitting stump to anchor his sled before starting for the door.

"Whew! She ees frosty!" he exclaimed, pulling off his mittens and raking at the ice in his mustache.

"Thirty-six below, according to my thermometer," Barker stated. "Spring is just around the corner," he added, grinning. He handed the mailman a mug of steaming black tea. The half-breed helped himself to a spoonful of sugar and began stirring it.

"Any news?" Barker asked, shrugging out of his sheepskin coat.

"When I left Seely Creek, there was one beeg ruckus."

Barker arched his eyebrows in silent query.

The half-breed threw his hood back and was standing as near as he dared to the hot stove. Melting snow dripped from his mukluks to the bare board floor. "Claim jumper," he replied. "Cheechako. Man name Arnold Klegg." Beaudoin sipped the scalding tea and Barker waited patiently for him to continue. "Gunnar Herbert caught him stealing from hees cache, too."

Barker gave a low whistle. "Trouble. Herbert isn't one to let that slide."

Beaudoin brushed his shaggy black hair from his forehead with stubby fingers. "Herbert ees a bad man."

"Intolerant, maybe," Barker said. "Never gives an inch. Did he send you to tell me so I can arrest Klegg?"

"Oh, no, m'sieur. They weell hold miners' court today or tomorrow."

"We know what the outcome of that will be," Barker mused, staring at the mug in his hand. "They'll hang him, sure. They should have sent for me."

"Ees eet not justice?"

"Only if there's no established law available. And, if Herbert is running things, it'll be more like vengeance. I've got to get there before it's too late." He reached for his coat. "You got time to help me hitch up the dogs?"

"Don't tell heem I sent you, *m'sieur*," Beaudoin said. "Herbert weel keel me."

"As far as he'll know, I'm just on routine patrol." On a sudden impulse he reached up to a shelf for his *sabretache*—the square leather case that hung from his saber belt when he was on mounted parade. The brass, convex badge of the Mounties was worn attached to this *sabretache*. The badge was beautifully wrought with the embossed head of a bull buffalo in the center. Surrounding this head were the words:

NORTH-WEST MOUNTED POLICE

and across the bottom:

Maintien le droit

The heading and inscription to "maintain the right" were enclosed in a cluster of maple leaves topped by a crown. He unfastened the badge, polished it on his pants leg, and pinned it prominently to the front of his fur cap.

Both man and dogs were fresh and the thirty-three-mile run to Seely Creek took only six hours. The sun had been covered by a gray pall of clouds almost as soon as it cleared the horizon and Barker guessed the temperature had risen to only ten below by noon. The sled was unburdened and the snow dry, so they made good time, following mostly in the back tracks of the mail carrier. He ran behind to keep warm, alternately riding the sled to rest. Several times, to make even more speed, Barker took the team off the trail onto the frozen river where the runners fairly sang along the ice, cutting through patches of powdery snow here and there. He rode the backs of the runners with the cold wind stinging tears to his eyes and blood to his cheeks. It felt good to be out on trail again after nearly a week indoors.

After two short stops to rest the dogs, he arrived at the cluster of cabins on Seely Creek about mid-afternoon. He rapped with the butt of his whip on the whipsawed plank door of the largest cabin.

The latch was lifted and a face thrust out. "Yeah?"

Barker had opened his long coat so that his scarlet tunic was plainly visible, to go along with the badge on his fur hat. "Constable Barker on patrol," he announced, although Gunnar Herbert knew him on sight. "Mind if I have a look inside?"

"Ain't nothing here to see," Herbert growled.

"Nevertheless, let's have a short chat, then. I've come a long way and my dogs need some rest," he replied evenly. "You wouldn't have something hot you could offer a man to drink, now, would you?" He knew Herbert couldn't refuse to provide the customary hospitality without incurring suspicion. The policeman moved forward to enter, but Herbert stood his ground in the doorway.

"We're kinda busy just now, Barker. Maybe on your way back through. . . ."

"This won't take long," Barker persisted.

Herbert squinted at him in the long rays of the declining sun shooting through a break in the clouds. The Swede was ruggedly handsome, blue eyes, angular jaw, and strong nose, eyebrows so blond they were almost invisible against the pale skin. Blond hair with a reddish tint. A big, raw-boned man at least three inches taller than Barker and probably tipping the scales at more than two hundred pounds. His clean-shaven face was flushing pink in the biting cold.

"Shut the damn' door! We just got it warmed up in here!" a voice yelled from inside.

Reluctantly Herbert moved aside for the Mountie to enter. "Well, if you have to."

Before his eyes adjusted to the dimness, Barker's nose sensed a miasma of unwashed bodies and damp wool, mingled with wood and tobacco smoke. He slid along the wall, just inside the door, hand inside his coat near the flap of his holster. Slowly his eyes adjusted and he counted nine men in the room, most of whom he recognized—bearded miners he'd favored with help at one time or another. But now their eyes were hostile and suspicious. Then he saw why. He'd apparently interrupted preparations for a hanging. A thin man with black, curly hair was bound with rope and was being escorted toward the door by two miners. A third man carried a coil of rope with a hangman's noose fashioned in one end of it.

"What's going on, boys?" Barker asked, a hard edge to his voice.

No one answered at first. Then Herbert said: "We just had a trial. This Cheechako was convicted and is about to hang for robbery and claim jumping. Caught in the act," he added, as if that eliminated any doubts.

"If he's a newcomer, it might've been an honest mistake," Barker suggested blandly.

"He ain't *that* new!" Herbert snapped.

"I thought the usual punishment for thievery was banishment," Barker suggested.

"Robbin' a cache can leave a man to die in the wilderness.

You know that. Same as stealin' a man's horse. And that's a hangin' offense.'"

"Since I'm here, I'll take custody of him. You can press charges at his trial in a Canadian court." He looked at the prisoner. "What's your name?"

"Arnold Klegg," the man answered. Barker thought he'd never seen such a piteous look of gratitude.

"Too late, Barker. A miners' court has duly tried and convicted the sneaky son-of-a-bitch. Everything legal and above board. Bring him outside, boys."

"Hold it!" Barker's voice cracked like a shot and the stirring among the miners instantly stopped as they looked from the policeman to Herbert. "Let's talk outside," Barker said, edging toward the door. "I need to check my team."

The door closed behind the two men. Barker noted it was already dusk as the lowering sun had disappeared behind the leaden overcast. "I'll arrest that man, Klegg, on your say-so and take him with me," Barker said.

"We'll deal with him in our own way."

Barker shook his head. "I represent the law here. You or any of the others can come and testify when the time comes. Or, you can write out your statements, sign 'em, and I'll take your affidavits with me."

"How much do they pay you, Barker?" Herbert looked away from him. "Last I heard a constable got about a dollar-fifty a day. Why, hell, even a miner on wages or a laborer gets at least three times that much. Is it really worth it . . . all the work and danger and responsibility . . . for starvation pay?" He shook his head. "Tell you what." He slipped a rawhide bag half the size of his fist from his coat pocket. "Here's a poke of gold dust that will more than compensate you for your time and work. Call it a little bonus for all your trouble. But we don't need you here. Take it and go." He looked directly at Barker. "We'll feed and water your dogs and you can push on tonight. Or you can go on down the trail a ways and camp. Get a fresh start in the morning."

"I'll pretend I didn't hear that offer of a bribe," Barker said quietly, wondering how far he should push this man. He sniffed the breeze that had sprung up from the northwest. A definite smell of snow was on the air. Even though he had a Winchester carbine on the sled and a Smith & Wesson .38 on his hip, he was outnumbered and outgunned. But the history of the Mounted Police, with the exception of the uprising of the *Métis,* was not written in blood. It was a history of good accomplished and crime deterred mostly by force of personality and a calm insistence on fairness. He made a quick decision. "Postpone the hanging and I'll camp out here with my dogs. We'll talk again in the morning when we've had a chance to sleep on it."

Herbert looked almost relieved to have avoided an immediate confrontation. Barker knew that Herbert wasn't personally afraid of him. It was the uniform, the force of law represented by the badge, which made the Swede hesitate.

Herbert nodded, opened the door, and announced the delayed execution. The men dispersed, grumbling, to their cabins. Then, at Herbert's invitation, he and Barker sat down to supper, waited on by Herbert's half-breed wife, Tanna. She was a plain, dark-skinned woman who looked to be in her twenties. Barker guessed that her figure, under the shapeless wool dress and leggings, was stunning. She served them from a pot of caribou meat and beans on the stove, and cut thick slices of sourdough bread. Herbert must have planned ahead, or rationed his supplies carefully to still be so well supplied this late in the winter season.

The men ate and discussed topics of mutual interest as though nothing had transpired between them. They ignored the prisoner who sat tied to a chair on the other side of the room near the stove. Herbert had a reputation as a violent man when aroused. But he could be most amiable, if he chose, and Barker realized once again why this man, in addition to his physical strength and endurance, was a natural leader of men.

After supper, they smoked their pipes, then Barker said good night and went to make up his camp. He didn't go far— only a few yards into the trees behind the cabin, to be certain Klegg wasn't executed before dawn. He took a tarp from his sled and made a lean-to between two trees to block the wind and reflect the heat of a campfire he built with the Swede's wood. He cut some low-hanging pine boughs to form a dry, springy base for his bed, then sat for nearly an hour, staring into the flames and thinking. Whether Klegg was guilty or not, he deserved to have his day in a real court. But if persuasion failed, how would he get custody of the prisoner? It would have to be at gunpoint. But that would be a last resort. If Herbert and the other miners were adamant about hanging this man, blood could be shed, and it might very well be his own. As Herbert had put the question, was it really worth it?

He sighed and loosed the collar of his tunic, nodding wearily after hours on the trail. He pulled the wolf-skin cover off his nearby sled and spread it on the pine boughs, then stretched out and covered himself with the long, sheepskin coat, his feet toward the fire. Just as he turned down the flaps of his fur hat and prepared to sleep, he noticed some snowflakes drifting down in what light there was. From somewhere in the distance came the mournful howl of a wolf. Then he remembered no more as sleep took him.

The next thing he knew he was awakened by some movement close to him. He opened his eyes in the dark. The fire was nearly out. Instantly alert, his hand went for the pistol still strapped to his hip. A dog, a wolf, a prowling wolverine perhaps? A chill went up his back and he lay perfectly still, senses straining to identify the presence. He caught a faint musky scent, then some essence of grease and old wood smoke.

"Meester Barker," a low voice hissed.

"Who is it?" His eyes couldn't penetrate the blackness, but a figure moved in front of him, blocking the red glow from the few remaining coals in the fire.

"Tanna."

He sat up, keeping a hand on the butt of his revolver. "What do you want?"

"How long since you had a woman?" she asked, moving closer until he could feel her breasts rubbing his arm and shoulder.

His mind was in a sudden whirl. Now was not the time or place. Was this some kind of trap? Had Herbert sent her out here so the Swede could catch him in the act of seducing his wife and have an excuse to shoot him?

There was a slight gust of wind and he could feel wet snowflakes on his face. He thought the temperature had moderated.

"You make love to me?" she asked, taking his free hand and drawing it to her. She was wearing a cotton shift of some sort under a heavy fur coat thrown over her shoulders. He caught his breath at the touch of her warm flesh.

"Why do you want me?" he asked. The question sounded stupid, but he could think of nothing else to say.

"He theek maybe you go 'way. Leave prisoner."

What gold couldn't buy, maybe sex could. Herbert was willing to try everything.

"Where's Gunnar?" he asked in a low voice.

" 'Sleep."

"Did he send you out here?"

She ignored the question.

Barker felt himself stirring at her touch. What did it matter? He could have this woman and still arrest Klegg and take him back. Yet, deep down, he knew his honor would not allow him to take her body, any more than his honor had allowed him to accept the poke of dust. But the gold dust was only cold metal. Here was a warm woman who was his for the taking, right here, right now. The desire was strong and he wavered, considering, his heart beating faster. Then an idea flashed into his mind. How loyal was Tanna to Herbert? Maybe Barker could enlist her help in getting the prisoner. But he remembered the intensity of her silent regard for Herbert during supper. She had shown him fawning looks of love. Or had Barker completely misinterpreted what was really submissive servility? He wished he'd been more attentive. Herbert was a strong, rich man. Did she really love him, or had he just purchased her from some tribe as an unwanted, half-breed girl child of a French trader?

"No," he managed to articulate. "You are a very attractive woman, but you belong to Herbert," he said. "I am the law. I must arrest Klegg." If this made any impression on her sense of loyalty or duty, he couldn't tell. He suspected her standards were far different from his own. He had nothing to offer her as an inducement. "You help me get Klegg?"

There was silence for several seconds, as she finally let go of his hand and he withdrew it into the warmth of the sheepskin. He could feel the snow falling harder. In spite of the fact that she was lightly clad under the coat, she didn't seem to be shivering.

"I get Klegg . . . you take me weeth you?" she whispered in a husky voice.

He was stunned at this stroke of luck. Apparently her life

with Herbert wasn't as happy as Barker had assumed.

"Yes," he heard himself saying. "You help me get the prisoner and we'll all leave here together . . . now." It was a terrible gamble. Not only was he taking Herbert's prisoner, but also his woman—enough to enrage the hot-tempered Swede twice over.

He stood up, stretching his stiff muscles, and stamped his feet to restore circulation. Without a word, Tanna was gone, and Barker set out to rouse up his dogs from where they lay curled in the snow, bushy tails over their noses.

A strong gust whirled the dry snow up around the cabins, and he hoped the wind would carry away the sound of the snarling and whining as he rousted the dogs, one at a time. They had finished a run of more than thirty miles only a few hours before and were in no mood to be harnessed again. But he'd hitched and unhitched this team in the dark so often that he managed it now with little trouble. While he worked, the snow squall passed, and he looked up. The night sky glittered with stars like millions of ice crystals.

Suddenly he saw two ghost-like figures coming toward him, silhouetted by the aurora borealis that wavered its eerie, silent light just above the horizon. It was Tanna and a very willing Arnold Klegg.

"By God, let's get out of here," Klegg said in a loud whisper. "I'm sure as hell not hankering for a rope in the morning."

"I'm arresting you for claim jumping and robbery," Barker said. "You're not going free."

"Fine with me, Constable. I'll take my chances. I didn't have *no* chance with them."

"You got enough clothes on?" Barker asked.

"Yeah. Let's go." Klegg flung the hood of his parka up over his shaggy head.

"You ride," Barker said to the girl. "Klegg, you travel afoot for now to save the dogs."

"I weel walk," she replied with pride in her voice. "Strong."

"OK," Barker replied, appreciating her more all the time. "But stay close. I don't want to lose either of you."

The stars were blotted out as another heavy snow squall gusted down on them. The snow was falling so thickly that, even in daylight, the visibility would have been only a few yards. He grabbed the handles of the sled and rocked it to break the frozen runners loose from the snow. "H'ya, Soot!" he called softly to the big, black leader, and the dogs lunged into their harnesses. He held the coiled whip in one mittened hand, but didn't use it for fear of the noise. Guiding the team down around the cabin toward the river, he guessed at the location of the trail and started. Barker jogged behind the sled, one hand on a handle while the other two followed, single file, behind him. The snow was already very soft underfoot and it wouldn't be long before the wind would cause the trodden trail to be drifted over completely. Barker briefly considered traveling the river where the ice alongshore was smoother from partial thawing and refreezing, but he dared not risk the danger of springs or other faults in the ice.

The weather suddenly ceased to be his main concern as a clamor of barking and howling erupted behind them. Somehow Herbert's dogs had been aroused and were setting up a racket that couldn't fail to awaken the men in the camp. The noise gradually faded into the distance as they rounded a bend and the moaning of the increasing wind blotted out the barking.

Barker estimated they'd gone less than a mile when he drew the dogs to a halt to wait for Klegg to catch up. Tanna was right on his heels with no apparent distress, but the prisoner finally came staggering up, gasping. Barker knew immediately that Klegg was going to slow them and he had a decision to make. The snowstorm was intensifying to a full blizzard, the wind roaring through the giant spruce and fir trees, the snow blowing sideways, stinging their faces. The dogs were having a difficult time keeping to the trail and had floundered off into deep snow several times. Twice the sled had upset.

Barker looked back. As yet, there was no sign of the pursuit he knew was coming. If he put Klegg on the sled, it would only burden the dogs even more. But Klegg was the reason for this trip, and Barker was paying a high price for him, so he had to insure he got the prisoner back to the outpost.

"Get on the sled, Klegg."

Breathing hard, the man obeyed, covering himself with the wolf pelt.

"Mush!" Barker popped the whip over the dogs, and they surged ahead. He was unable to see and so had to trust the dogs somehow to sense the grooved trail. Protected from the wind by the side of a hill, they were able to keep the trail for about an hour longer. Then they dipped down into a swale and the running dogs floundered into deep snow. Barker, jogging with his head down, was caught off guard and pitched over the sled as it careened sideways. Klegg staggered to his feet. "I'm fr . . . freezing," he chattered.

Barker struggled up in the thigh-deep drift, brushing himself off, feeling the icy pack of snow down his neck and up his sleeves. He snapped with no sympathy: "Run alongside for a while. That'll get your blood pumping!" Barker was perspiring from exertion and knew he couldn't stop long for fear of becoming dangerously chilled. He waded in among the snapping dogs, beating them away from each other with the butt of his whip as he strove to untangle the snarled harnesses in the dark. When he finally got them lined up again, he realized he could see the vague shapes of the dogs and the sled as the light of dawn struggled to penetrate the heavy snow clouds and the thick, swirling flakes.

The half-breed woman still showed no signs of fatigue as she averted her hooded face from the stinging blast and waited patiently for them to continue. He could see her now in the half light and noticed a dark bruise on her left cheek bone. The mark had not been there the night before at supper and he began to sense her desperation.

Day sneaked up through the flying blizzard, but it was only a gray pall to show that night was gone. The party moved at a slower pace now as the deepening snow slowed the tiring dogs. The trail was completely obliterated. Barker could only stay roughly between the white expanse of frozen river to his left and the irregular line of dark evergreens on the slope to his right. Finally he saw that he would have to break trail. He pulled his snowshoes off the sled and put them on, at the same time instructing Tanna to take the whip and be ready to drive the dogs, if they needed any urging.

Barker went out front to break trail for the animals that were unable to make any progress against snow now above their bellies. He dreaded the ordeal that was coming—a test of man's conditioning and endurance, and ultimately of his heart and will. The snow was now more than knee-deep and with each step he had to lift his leg straight up, swing his foot forward, and set it down, flattening the soft snow and creating a path the dogs could negotiate. Then he repeated the process with the other leg—up, forward, and down; up, forward, and down—with his feet far enough apart to keep from stepping on his snowshoes. Ten steps, forty steps, a hundred steps. He slitted his eyes against the biting wind that froze his eyelashes and numbed the exposed skin of cheeks and nose.

In spite of this, sweat was soon soaking his inner clothing. Cold air whistled through his clenched teeth, searing his straining lungs. He'd always been blessed with great lung capacity. The doctor who'd examined him when he enlisted in the Mounted Police had even commented on his unusual chest expansion. It was a trait that had brought him through many exhausting ordeals.

But he floundered to a stop after only a few hundred yards, realizing he could not keep up this pace. He stood for several seconds, head tucked down into his fur collar, sucking air into his burning lungs, legs trembling. The bitterest thought was the realization that he was also breaking trail for Herbert and his team of rested Huskies. The big Swede had a reputation as one of the best sled-dog travelers in the territory. Barker knew he would have to make a stand and fight. It was too much to hope that the storm had discouraged pursuit.

He staggered back to the sled and reached under the wolf skin for the Winchester in its leather scabbard. He worked the lever to be sure the action wasn't frozen. It was stiff, but still operable. He let the hammer down and shoved the weapon back under the cover. As his breathing slowly steadied, he considered stopping for a rest, possibly building a fire and making tea to restore their energy. He estimated they'd covered barely ten miles—hardly a third of the distance. No. He would just keep going until they had to stop and camp for the night. It didn't appear they would be able to reach his cabin while daylight lasted. His strength was ebbing and the falling snow had not let up. If anything, the storm had grown fiercer, with very diminished visibility. It had become a silent world from which all wildlife had fled to shelter.

Then Barker thought he heard something unusual. He raised the earflaps of his fur cap and turned his head this way and that. He knew heavy snow was like thick fog in its ability to deflect, muffle, and confuse sounds. He heard nothing. Probably a tree limb snapping under its weight of snow.

Then he heard the distinct *crack,* and he instantly knew it for what it was—the popping of a dog whip. This was followed by a faint shout, and he looked back to see, through the whirling white, a dog team and sled.

"It's Herbert!" he shouted. He reached down and quickly yanked off his snowshoes. "Make for the river! That way!" He pointed left. "Haw! Soot! Haw!" He grabbed the handles and threw his weight against the sled, tilting it, muscling it around as the team followed the lead dog and plunged away to the left. The unseen river was out there in that swirling whiteness. But how far? Two hundred feet? Two hundred yards? The trail roughly paralleled the water but never at a constant distance. If they could reach it quickly, they could make faster time, especially if the wind had swept the ice clear of snow in places. He knew there were dangerous faults in the ice that covered a swift-flowing current, but they would have to take that chance. What was coming from behind was no chance—it was a sure thing. He heard the boom of a heavy rifle. He yelled at the dogs and cracked his whip over their heads, leaning forward on the handles and running.

Suddenly there was the river, like a wide, white highway. The dogs' tongues were lolling out of open mouths, but they seemed to sense the desperation of the chase and lunged into their collars, the sled bouncing crazily over the steep lip of the riverbank and out onto the ice.

"Both of you—get aboard!" He grabbed Klegg by the back of his coat and flung him headfirst across the sled while Tanna leaped nimbly onto the backs of the runners and held on. Free of the deep snow at last, the team burst ahead, stretching their stride with renewed vigor. At the last instant, Barker dove and caught the wooden side of the sled, dragging alongside. He scrambled to pull himself up, losing his whip, but managed to snatch the Winchester from the sled before letting go. Tanna was yelling at the dogs, urging them on, as his sled disappeared into the whirling flakes.

Barker slid to a stop on his knees. He turned around, thumbing back the hammer on the rifle. He wiped a sleeve across his face just as the wind tore a massive rent in the curtain of snow for several seconds. He saw the team coming, bushy tails bobbing over their backs, the sled yawing from side to side on the ice behind them. The figure of the broad-shouldered Swede showed above the back of the sled. He was trying to hold on and raise his rifle for another shot. Then the curtain of snow fell again, blurring the image.

Barker scrambled, slipping and sliding, toward the river-bank as Herbert swiftly approached. He slid behind a tangle of driftwood frozen in the ice. His eyes were watering as he squinted down the barrel at the dark, fast-moving figure. Herbert, now lying across the top of the sled, raised his rifle just as Barker drew a bead. Both weapons roared simulta-neously.

Barker felt as if an invisible fist had hit him in his left side, knocking him backward. Then came the searing pain. Gasping, he fumbled with the fastenings on his sheepskin coat. Then he unbuttoned his tunic and saw the red wetness staining his white long johns. With his knife, he slit the under-wear and examined the wound in the half light. He let out his breath in a long sigh of relief. From the soreness and the look of it, the bullet had apparently been deflected by a rib and grooved a path along the flesh without entering his body. He blotted the blood with his cotton bandanna and padded the rib that was probably broken. The blood was coagulating quickly in the cold as he gingerly fastened his clothing back over it.

Picking up his rifle, he went to look for Herbert. He found him unconscious on the ice, his sled and team gone. Barker's bullet had apparently hit the brass receiver of the Swede's rifle, throwing the weapon back against his head and knocking him out. He had a gash and a purpling bruise on his forehead. He flung the ruined rifle away, then pulled the big man's belt off, looped it around Herbert's neck, and began dragging him. The pain in his side was excruciating and his breath was coming in short gasps, but he didn't have far to go before he came upon the Swede's winded team that had slowed and finally stopped.

Barker was checking the sled for some rope when he heard a grunt. He turned and swung the stock of his carbine. But Herbert was already up and rolled a shoulder into the Mountie's legs, knocking him to the ice. Barker gasped, momentarily stunned by the stabbing pain in his side. Herbert clumsily, groggily, crawled up onto him like some shaggy beast. His assailant was too close for Barker to use the rifle and Herbert pinned him down, preventing Barker from reaching under his coat for his revolver. He gasped for air as more than two hundred pounds crushed him. Piercing pain in his lower rib cage screamed the message that jagged ends of bone were jabbing the muscle sheath. Herbert slowly slid his hands up to Barker's throat and clutched for a choke hold. The Mountie was powerless against the big man's strength. Desperately Barker twisted his head from side to side to break the deadly grip. This movement, along with Herbert's bulky gloves and Barker's thick collar, saved him from being strangled.

Suddenly the ice under them cracked with a report like a pistol shot. Herbert raised his head. Another loud *crack* and Barker felt the ice give slightly. Herbert let go and pushed himself up, eyes wide with alarm. Barker jerked his arms free and swung the carbine with all his strength. Herbert caught the force of the blow on the side of his bare head and fell sideways. Barker rolled to his knees and leveled the weapon, jacking a shell into the chamber. "Get on that sled!" he rasped. "On your back!"

The Swede obeyed with a dazed look. Barker jerked the lashings off the Swede's bedroll and secured Herbert's wrists and ankles to the sides of the sled.

The dogs were whining and lifting their paws gingerly as if sensing the rotten section of ice beneath their feet. Barker carefully drove the team close to the bank, then cracked the whip, and pushed the dogs as fast as he dared. But it took another half hour before he glimpsed his own sled in the distance through the thinning snowfall. He shouted and waved to Tanna. She stopped to wait.

"We heard shots. Figured he'd got you," Klegg said. "Damned glad it's the other way around."

"Let's get moving," Barker replied through gritted teeth, hoping no one would notice how he was favoring his left side. He pointed with his carbine. "We've still got a long way to go."

Sergeant Cecil McKee smoothed his mustache with the back of his hand and looked at the half-breed girl massaging her bare toes in front of the stove. "One helluva tale," he muttered to himself. Two men arrested and shackled to the bedpost. Both lay on the floor sound asleep under Hudson's Bay Company blankets. His partner, Derek Barker, wounded, had been bandaged and fed and was now lying exhausted in his bunk.

Both prisoners would likely spend some time in jail, but no one had been killed in the fray—thanks mainly to Barker. McKee resolved, as soon as he got all the details, to write up a report, commending Barker for his actions. The report would go to their superiors by the following week's mail. It was the kind of thing that men of the Mounted Police were expected to do all the time, but McKee felt that such deeds should be recognized. He glanced at Barker's fur hat that had been tossed on the table. The brass badge pinned to the front of it glowed dully in the light of the coal-oil lamp. *"Maintien le droit . . . ,"* McKee muttered thoughtfully. The motto fit the man.

About the Editor

Jon Tuska is the editor of several anthologies of Western stories, including *The Western Story: A Chronological Treasury* (University of Nebraska Press, 1995). With Vicki Piekarski he co-edited *The Max Brand Companion* (Greenwood Press, 1996), *The Morrow Anthology of Great Western Short Stories* (Morrow, 1997), and *The First Five Star Western Corral* (Five Star Westerns, 2000). He has been editing a series of short novels in the Five Star Westerns titled *Stories of the Golden West*.